The Firefly Summer

The Firefly Summer

MORGAN MATSON

Simon & Schuster Books for Young Readers
NEW YORK   LONDON   TORONTO   SYDNEY   NEW DELHI

SIMON & SCHUSTER BOOKS FOR YOUNG READERS
An imprint of Simon & Schuster Children's Publishing Division
1230 Avenue of the Americas, New York, New York 10020
This book is a work of fiction. Any references to historical events, real people, or real
places are used fictitiously. Other names, characters, places, and events are products of
the author's imagination, and any resemblance to actual events or places or persons,
living or dead, is entirely coincidental.
Text © 2023 by Morgan Matson
Jacket illustration and interior maps © 2023 by Celia Krampien
Jacket design by Lizzy Bromley © 2023 by Simon & Schuster, Inc.
All rights reserved, including the right of reproduction in whole or in part in any form.
SIMON & SCHUSTER BOOKS FOR YOUNG READERS
and related marks are trademarks of Simon & Schuster, Inc.
For information about special discounts for bulk purchases, please contact
Simon & Schuster Special Sales at 1-866-506-1949 or business@simonandschuster.com.
The Simon & Schuster Speakers Bureau can bring authors to your live event.
For more information or to book an event, contact the Simon & Schuster Speakers
Bureau at 1-866-248-3049 or visit our website at www.simonspeakers.com.
Interior design by Hilary Zarycky
The text for this book was set in Adobe Garamond Pro.
Manufactured in the United States of America
0323 FFG
First Edition
2 4 6 8 10 9 7 5 3 1
Library of Congress Control Number: 2022932555
ISBN 9781534493353
ISBN 9781534493377 (ebook)

For Jane Finn
with love and gratitude

Van Camp Family Tree

<u>Grandpa & Grandma</u>
Cal & Vivian

<u>Aunts & Uncles</u>
Abby
Benji
Casey
Dennis
Quinn

<u>Kids</u>
Pete, 15
Diya, 12
Ryanna, 11
Max, 10
Hattie, 9

Abby Van Camp & Neal Kharkar
Pete
Diya

Benji Van Camp & Katie Lowenstein
Hattie

Casey Van Camp (deceased) & Dave Stuart
Ryanna

Dennis Van Camp & Byron Harris
Max

Quinn Van Camp

The Hollywood Edit
GREENLIGHT ALERT!

The long-in-development movie *Frank N. Stein* is finally coming to life! This adaptation of Mary Shelley's novel imagines Frankenstein's monster as a superhero whose powers are awakened when he is reanimated. The script was written by Dave Stuart.

Stuart's first movie was the summer camp feature *Bug Juice*, based on the award-winning play. (The film won no awards and was roundly panned.) He's more recently known for his high-concept scripting work (the Alien Rebels franchise and the Ghost Robot franchise). Stuart is also a director, but following the box office bomb of *Annul and Void* five years ago, he has not directed since.

Filming will take place this summer in Budapest, Hungary.

The Pocono Eagle
A Groundbreaking Autumn?

It seems as though, after years of legal wrangling, construction will finally begin on a former summer camp in Lake Phoenix. The 40-acre plot of land was formerly the site of two summer camps that sat across a lake from each other—Camp Somerset for Boys (closed in 1987) and Camp Van Camp (closed in 1993). The two owners of the overlapping plots of land have been in and out of court for the past few years, with the owners of Camp Van Camp fighting any development. But while it is currently unclear what is happening with the Camp Van Camp land, the owner of the former Camp Somerset, Rick Andersen, has procured permits to begin construction on his land in September—with six planned lakefront condominiums.

We reached out for a comment from Andersen, who inherited the former Somerset property five years ago when his father, beloved community figure Robert Andersen, passed away. "I'm thrilled to begin construction in the fall. It's a very exciting phase," Andersen replied in an email. When asked about pushback from his across-the-lake neighbors, and the community, he replied, "I have every right to build and don't listen to anyone who says otherwise."

We were unable to get Cal Van Camp, owner of the Camp Van Camp property, on the phone. But when we called at his house, the person answering the phone (she did not identify herself but sounded young. And like she was putting on a British accent) said, "This entire thing is a tragesty (?) and will not be allowed to stand! We don't want to have to see terrible condos and construction! We shall fight on the land! We shall fight in the lake! We shall fight, um, near the lake! We will never surrender, and we will—*Mom!* I'm giving an *interview!*" And then there was the sound of a muffled argument and the phone was hung up.

More to come on this developing story.

PART ONE
THE CAMP

CHAPTER 1

I could tell something was wrong the second I came downstairs.

First of all, my dad was sitting at the kitchen table.

I know for most people, this might not be weird. Normal dads probably sit at kitchen tables all the time.

But we live in Los Angeles, and my dad is a writer—he writes screenplays. Not just everything the actors say—all the action and settings and everything else that happens in a movie has to be written down too. (Not everyone knows this. Nana, my dad's mom, still thinks that the actors make up their own lines, no matter how many times my dad tells her otherwise.) He also used to direct movies, until his last one did so badly that now he's in movie jail, and when we go on hikes, producers pretend they don't see him when he waves.

But because of this, my dad was normally always busy writing something, and always in motion—pacing around our pool as he tried to figure out a story problem, or working in his office, or in meetings. He was almost never just sitting still at home. So right away, I knew something was up.

"What's up?" I asked as I came into the kitchen.

I'd been upstairs reading, which was pretty much what I'd been doing since school let out last week. I'd managed to make it through the sixth grade, even though I barely passed PE. (My PE teacher didn't seem to get that some people can climb ropes and some people can't. And that no amount of encouraging me to do it would magically give me the ability as I spun in circles a few inches off the ground and everyone snickered.)

I'd been deep into a mystery—my favorite type of book to read. My current favorite series was Miss Terry's Case Files, where the heroine, Terry Turner, is a seventh-grade detective who people hire to get to the bottom of things. Whenever I was reading those books, I couldn't help wishing that I, too, lived in a small town in Vermont with lots of mysteries. Stupid Los Angeles had a lot of private detectives already, so nobody needed to turn to middle schoolers to solve their crimes.

"Why aren't you working?" I asked my dad.

"I want to talk to you about something," he said.

"Okay," I said, sitting across from him, studying his expression and noticing that he looked pale. I frowned. "Are you remembering to take your B-12?"

"Ryanna," my dad said, shaking his head. "Keeping track of vitamins is supposed to be my job. I should be asking you that."

"Of course I'm taking all my vitamins. *Are* you taking your B-12?"

My dad sighed. "No."

I nodded, satisfied, and headed to the cabinet, where I pulled the white bottle down. I knew most of my friends would not have any idea if their dad was taking his vitamins, and would probably be alarmed that this was something they were supposed to keep track of.

But it had been just my dad and me, ever since my mother died when I was three.

I'd basically grown up on movie sets with my dad all over the world. I loved everything about being on set—getting snacks at craft services (aka "crafty"), hanging out in the hair-and-makeup trailer and learning all the best gossip, the friends I'd make with the child actors, who were usually the only other kids around.

But mostly what I loved was that a movie set was a tidy, orderly universe. The day's schedule was printed every morning and handed out—and it told you everything. The shot list and the time the sun would be coming up and setting. The times that different crew and actors would be arriving. When lunch would be and what we were having.

While there were often a lot of surprises that cropped up while making a movie, the basic structure of the day was never in question. Everyone had a job, and if there was ever an issue, there were always lots of production assistants with walkie-talkies who could answer any questions for you.

But especially when my dad was directing, he was the one who was responsible for knowing everything, which meant it became my job to make sure that he was eating and drinking water and remembering to call Nana back so she wouldn't panic and call his agent over and over again. When I started middle school, my dad said that he wanted to be home more, and we hadn't spent much time on set since. But some habits were hard to break.

I handed him his vitamins. "Here."

"Thanks. But I do need to talk to you, Ry. This is serious."

"Okay," I said, starting to get worried I was in trouble. But we'd already gotten my report card, which was fine except for the PE grade. "Is everything okay with Ginger?"

Ginger was my stepmother—she and my dad got married eight months ago in Ojai, which is a town two hours outside Los Angeles. (It's pronounced "oh hi," and my dad and Ginger made shirts to go in everyone's welcome bags that read OJAI THERE, WELCOME TO THE WEDDING!)

They'd only dated for about a year before they got married, but it hadn't come as a surprise to me. Dr. Ginger

Kang was my pediatrician, and for once my dad came to my appointment, not my babysitter, and I watched them get googly eyes at each other right there in the office. They were talking so long that I finally left and went out into the waiting room to read an old issue of *Highlights*. (I still enjoyed the "What's wrong with this picture?" puzzles, after all.)

And by the time my dad came to get me, with a dazed look on his face, I was pretty sure I knew where it was going.

I felt like everyone—my dad; my teachers; my old therapist, Dr. Wendy—had been expecting me to have a harder time with Ginger joining our family. But while it was definitely different, it mostly felt like things were pretty much the same, just with some added improvements. It helped that we moved into a new house right before the wedding so that, according to my dad, we could *all start fresh as a family*. I was thrilled because my new room had a window seat, something that I'd wanted ever since I'd read *The Mystery of the Haunted Homestead*, where someone finds a dead body in one. (When we moved in, there was nothing but dust bunnies in mine. I checked.)

And despite some small bumps along the way—Ginger organized the spice rack in a way I hated and kept changing back (she told me that eleven-year-olds shouldn't have opinions about the spice rack)—things were definitely better now. My dad laughed more, there were plants all over the house, and we now had a cat, Cumberbatch, who spent all his time sleeping in sunbeams except when he woke up to yowl at us for food. Ginger had insomnia, so she was always online shopping late at night, which meant that clothes she'd picked out for me were constantly showing up (even if Ginger usually had very little memory of buying them). But even Insomnia Ginger had great taste, and when the packages arrived, we'd do fashion shows and try-ons in my room. She was great at braiding hair; she saw kids all day, so she knew about the cool sneaker trends; and she'd taught me about stuff like leave-in conditioner.

And best of all, she didn't try to be my mom, or take over my life. It was like she understood it had just been me and my dad for a long time, and she was going to ease in rather than barge in. It had been so drama-free with Ginger that it made me wonder if all the fairy tales with evil stepmothers had been lying.

"Everything's fine with Ginger," my dad assured me.

"Talking about me?" Ginger asked as she came into the kitchen, a cover-up over her bathing suit. She grinned at me. "Want to go swimming, Ry?"

"I was just talking to Ryanna about the . . . conversation," my dad said to Ginger, widening his eyes at her.

"Oh," Ginger said, widening her eyes back. She opened the fridge and pulled out a water, then came to sit next to my dad. "Right."

"What conversation?" I demanded. I felt out of the loop, which always made my mouth get dry and palms sweat.

"I received a letter last week," my dad said. He reached into his pocket and pulled out an envelope, and from that, a folded piece of paper. "It was sent over a month ago, but it went to our old address." He handed the paper to me, and I opened it up and smoothed out the creases.

> Hello, David
> We know it has been a while. But we feel it's time Ryanna gets to know where she comes from while she still can. We'd love to have her in Lake Phoenix for the summer.
>
> If this is acceptable, please call.
>
> Cal & Vivian Van Camp

I stared down at the letter. Where was Lake Phoenix? What did *while she still can* mean? But most importantly—"Who are Cal and Vivian Van Camp?"

My dad winced slightly, and Ginger reached out and gave his hand a squeeze. "Your grandparents. Your mother's parents."

"Oh." I just blinked at him for a second, then looked down at the letter again. I knew Nana, my dad's mom, who lived in New York City. (My dad's dad died when he was in college.) And I'd gotten to know Ginger's parents, who lived in the Bay Area and had taught me poker. But I had never once heard from these other grandparents before.

My dad never talked about my mom's family, so I only knew the basics. She was one of five siblings, the middle one. She had two brothers and two sisters. But mostly, all the facts I knew about my mom were from when she was older: Her name was Cassandra, but everyone called her Casey. She was gorgeous, with long blond hair and a big smile. She died when I was three. She was crossing the street in New York City when a taxi had run the light, and hadn't seen her in time. And she was an actress who'd met my dad on the set of *Bug Juice*, the first movie he wrote.

"I called them," my dad said, making this sound like *And then I went to the dentist.* "They want you to come and spend the summer with them. And I told them I'd check with you."

"But . . ." I looked between my dad and Ginger. Ginger had her serious face on, which was a real contrast to her cover-up, which had embroidered rabbits on it and read SUN'S OUT BUNS OUT. "The summer's already started. We have a whole plan in place."

I glanced over to the color-coded calendars that hung on the wall. I was going to go to a local day camp for June and half of July. Ginger had her practice, and my dad was going to be on set working. A movie he wrote, *Frank N. Stein*, was filming in eastern Europe this summer. It was a retelling of *Frankenstein* in which the monster was a zombie but also a single dad and somehow also a superhero? The last draft my dad let me read had been really confusing; he blamed the notes he was getting from the studio.

And then in mid-July, Ginger and I were going to fly out to Hungary and spend a few days on set, and then the three of us were going to tour around eastern Europe before heading home. It was the plan we'd worked out over weeks, and nowhere in that plan did I see room for hanging out with grandparents I didn't even know.

Ginger looked at me with a sympathetic smile. "I know it's a lot to take in."

"Why haven't we heard from them before?"

My dad and Ginger looked at each other without speaking. Finally, my dad said, "We had an argument a long time ago. And we all decided it would be better not to be in contact."

"Nobody asked me."

"You were three," my dad said with a smile.

"Still."

Ginger's phone rang. Her eyebrows rose, and she got up to answer it, sliding her finger across the screen. "This is Dr. Kang," she said, her voice going more serious and professional. *Sorry!* she mouthed as she headed out the back door, walking toward the pool. "Well, are you *sure* he ate it?" I heard her ask before the door slammed shut.

I picked up the letter again, trying to sort out what I was feeling. "Where is this?" I asked, tapping my finger on *Lake Phoenix*.

"It's in Pennsylvania. About three hours from New York City."

"I thought Mom was from Philadelphia." The word "Mom" caught on my tongue, like it was rusty from lack of use. Sometimes when I'd be with friends, I'd notice the way they tossed "Mom" around, so carelessly, like they didn't even realize that some people never got to say it. I was sure I must have said it when I was little, but since I couldn't remember, did it even count?

"She was. But she always spent summers in Lake Phoenix. So when we were back east, we used to go."

"*We* who? You and Mom?"

"You too," my dad said. "We brought you a few times. You don't remember?"

I shook my head. Somehow adults always expected you to remember things that had happened when you were two years old. Even though they could never remember where they put their keys five seconds ago.

"You—your mother brought you up there when you were three. You spent almost the whole summer up there."

"I did?"

"We actually met there. Your mom and me."

I frowned—this didn't sound right. "I thought you met on the set of your movie. That's what you always told me."

"But *Bug Juice* was filmed at their summer house. Casey was an extra until the director realized how good she was, and then her part got expanded."

"Because you expanded it," I said with a smile. I'd heard this part of the story before, and it always seemed so romantic to me. "Because you were falling in love with her."

My dad smiled the sad smile he did whenever he talked about my mom. "Exactly."

"But wait. *Bug Juice* is a movie that's set at camp. How was it filmed at their house?" I'd never seen my dad's first movie— it was adapted from a play, but the movie was changed a lot so that the characters were teenagers, and since it was PG-13, I was not allowed to see it. He'd shown me some clips of my mom from the movie, dressed in shorts and a polo shirt, herding campers into a cabin, but apparently I wasn't going to be allowed to see the whole thing until I was thirteen.

My dad took a breath and explained how my mother's family had run a summer camp in Pennsylvania until the nineties, when it closed down. But they still spent summers up there. And so when the *Bug Juice* production was scouting for locations, an unused summer camp was the perfect setup.

"So they want me to come to a camp for the summer?" It was like finding out that someone lived at a zoo. Who lived at a *camp*?

"It's not a camp anymore. It's more like . . . a house with a lot of archery targets."

"Why didn't you tell me any of this?" It felt strange. Like there was a whole part of my life that had been shut off from me.

My dad looked down at the paper. "Like I said, I don't . . . have a great relationship with your grandparents. And I don't have the best memories of that place. But if you want to go, Ryanna, you can. Ginger and I think you're old enough now to decide for yourself."

"Of course I'm not going to *go*," I said immediately, folding the letter up. The summer had been planned out already, after all. The calendar was all filled in.

A look of relief passed over my dad's face. "Well, it's your decision. Do you want to talk it through with Dr. Wendy?"

Dr. Wendy was the therapist I used to see once a week—my dad had found her for me after my mom died. He'd been worried about me processing my mother's death, which I didn't really understand, since I couldn't even remember my mom. But I liked Dr. Wendy, even though half the time I wasn't really sure *why* we were talking. And while it was nice to have someone to talk to about friends and grades and the current Miss Terry mystery I was reading, I'd asked my dad if I could stop seeing her this past year. He'd agreed but let me know that she would always be available in case of an emergency.

"No—" I started, just as my dad's phone rang. He winced as he looked at it.

"Gotta take this," he said. "It's Annabeth." Annabeth was my dad's agent. She gave great holiday presents and terrified everyone around her, including my dad. He jumped to his feet and headed down the hall to his study.

I sat at the kitchen table in silence for a moment, then picked up the letter and the envelope—I figured that maybe it would be another eleven years before I heard from these grandparents again, so I might as well preserve a keepsake—and headed back up to my room.

As soon as I stepped inside, I could tell that something was off. I looked around, trying to see what it was, then noticed four books that had been knocked off my bookshelf onto the floor. "Cumberbatch!" I scolded. Cumberbatch was round and gray and fluffy, with a white splotch on his back, like someone had dropped paint on him. He was kneading my comforter with his paws, what Ginger always called "making biscuits" for some reason. He paused long enough to give me a withering look before going back to it.

I sighed and picked up the books. I had a system—it was why my dad and Ginger weren't allowed to put things away in my room. I put the books back in their spot—alphabetically but also color coded—and I was grateful, for the thousandth time, that I didn't have to share a room like some of my friends did. I knew I wouldn't be very good at it.

I decided to forgive Cumberbatch, crossed over to my bed, and hopped up next to him. I gave his chin a scratch as he stretched out with a rumbly purr.

I rubbed the spot on his head he liked and glanced over at the framed photo on my nightstand—it was where I kept the last picture I had of my mother and me. We were in New York City, posed next to a serious-looking stone lion, both of us laughing so hard, our eyes were closed. I traced my finger over the glass, looking at my mother's bright blond hair, how her hand was holding tight to mine.

I turned away from the picture—it was starting to make me sad—and folded up the note from my grandparents. I went to put it in the envelope . . . which was when I realized something else was in there.

I lifted out a photo, a printed-out one. Something about the colors—well, and the fact that it was a printed-out photo—made me think it was older. It was of a girl who looked my age. She was in a one-piece bathing suit with jean shorts over it, sitting under a picnic table. In the background, I could see a dock. She was holding what looked like a tackle box for fishing, but it was pink and purple and locked with a padlock. And she was raising one hand in a peace sign.

I looked closer—this girl looked a *lot* like me. She was blond, and I had dark red-brown hair, but besides that . . . I turned the picture over, holding my breath. Written on the back was:

Casey, Camp Van Camp.

12 years old.

I turned the picture over, my breath catching in my throat. This was my mom when she was around my age.

My mom looked like me. I looked like *my mom*.

I stared down at the letter my grandparents had sent. My thoughts were whirring. What did *while she still can* actually mean? Did it mean that this was a onetime offer? My only chance to go to Pennsylvania—wherever that was—and see more pictures like this of my mom?

Because suddenly that was all I wanted. I wanted to know more about her—much more than just the same stories I'd heard so often from my dad. And I wanted to know what had happened. Why hadn't I heard from my mom's family? What had gone on between my dad and my grandparents to cause a rift this big?

My eyes drifted over to my bookshelf. All my Miss Terry

mysteries were neatly lined up—and it felt like they were scolding me. Because all this time, I had been living inside an *actual* mystery and I hadn't even realized it, much less cracked the case.

But this was my chance to. I could go to Lake Phoenix—I could find out more about my mom. Because if there was this photo, there were *more*. Whole albums and lots of stories—stuff my dad probably didn't even know. I'd get to hear all of it. And as an added bonus, I would get to the bottom of the feud.

It would mean upending all my summer plans—but the same thing had happened to Terry in *The Hound of the Baskin-Robbins*. She was supposed to go to Maine but then got pulled into a mystery about stolen ice cream scoopers. You always had to answer the call. And this was mine.

I jumped off the bed—Cumberbatch yowled at me, not happy that I stopped petting him—and took the steps downstairs two at a time.

The kitchen was empty, but my dad and Ginger were sitting on loungers by the pool, and I hurried out to join them.

"I've made a decision," I said before I'd even reached them. I needed to say it before my mouth went too dry to talk. Before I started wondering if this was actually a good idea. "I want to say yes. I want to go to Lake Phoenix for the summer."

CHAPTER 2

L ooks like we'll be there in twenty," Kendra called from the front seat. Kendra was our driver who'd picked us up at JFK in a big black SUV.

We'd flown from LA to New York that morning. And even though we were on the early flight, I hadn't been able to sleep on the plane. Neither had my dad—he spent the flight either working or reading *The Stockholm Syndrome* by Sven Svensson, the Swedish crime author he was obsessed with.

I'd spent the flight alternating between reading *Ex Marks the Spot*, the latest Miss Terry book, and looking out the window, imagining the summer—just me and my grandmother and grandfather. I figured it would be quiet and peaceful. I was picturing reading in a hammock by a lake (because what else was I going to do, with just me and two old people?). I'd get all my questions answered about my mom, and get all the stories about her that I could. I had a feeling it might be kind of a boring summer, but that was okay. I was there for a greater purpose, after all.

"Thank you!" I said now to Kendra. I reached across the back seat and tapped my dad's arm—he was in the middle of a work call. *Twenty minutes*, I mouthed, and he nodded.

In the two weeks since my dad told me about the letter, things had moved really fast.

Since my dad didn't want to speak to my grandparents unless he absolutely had to (I noted this as a potential clue to work out later), he turned all communication over to his assistant. His assistant got all the information about the trip from my grandparents, including a packing list of what to bring, and Ginger had followed it to the letter. She'd been very excited about getting me all-new summer clothes, even ordering me a trunk with my initials painted on it to put all my stuff in. We'd packed shorts and T-shirts and sweatshirts and bathing suits and sneakers and flip-flops and one nice dress. Ginger had insisted, even though it hadn't been on the packing list. *Always pack a nice outfit,* she'd told me with a wink as she'd placed it in my trunk. *It's a rule. You just never know when an occasion might arise.*

My dad had organized it so that we could fly to the East Coast together. He'd drive with me to Lake Phoenix, then find a coffee shop or diner or something to hang out in while Kendra drove me to my grandparents', and then he'd go back into New York City. *I'll stay with Nana for the night,* he'd explained to me as we were going over the itinerary—I was looking at it with a pen in hand in case I had notes. *Just in case you change your mind. I won't fly to Budapest until the next day. So if it's not what you want, I can still come get you, make arrangements.*

I'm not going to change my mind, I'd assured him. I was pretty sure he wasn't thrilled about me going. He never said anything, but I could pick up on the general vibe. Ginger also seemed sad, bursting into tears regularly, bemoaning the fact that we were leaving her all alone in the house with nothing but the cat for company.

I had been worried that I'd also start to get homesick in the lead-up to leaving, but this was helped when a few days before I left, Ginger came down with the flu. Suddenly she was barfing all the time. She stayed in bed most of the week, and I tried to give her some space—not wanting to catch it.

But I'd made an exception to give her a hug that morning before we got our super-early flight. She'd sat up in bed and hugged me hard, whispering in my ear, *If you don't like it, just call me. You don't have to stay if you're not happy. We'll figure it out. Okay?*

I'd nodded.

She'd smoothed her hand over my head. *Love you, kid.*

Love you too. I'd given her a smile, then run out of the room before too many of the germs could get me.

"Okay," my dad said now, closing his computer and turning to look at me in the back seat. "You said twenty minutes?"

I nodded, then pulled out the itinerary that I'd made when I'd found three errors on the one his assistant had sent. "So just to remind you, your flight tomorrow is noon, so you'll want to leave for JFK around nine thirty. . . ."

"Ryanna. You're not supposed to tell me my schedule. That's supposed to be *my* job."

"It can't hurt to double-check."

"I think I'm good. But that reminds me . . ." He reached into his messenger bag and pulled out a padded envelope. "Here." He held it out to me. I peered inside—a white envelope, papers, and—

"A *phone*?" I picked it up reverently. My dad and Ginger had told me that I wouldn't get a cell phone until eighth grade. (This was also the year that I would be allowed to see PG-13 movies and get my own real social media accounts— ones without penguins and kittens as avatars. At some point, they'd decided everything important would happen in eighth grade.)

"Just for emergencies," my dad said in his *I'm serious, Ryanna* tone of voice. "If you want to leave early, or need to talk to us, I want you to feel like you can without having to ask to make a call."

"Uh-huh," I said, barely listening as I turned the phone over in my hands.

"Plus, if it's the same as it was eight years ago, there might not even be reception—*Ryanna!*"

"Right." I tried to look responsible. "I'm listening."

"I mean it. The phone is a privilege, and it's for emergencies only. Promise?"

I nodded. "Promise."

"Hold on to those documents." He explained they were signed medical forms in case of emergency, and contact information for where he would be.

I lifted out the small white envelope and opened it, and my eyes widened again. There was cash inside, and a credit card with my name on it. "Whoa."

"The card is also for *emergencies only.*"

"And the cash?"

"Well," he said, and gave me a small smile. "I wanted to make sure you had some spending money. I don't want you to need to take any from Cal and Vivian, okay? No matter what they say, I can certainly . . ." My dad's voice trailed off, and he cleared his throat. "Never mind. Just don't spend it all in one place, okay? I'm not sending more from Hungary."

"Got it." I tucked the envelope inside my canvas bag, the

one with RYANNA stitched on the front. Ginger had gotten it for me for school last year. She'd had to special-order it—the way anything with my name always had to be ordered.

Knowing that I had a phone, and cash, and a credit card, and medical forms that I had to be responsible for was making me feel very grown up, and I sat up a little bit straighter.

"If it starts to feel too long, I'm back in New York in the beginning of August for meetings. You can always just leave and come stay with me at Nana's. You don't have to stay for the whole summer."

"Okay," I said, filing that away in the back of my mind. Maybe by early August, I would have gotten all the information about my mother that I could and would be more than ready to head back. "But no matter what, we'll be home to celebrate your birthday together."

"I should hope so," he said, laughing—his birthday was at the beginning of September.

"Good," I said with a grin. "Because I didn't pack any string."

The birthday string was a tradition with us. My dad had done it for me when I was little, and when I was six, I started doing one for him, too—and now we collaborated to plan Ginger's, which was really fun.

Basically, you woke up on your birthday to find a string tied somewhere in your room—the bedpost, your foot, your doorknob. (When my dad and I did Ginger's, we tied it around Cumberbatch's collar. He was *not* a fan of this.) You had to follow the string all over the house, and there would be little presents tied to it, and it would lead you to other presents. When my dad did it, he always had the string go through the fridge, where there were always birthday donuts waiting for me. And there were at least three clues on the string that would hint at what the string was leading to—the *big* present.

Last year for my birthday, there had been a bell tied to the string, and a mini personalized license plate, and a picture from my dad's favorite old movie, *E.T.*—all of which meant that by the time I followed the string into the garage and saw it ended at a bike, I had already figured out what it would be.

"You know your mom started the birthday string tradition, right?"

"She did?"

"Yeah. She started doing it for me when we were dating, and then I started doing it for her. So then of course we started doing it for *you*—even when you were a baby and more interested in eating the string than following it."

"Why did she start it?"

My dad shook his head. "No idea. But your mother always loved a treasure hunt."

"Okay, sir," Kendra called from the front seat. "It looks like we've reached the downtown area."

I turned to look out the window, wondering if "downtown" was maybe too strong a word. We were on a street with a single stoplight and a handful of stores and restaurants on either side. Sweet Baby Jane's looked like an ice cream parlor. Borrowed Thyme looked like a bakery. There was a pet store and a small supermarket and a souvenir shop.

"Just up ahead," my dad said, pointing to the end of the street. The sign read POCONO COFFEE SHOP, and then in smaller letters under it, WALK IN. ROLL OUT. "You can just let me off there."

Kendra swung into the parking lot, and when she put the car in park, my dad got out, and I did too. I shut my door and looked around, blinking in the sun. The sky was a vibrant blue, with a few lazy clouds trailing across it. And there was so much *green*. There was green grass, and the trees had bright green leaves on them—there wasn't a palm tree in sight.

And also—the air felt . . . wet? Like I'd wandered into a bathroom right after someone had turned off the shower. It was almost never humid in California, and I wasn't used to it.

"It's humid."

"Welcome to the East Coast."

"Wow," I said, trying to take a deep breath.

My dad gave me a sad smile. "So I guess this is it, kid."

"Yeah," I said. I nodded a few too many times. I fought down the lump that was starting to rise in my throat. I was seized by a sudden urge to tell my dad I'd changed my mind. I could get back in the car and have Kendra drive us both to New York and not have to do this really scary thing all by myself.

But then I shook it off and focused on why I was here. I was going to learn everything I could about my mom. I was going to meet my grandparents. And I was going to get to the bottom of a mystery.

"Just call if you need anything. And if things get too much, or you ever need to talk . . ." My dad paused to lift his messenger bag over one shoulder. "You know you can reach out to Dr. Wendy, right?"

"Oh." I was suddenly disappointed but wasn't sure why. "Okay."

"I put her number in your phone, along with the info for where I'll be in Hungary. I'm always just a phone call away."

I nodded, and he pulled me into a hug. "Bye," I said, the word catching in my throat. "Don't forget your vitamins! And bring a sweater to set; you always forget it's cold. And remember to charge your phone!"

My dad laughed and stepped back. "Have a good time. And tell Cal and Vivian that . . . that . . ." His voice trailed off, and finally he just shook his head. "Anyway, have fun. I can't wait to hear all about it."

He turned and headed into the Pocono Coffee Shop. I got back in the car, noticing just how big the back seat was now that I was the only one in it.

"Okay," Kendra said. She turned around to give me a smile. "I'm going to make a quick stop for gas, and then we'll drop you off with . . ." She paused and squinted at her clipboard. "Cal or Vivian Van Camp."

"Sounds good."

She put the car in gear, and we were only driving for a few moments before she pulled into a gas station—it looked like we were just up the road from where we'd let my dad off. She stopped at a pump, and I looked around. There was a building just ahead—pocomart was printed on the awning.

"I'm just going to fill up," Kendra said. She cut the engine and turned around to look at me. "Want to stay in the car?"

I glanced down at my bag, and the envelope with the cash in it, then back at the mini-mart, exciting possibilities occurring to me.

"I might go into the store." I tried to make my voice sound casual, like I wasn't secretly gleeful inside.

"Don't be too long."

"I won't!"

It seemed like PocoMart was a regular mini-mart—except for the wall of firewood along the back. And as I walked through, I saw a section just for s'mores fixings—marshmallows, chocolate, more graham crackers than I'd ever seen in one place.

I looked at them for just a moment before moving on. I'd had s'mores at restaurants, and occasionally we'd be at someone's house with a firepit and would try to make them. But this usually came with so many warnings about not getting any marshmallow drippings on the fake firepit rocks that it had always seemed like more trouble than it was worth.

There was an electronic *ding* as the door opened and I saw two kids come in—a boy and a girl. The boy wore glasses and was talking a mile a minute. "We need something befitting the occasion. Something *somber*."

The boy was Black, and the girl looked South Asian—but I wasn't sure if they were siblings or just friends. I tried not to make assumptions. Since Ginger had become a part of my life, I'd noticed that when we were together, people would look around for the adult that was supposed to be with me—and overlook her, just because I was white and she was Korean American. These kids seemed like they were near my age—the girl maybe a little older, the boy a little younger.

The girl shook her head. "What's a somber snack?" She was dressed all in white, with her dark hair in a high messy bun.

"Well—maybe just nothing too happy, then. No Laughing Cow. Or Almond Joy. Or Snickers."

"You're taking this too far."

Knowing my time was limited, I hurried over to the candy aisle and debated my options. M&M's? Peanut M&M's? Peanut *butter* M&M's? Or maybe I wanted to go sour—Sour Patch Kids, sour gummy worms, super-sour straws. I was on the verge of reaching for a pack of Skittles—which somehow seemed like a compromise—when I saw it on the back wall.

The Icee machine.

There were three flavors: cola, cherry, and blue raspberry. I grinned as I hurried over and grabbed a jumbo cup. I was *never* allowed Icees. *It's just pure sugar,* Ginger would say, shaking her head whenever I'd ask if I could have one at the movies or Dodgers games. *It'll go straight to your brain.* She wasn't convinced when I told her my brain was where I *wanted* the sugar to go.

But now I had spending money in my pocket and nobody to tell me no. I started filling my jumbo cup with cherry, and occasional hits of blue raspberry.

I filled it all the way up, the last swirl rising above the

cup, then wondered if I should have put the lid on first, the way I'd seen the people at concession counters do. But whatever—I was sure it would be fine. I spotted the lids at the end of the counter. I turned around quickly to grab one—and crashed right into someone.

The Icee went flying out of the cup and landed all over the person I'd just bumped into.

I stared in horror at what had just happened. It was the girl I'd noticed before. She was looking down at herself, her expression equal parts shocked and furious.

But this was understandable, because her outfit— which moments before had been white—was now, almost entirely, red.

CHAPTER 3

O h *no*," I gasped. I clapped my hand over my mouth. I'd always read about characters doing that in books but had never quite understood why until that moment.

If I had ever needed a ten-second rewind (like in my dad's terrible movie, *Ten-Second Rewind*), it was now. Because this was *bad*.

The girl in front of me was covered in red. *Covered.*

She stared down at herself, then at the empty, dripping jumbo cup in my hand. "What . . . ?" she started, then glared at me. I instinctively took a step back. "What did you *do*?"

"I'm so sorry," I said. I looked around for anything that could help. There were brown PocoMart napkins in a nearby dispenser, and I grabbed some and held them toward her, even though I knew this was way beyond the help of a napkin. "It was an accident—"

"Everything is ruined!" she cried. "This isn't even mine; it's Quinn's. And I'm not supposed to borrow it. She's going to kill me!"

"Oh. So—why are you wearing it if you're not supposed to?"

"Because I didn't realize that someone was going to throw a Slurpee on me!"

"Technically, it's an Icee. And I didn't *throw* it on you. It was an accident."

"What is happening?" The boy she'd walked in with was hurrying up. His eyes widened behind his black thick-framed glasses. "You've been shot!" he wailed.

"No, I haven't," the girl said irritably. "Calm down."

"Stabbed, then?" He looked at her fearfully. "Who did it?"

"Her," she said, pointing at me. The boy gaped at me. "Well—she didn't stab me," the girl added after what felt like far too long a pause, and very grudgingly.

"My Icee spilled," I said quickly, since I noticed that everyone else in the mini-mart was now looking over at us. Apparently if you yell the word "stab" repeatedly, it gets people's attention.

"Oh," the boy said. He looked relieved and maybe—unless I was imagining it—a little disappointed. "Well—I'm glad you're not dying."

"Except that I *am*." She pointed down at her sweatshirt.

A second later, the boy gasped again. "Quinn is going to kill you!"

"I know. I'm a dead girl walking."

"RIP, you."

"Exactly. Say nice things about me. I'm gone."

"Is there a problem?" A teenager in a PocoMart polo shirt ambled up to us. He looked at the puddle of red on the floor and sighed. "I'll go get the mop."

"Um—should I . . . ?" I asked. I held up my empty cup. Was I supposed to pay for the Icee that I'd spilled? The last thing I wanted was to get in trouble.

"Don't worry about it," he said, turning and heading toward the back. "If you still want one, just get a fresh cup."

"I'm okay," I said, carefully stepping around the red puddle to throw the crushed cup away. An Icee no longer sounded good.

"What about me?" the girl demanded.

"What do you mean?" I asked, genuinely confused.

"How are you going to make this right?" she asked. The boy also turned to look at me, folding his arms across his chest.

"Um . . ." I looked around for a solution. I was all too aware that Kendra was probably waiting for me back at the car. "Want me to buy that for you?" I nodded at the box of Junior Mints in her hand.

"Sure!" the boy said eagerly.

"No," the girl snapped, shaking her head, and the boy's face fell. "You can't fix this with Junior Mints."

"Look . . . ," I said. I shook my head. I was feeling my patience starting to wear thin. "I apologized. I said I was sorry. I offered to buy you candy. I don't know what you want."

She narrowed her eyes at me, and I narrowed mine right back. I wasn't sure what happened next, but then she spoke. "I will not," she said, emphasizing every word slowly, "forget this. You watch your back."

"Yeah," the boy piped up next to her.

I took a breath—but then couldn't think of anything to say back. We'd gone so far outside the normal interactions I was used to having that I had no idea how to respond.

I pulled the door open and hurried outside, leaving PocoMart empty-handed. I'd only been in the Poconos a few minutes, and somehow I'd managed to make an enemy.

I got into the car and was surprised to see that Kendra had a map spread out on the dashboard—like, an actual paper map. I stared at it. I couldn't remember the last time I'd even seen a map, outside of movies with elves who go on quests. Terry had used an old map to find a buried time capsule in the backyard of her former best friend in *Ex Marks the Spot*, but I'd had very little personal interaction with them.

"Everything all right?" I asked.

"I'm not getting great service here, so my GPS is having trouble. Just wanted to confirm I'm heading in the right direction."

"Okay, cool."

Kendra looked at the map for a moment longer, then nodded and met my eye in the rearview mirror. "Here we go. Need anything, Ryanna?"

"I'm good."

Kendra nodded and pulled back onto the road. "It's a really unusual name," she said, reaching out and turning up the AC. "Where's it from?"

My name was always an issue. People either didn't know how to pronounce it ("Rye" like the bread, then the "Anna" that rhymes with banana, not "Anna" like sauna) or thought I was saying Rhiannon. When they finally got their heads around Ryanna, it was usually the first time they'd heard the name—and always wanted to know where it came from.

Whenever I asked my dad why I had my name, all he said was that it was my mother's favorite name. And that she had told him, even before they were married, that if she ever had a daughter, she was naming her Ryanna. *And you didn't ask her why?* I would press him, hoping that maybe he'd suddenly remember a different facet of the story. *Or where it came from?*

Your mom was stubborn. Once she wanted something, she was going to get it. She wanted to name her daughter Ryanna, and she was firm on that. And by the time you came along, it just seemed like a given.

But now, I realized, I was heading to a place where I might finally get an answer. Maybe my mother had told her parents where the idea for my name had come from.

"My parents just liked it," I said, realizing that Kendra was waiting for an answer. I never got to say "parents," so I liked to break it out when I could.

I smoothed down my hair and then my clothes and wondered if my grandparents would be standing outside to greet me. Maybe my grandmother would have baked cookies. And I'd get to see their house, and unpack my things in the room they would have set aside for me, and . . .

"I think we're here!" Kendra shook me out of these thoughts.

"We are?" I looked around. We were rolling up a long gravel driveway, the tires crunching over it. There were tall green trees on either side and, halfway up the driveway, a large sign arcing over it. CAMP VAN CAMP was spelled out in wooden capital letters. "I guess we are," I agreed. My heart was thumping in my chest. I rolled down my window and leaned my head out to get a better look.

It was like a summer camp straight out of the movies. There was a huge grassy expanse carved out among the trees, which were dense on either side. I could see small wooden cabins dotted around the property. And in the distance, through the trees, I was pretty sure I could see a gleam of sunlight hitting a lake.

There was a flagpole, with the American flag flying, and underneath it a blue-and-white flag that looked handmade and just said CAMP on it.

To my left was the biggest building I could see, dwarfing the smaller cabins that were scattered behind it. It had a peaked roof and was made of stone and round wooden beams, and there was a wide, open porch that wrapped all the way around it. LODGE was carved into a wooden sign that hung crookedly from the front and swayed back and forth in the breeze.

"How fun," Kendra said as she got out of the car. I got out too. "I didn't realize you were going to camp."

"I'm not—"

"Looks like there's already some kids here!" She crossed around to the back of the car.

"What?" I asked. But then I looked again and started to see things I hadn't before. It was like a "What's wrong with this picture?"—but in real life.

There was a lot of *stuff* hanging over the front porch railing—at least five beach towels and assorted bathing suits hung out to dry. There were three cars parked farther down the driveway, closer to the detached garage—a pickup truck, an old-fashioned station wagon with wooden panels on the sides, and a beat-up SUV with plates that read SOLV4X.

I knew I wasn't in the wrong place—the Van Camp sign above the driveway was proof enough of that. But maybe we were here at the wrong *time*? Maybe my grandparents had rented it out to people with lots of stuff and towels and cars?

I was about to take out my new phone and text my dad when two kids on bikes, riding fast, turned into the driveway and started coasting down it—slowed down a little bit by the gravel. They came to a stop in front of the car, got off their bikes, and stared at me.

I stared back—it was the girl and boy from PocoMart. Had they followed me here? Was this girl really *that* mad?

"What are you doing here?" I asked, folding my arms across my chest.

"What are *we* doing here? We live here. What are *you* doing here?"

"You . . . what?"

"Ryanna, you just had the one bag, right?" Kendra called, poking her head around the back of the car.

"Yeah, the trunk," I called back to her.

"Ryanna?" the boy asked, his eyebrows flying up. He looked at the girl, who seemed equally surprised. "You're . . . Ryanna? Ryanna Stuart?"

"Yeah," I said slowly. "How did you know that?"

"I'm Diya," the girl said, like she was expecting me to recognize her name. But I just blinked at her. The name didn't mean anything to me. I could tell that this annoyed her—her cheeks flushed. "I'm your *cousin*," she snapped.

My eyes went wide as I realized what this meant.

It meant this summer had just gotten a lot more complicated.

CHAPTER 4

Y ou—what?" I was trying to figure out if this was some kind of prank—or revenge for the Icee mess. Because I didn't have any cousins. My dad was an only child, so I didn't have any aunts or uncles on his side. But if these kids weren't related to me, how did they know me? "How . . . did you know my last name?"

"Um, because *I'm your cousin,*" the girl—Diya—said slowly, like I was too dumb to understand her. Right now, though, that was how I felt. Like my brain was currently covered in maple syrup and refusing to move quickly.

"Hi there," the boy said cheerfully, holding out his hand. "I'm Max." Diya slapped his hand down.

"What are you doing? We're mad at her!"

"We are?"

"She ruined Quinn's sweatshirt!"

"Ah," the boy—Max—said. He started to edge away from

Diya, like he was distancing himself from her situation. "But, see, that's really more of a *you* issue. And Gramps told us to be welcoming, remember? Or no dessert."

"Are you . . . ?" I looked between Max and Diya, trying to make the *Gramps* part fit with what was happening here. "Are we . . . ?"

"I'm your cousin too," he said. He took a big step away from Diya and held out his hand again. "Max Harris–Van Camp. That's Diya Van Camp–Kharkar."

I shook his hand, feeling dazed. I *did* know that my mother had had siblings—two brothers and two sisters. But it had never crossed my mind that they'd have had kids of their own. Much less that they'd *be* here. Shouldn't my grandparents have mentioned this? Shouldn't . . . my dad have told me I had cousins? "So—wow," I said, taking a deep breath. "I've got two cousins. Okay. That's bananas."

"You've got more than two," Diya said.

"I—what?"

"Here you go!" Kendra walked around from the back of the car, carrying my trunk. She set it down next to me. "I take it this is the right place?"

I bit my lip. I wanted to yell *no*. I wanted to get back in the car and have her take me to the place I thought I'd be spending the summer, the place where my grand-parents would be there, standing out front to meet me.

Possibly with a plate of cookies. Not this. "I guess so."

Diya scoffed. "Don't sound too excited."

Max looked down at his watch. "We need to go," he said, tugging at her arm. "The service was supposed to start at four."

"Great," Diya huffed. "And now we're late for the funeral."

"Did you say 'funeral'?" I asked as Max retrieved some candy from the front of his bike basket—apparently he'd gone with Swedish Fish.

"Yeah," Diya said, and they both started walking toward the cabins.

"Wait," Kendra said. "A funeral—here?"

"Uh-huh," Max said, pushing his glasses back into place. "In the lake."

"The *lake*?" I was starting to get really unnerved.

"It's a Viking funeral," Diya said. "Where else would you hold it?"

"A what, now?" Kendra asked.

"You float the body out in a shallow boat," Max explained. "Then you fire a flaming arrow onto it so the whole thing catches fire and then the spirit can go up to Valhalla. You know, standard stuff. Hattie always said Karma had a Viking spirit."

I had lots of questions, including who Hattie and Karma

were. But mostly about the fact that someone had *died* and they were going to set the body on *fire* in a *lake*?

They started walking again, Max turning to give us a small wave before hurrying on. Kendra looked down at me, her brow furrowed. "I'm . . . not sure I should leave you here."

I tried to give her an *it's fine* smile, even though I wasn't sure it was.

"Your dad gave me instructions—I'm only allowed to leave you with two individuals, and I need to see ID first. But nobody said anything about a *funeral*." She looked around, like she was waiting for someone else to show up. I knew how she felt—this was *not* what I'd had in mind for this summer.

But then I thought about my mother, and how this might be my only shot to find out about her. And that trumped unfriendly cousins and Viking funerals. So I took a deep breath and made myself stand up straighter, which was always Ginger's suggestion when you needed a little infusion of confidence. "Well—there have to be adults here somewhere, right?"

Kendra nodded. "Let's go find them." She headed in the direction Max and Diya had gone, leaving my trunk next to the car.

I followed behind her, passing cabins as we walked the

path laid out with flagstones and gravel. We were going slightly downhill—the lodge was at the top of the property, with everything else sloping downward.

The cabins we passed all had screen doors, some banging open and shut in the breeze. There were towels and clothes and bathing suits hung over the front porch railings, flip-flops and sneakers scattered outside the doors.

Kendra passed out of sight, and I hurried to catch up. I rounded a bend in the path—and then stopped short.

There was suddenly a lake in front of me.

It sparkled when the late-afternoon sun hit the surface. It was big, stretching out in a kind of lopsided oval, sur-rounded on all sides with green trees. There was sand lead-ing up to the lake, and a square floating dock in the middle. It had a ladder going up one side and a blue-and-white buoy bobbing cheerfully next to it. The lake wasn't so big that I couldn't see across it—but there was just one house on the other side. It was big and modern—all right angles and steel and glass. It looked like some of the beach houses I'd seen in Malibu—which meant it really didn't fit here, in the woods in Pennsylvania.

There was a dock that extended out over the sand and partway over the water. I could see two kayaks and a stand-up paddleboard pulled halfway onto the sand. And there were lots of boats either tied to the dock or pulled onto it. The dock was long and narrow, and then widened out at the end like a *T*. And this was where I could see there was a group of people gathered.

Kendra stepped onto the dock and started walking down it with purpose. I followed, dreading what I was going to see at the end of it. Because from everything that my alleged cousins had said, there was going to be a dead body waiting for me. Possibly in a boat.

As we got closer, I could see more clearly the people standing at the end of the dock—or at least their backs. The *T* part of the dock was big, but this group still took up most of it. There had to be ten people standing there, a mix of adults and kids.

I saw Kendra open her mouth like she was going to say something, just as a voice—a kid's voice—said, "Dearly beloved, we are gathered here today . . ."

Kendra paused and took a step back. I wondered if she was feeling what I was—that it was probably really bad manners to crash a *funeral*.

"We'll just . . . give this a minute," she murmured to me, and I nodded, setting my canvas bag on the dock. Nobody seemed to have noticed us yet, the group forming a loose semicircle and facing the water.

"Dearly beloved," the kid said again, louder this time. She stepped out of the circle, and I could see she was wearing a long black dress that was way too big for her—it was pooling at her feet. She looked maybe a few years younger than me and was holding a ukulele.

"That's for weddings," a tall teenager said. He was standing next to Diya—it looked like maybe they could be brother and sister—and he was doing foot drills with a soccer ball, which frankly seemed a little disrespectful.

"It's for funerals, too," an adult across the dock said. He wore glasses—and looked like he could have been Max's dad.

"Are you sure?" the teenager asked.

He paused, then shook his head. "Actually, no."

The girl with the black dress started strumming the ukulele, a song that sounded a little bit familiar.

Kendra frowned. "Is that Boy George?"

"Who?" I asked.

The girl finished the song with a flourish, then cleared her throat and said, her tone serious, "Karma. Karma, Karma, Karma. Karma the chameleon. We are here to honor your brief but wondrous life."

I suddenly felt relief flood through me. It seemed we weren't at a person's funeral after all—this was apparently a lizard funeral.

The girl started talking about how great Karma the chameleon was. About her loyalty and gentleness and fly-hunting prowess. When she started detailing the lizard's sense of humor, I noticed some of the adults in the group checking their watches.

"Thank you for showing me your true colors," the girl finally said, wrapping it up, her voice choked. "Good night, sweet lizard. And may flights of crickets sing you to your rest." She nodded to the teen with the soccer ball. One of the adults—it looked like a guy with white hair; I could only see his back—handed him a bow and quiver of arrows. The group parted slightly—letting me see, resting on the dock, a small boat with a sheet over the top.

Everyone bowed their heads in respectful silence—even as I caught another one of the grown-ups looking at their watch again—as the boat was lowered into the water and pushed out. It started drifting toward the middle of the lake, and the teenager pulled an arrow from his quiver and looked around. "Who has the matches?"

The adults started patting their pockets, but nobody came up with anything. "Seriously?" the girl asked, sounding scandalized. "Nobody brought matches?"

"I could go get some from the house," the white-haired man suggested.

"Karma is just floating out there!" the girl cried. "All not-aflame! What kind of Viking funeral is this?"

"It's okay, I have some." A woman stepped forward. "From s'mores last night."

The teenager nodded and took the matches, then squinted at the boat, which had drifted almost to the floating dock by now. "It's too far for me to hit it."

"Are you sure?" the girl asked, sounding tearful. "Now Karma will never reach Valhalla!"

"Don't worry, Hattie," the man with the white hair said. He took the matches, kicked off his sandals, then jumped into the lake. He swam, with one arm holding the matches up out of the water, until he reached the small boat. He stopped, treading water until the little boat caught fire. Everyone on the dock clapped, and he started to swim back—only to have the boat flip over and a small plume of smoke rise from where the fire had gone out.

And that seemed to be the end of the funeral. The group started to break up and turn back to the house, which was when Kendra stepped forward, clapping her hands together to get everyone's attention. "Hello," she said, her voice authoritative and carrying. "I have a young lady, Ryanna Stuart, with me. We've had a very long journey, and I'm sure we both want to be going our separate ways. But I cannot leave until I have placed her in the company of a responsible adult."

"Well." I looked over to the end of the dock, where the white-haired man who'd swum out was pushing himself up out of the water and clambering, dripping, onto the dock.

He looked like a wet, off-duty Santa Claus. He was just taller, and without a belly like a bowlful of jelly. But he had longish white hair and a white beard, both of which were currently very damp. "I don't know about *responsible*, but I'm certainly an adult." He took a few steps closer to us, and I could see that his eyes were twinkling, like this was just the most fantastic joke. "I'm Cal Van Camp," he said, and he smiled right at me. "But call me Gramps."

CHAPTER 5

Kendra had verified my grandfather's identity, he'd signed a paper on her clipboard, and then she'd given me a smile. She'd looked back at the remnants of the chameleon Viking funeral and the group gathered on the dock and wished me good luck. I could read it clearly on her face, what she was thinking but not saying—*you're going to need it*. Then she'd waved goodbye and walked up the path back to the car, and a moment later I heard tires crunching over gravel. She was gone, leaving me alone with the Van Camps.

And there were a *lot* of them.

Everyone had helpfully grouped themselves by family, and my grandfather went around the dock, introducing me.

There was my aunt Abigail, my mother's sister, the oldest of the siblings. "Please, call me Abby," she said, giving me a quick hug and then straightening out my T-shirt, like the hug might have wrinkled it. She had brown hair pulled into a perfectly neat ponytail and was wearing running clothes and sneakers. She was married to my uncle Neal, who was South Asian and smiled vaguely at me, like his mind was somewhere else. "And these are our kids," Neal said, gesturing to them, "Pete and Diya."

Diya glowered at me—it was clear I was not forgiven for the Icee incident. Pete was the teenager with the soccer ball who'd tried to fire the arrow into the lake.

"Hi," I said, giving an awkward wave.

"Do you remember each other?" Aunt Abby beamed as she looked at us.

"Um," I said. I wasn't sure how to tell her that the very existence of cousins had been a revelation to me without insulting anyone.

"Of course," Pete said, surprising me.

"Oh, that's right," Aunt Abby said, nodding. "Petey, how old were you when Ryanna was here last? Seven?"

"Mom! Don't call me Petey!"

"Anyway," Gramps said, giving me another twinkly smile and steering me toward the next grouping. This was Uncle Benji, who was married to my aunt Katie. Aunt Katie was dark-haired and petite, the opposite of Uncle Benji, who was tall and bearded and blond. There was something about Uncle Benji that reminded me of pictures I'd seen of my mother—maybe it was the eyes. Aunt Katie and Uncle

Benji had one daughter—the one who'd been running the funeral and giving overly long eulogies.

"Henrietta Vivian Lowenstein Van Camp," she introduced herself, stepping forward with a flourish. I noticed that, in contrast to the black dress, her shoes were covered in sparkles, including the laces. She had red hair and her face was covered in a spray of freckles. She gave me an appraising look. "But call me Hattie. I'm nine, but I'll be ten in October. How old are you?"

"Um, eleven—" I started, but she was already continuing.

"Smashing! I'm *ever* so happy to make your acquaintance." For some reason, Hattie was now speaking with a British accent.

"Let's take it down a notch," Aunt Katie murmured to her. "We're all so glad you're here, Ryanna."

I heard what sounded very much like a scoff from Diya's direction, but my grandfather was already steering me to the final family group. This consisted of my uncle Dennis, my mother's younger brother, and his husband, Byron. Byron and Dennis were almost exactly the same height, and both were wearing dark T-shirts, probably for the somber occasion. Byron was Black, with cool square-framed glasses, and Dennis looked a lot like my grandfather, but with sandy brown hair. Max was their son, and he gave me a wave and a small smile as we were introduced.

"Your aunt Quinn is out right now, but she'll be back soon, and you can meet her then."

"Okay," I said, trying not to look as thrown by all this as I felt. I was already worrying that I'd forgotten someone's name. I really needed a piece of paper, or better yet, a spreadsheet so that I could keep track of this. It felt like I was drowning in new people, everyone looking at me . . . and all I wanted was some time to sort this out.

"I think that might be it," Gramps said with a nod as he looked around.

"Um. Mom?" Aunt Abby prompted after a moment.

"Ah yes, your grandmother," Gramps said. "She's out chasing down the white-winged tern."

I nodded even though I had no idea what that meant.

"Bird-watching," Uncle Benji supplied. "She's determined to have one of her finds published in the *Pennsylvania Birder Journal.*"

"So she wants to write a tern paper?" Uncle Byron asked with a grin. Everyone just looked at him. "Come on, that was good!"

"Ignore my father," Max said to me, shaking his head. "He's in advertising."

"So!" Gramps clapped his hands together. "Maybe we can head up to the house and leave all the kids to get acquainted."

"It's got to be *so* weird," Hattie said. "Meeting all your cousins at once like this."

"Well—I kind of met Diya and Max already."

"Really?" Aunt Abby asked, looking over at her daughter, her eyebrows rising. "When was this?"

"When we were driving into town," I explained. "At PocoMart."

There was a collective gasp on the dock. Diya's eyes narrowed while Max's went wide, and I realized I'd just done something wrong.

"What did you say?" Gramps asked. His voice was still genial, but there was a seriousness underneath it now.

"Um." I looked from Diya to Max. Both of them were giving me intense tiny hand signals, like we were suddenly in a baseball game and they were trying to tell me to steal home. "I . . ."

"You were in PocoMart?" Aunt Abby asked, looking down at her daughter. "After everything we talked about?"

Diya glared at me. She looked even madder about this than she had about the Icee. "Well . . ."

"We just wanted to bring something for the funeral," Max explained, his voice small.

"How many times have we talked about this?" Uncle Dennis asked.

"I know," Max said. "I just . . ."

"Wait." Hattie stepped forward, nearly tripping on the hem of her black dress, then recovering with a quick assist from Uncle Benji. She held up the box of Swedish Fish. "Are you telling me that this candy was bought at *PocoMart*?" She said the name of the mini-mart the way you might say *the toxic waste dump*.

"You said you appreciated it," Diya snapped.

"That was before I knew! Before I knew their tainted provenance."

"Nice word, honey," Uncle Benji whispered. Hattie gave him a quick nod, then turned and flung the box off the dock into the water, where it hit with a small splash.

"No," five adults on the dock said in unison.

"Sorry," Hattie said. "I'll get the net."

"I'll go," Pete said, then dove into the lake with a splash.

I opened my mouth, about to ask a question. But then I closed it when I realized I didn't know where to start—with why this mini-mart was forbidden, or why everyone kept jumping into the lake with their clothes on. I'd gotten pushed into a pool fully dressed at a birthday party when I was seven, and it was one of my least-favorite memories.

Pete emerged from the water, holding the sodden box of Swedish Fish above his head as he swam back over and climbed up the ladder on the right side of the dock.

"Here," he said, handing the dripping box back to Hattie.

"Thanks," she said, taking it with a grimace. "Sorry," she said to her parents.

"We'll talk about the littering later," Uncle Benji said.

"And PocoMart," Uncle Dennis added, looking at Max.

"Yeah," Uncle Neal said. He frowned at Diya, whose face was getting more and more flushed. "We'll have to discuss consequences, young lady. I think we should all go to the house."

"Good idea," Gramps said with a smile, even though he looked much less twinkly than he had a few moments ago. "Why don't we all head up and get Pete a towel, huh?"

"And you," Uncle Dennis pointed out. Gramps waved this off and started walking away, leaving footprints on the dock.

I turned to follow him when Diya yelled, "Wait!" Everyone stopped and turned to look at her. She was standing near the end of the dock, her arms folded across her chest. Even from a distance, I could see a gleam in her eye I didn't like. "What about Ryanna's initiation?"

"My . . . what, now?"

Aunt Katie shook her head. "We don't have to do that now. I'm sure Ryanna's tired—"

"No, we do." Diya raised an eyebrow at me. "Until she does it, the summer hasn't begun for her. Right? Max?"

Max nodded, even though he looked reluctant. "That is the tradition."

Hattie stepped forward with a dramatic flourish. "It's more than tradition! It's in the Camp Van Camp charter." Her voice was back to British again. "Not to mention the song based upon said charter." She cleared her throat, then sang:

> *"When first in summer you gaze o'er the lake,*
> *A flying leap you must to take.*
> *Into the waters deep you'll plunge,*
> *Your splash just the beginning of all your fun.*
> *For summertime, it can't begin*
> *Until you jump and then you swim!"*

Hattie raised her hands in triumph, then bowed deeply, even though nobody on the dock was clapping.

"I keep asking you to let me rewrite that last line," Uncle Byron said, looking pained. "It doesn't even rhyme."

"Well?" Diya asked, a challenge in her voice. She gestured toward the lake. "Go on. Jump in."

"Jump . . . in?" I echoed, staring at her, then the water. "I guess I could get my bathing suit—"

Pete shook his head. "No. It's the rules. Whatever you're wearing when you first see the lake, you have to jump in. It's why most of us wear our bathing suits when we drive here."

"Go on." Diya gestured toward the water again.

"But . . ." My heart hammered hard. I knew there was no way they knew I hated to get wet with my clothes on. But it felt like I was being punished for something when I hadn't even done anything wrong. "I don't . . ."

"What's wrong?" Diya asked, her tone mocking. I knew right then that she was exacting her revenge.

"I just . . . I don't . . ." I looked around at all the adults on the dock, waiting for one of them to step in, say that I didn't have to. But nobody said anything, and all at once I felt like I was going to cry.

I wanted my dad. He had left me here alone, and now I was expected to jump in a lake? I didn't understand the rules here, and nobody was explaining them to me, just telling me that I was doing the wrong thing. Tears pricked at my eyes, and I blinked quickly. I didn't want Diya to see and make fun of me.

"If she won't jump in, we get to throw her in, right?" Pete asked. He stopped kicking his soccer ball, suddenly looking interested.

"You what?" I whispered faintly.

"Well, *technically*," Uncle Dennis said, looking uncomfortable. "But we didn't really do that very often, right?"

"It is in the bylaws," Diya agreed. "What are you waiting for?"

Everyone on the dock had turned to look at me, which

was making everything worse. It was all just too much. I was only seconds away from crying, and there was a real possibility I was about to be thrown in a lake.

So I did the only thing I could think to do.

I ran.

CHAPTER 6

I ran through the woods, as fast as I could go.

Even as I crashed over leaves and snapped twigs under my feet, I knew running was the wrong decision. It wasn't practical, it wasn't logical, and it wouldn't help anything. But there also didn't seem to be anything else to do at the moment—everything in me was yelling *go go go*.

I hadn't intended to go into the woods necessarily—I didn't have anything close to resembling a *plan*. I was just running, passing cabins and what looked like a barn and a boathouse, then turning when the path curved. I suddenly found myself *in* the woods, not just next to them.

That probably would have been the moment to stop and gather my wits and turn around. But I didn't do that. I just ran farther in, like if I kept going, I could get away from the stress and disappointment and fear back on the dock. There was a faint path, but it was getting harder and harder to make it out. Finally, when the path seemed to disappear entirely, I stopped and braced myself against a nearby tree, trying to get my breath back.

I had a stitch in my side and scratches on my arms and ankles, and my hair was tangled where leaves had caught in it. I could hear the sounds of birds and the faint buzz of insects. It was a lot darker in the woods, and colder, too.

And as I looked around, totally unable to see the path anymore, I realized that I was lost.

I couldn't pull up a map—I had left my bag, with my phone in it, back by the dock.

I sat down on the fallen tree trunk and looked around. Maybe I'd just live here all summer? It seemed nice enough. Nobody was holding reptile funerals or threatening to throw me into a lake, so it was already better than the dock.

But after a few moments, I sighed and stood up again. I knew I was going to have to go back eventually, so I might as well start now. Before a search party was sent out to get me or something. And plus . . . didn't wild animals live in the woods? Like . . . *bears*?

I was just about to start walking when I heard a twig *snap*. I froze and looked around. My heart was hammering. Now that I'd thought about bears, it was all I could think about, and all I wanted was to get out of the woods.

I turned in a full circle, trying to retrace my steps. I started to go in one direction—then decided that didn't look right and went the opposite way. Why did woods look so much the same? Why weren't there more landmarks or something? I wondered if this was why fairy-tale characters were always getting lost and encountering cannibal witches and big bad wolves.

After a few minutes of walking—with nothing looking familiar—I realized that I was heading the wrong direction.

I sighed, turned around—and immediately tripped over a tree root. I went flying and hit the ground hard, landing on my arm. I lay on my back, dazed for a moment. "Ow," I muttered as I clutched my elbow. I sat up—I'd scraped my knee, too, as well as my other wrist. It was official. Today was the worst day ever.

"Are you okay?" a voice behind me said.

I pushed myself to my feet and spun around.

There was a boy standing in front of me—he looked around my age. He was wearing swim trunks with stripes and a Yankees T-shirt. He had dark red hair and blue eyes, and he looked surprised to see me.

"I'm fine," I said quickly.

"You said 'ow.' I heard you."

"I fell," I explained, nodding toward the tree branch. "Watch out for that guy."

"I will." He smiled. "Are you . . . I mean, what are you doing here?"

"I'm kind of lost, actually," I explained. "I'm looking for my way back to Camp Van Camp?"

His eyebrows flew up. "Really?"

"I'm staying there. With my grandparents. And my . . . cousins."

"Oh! You must be the cousin from California."

I nodded, even though I wondered what that meant. What had they said about me? It was weird that I only just found out I had cousins, like, twenty minutes ago, but random kids in the woods knew about me. "I'm Ryanna Stuart."

"Nice to meet you. I'm Holden Andersen."

"So I guess you must be friends with them, huh? All the Van Camps?"

A guarded look crossed over Holden's face. "Well . . . kind of? We used to be . . ." His voice trailed off. "It's kind of a long story."

I nodded, like I understood this, even though all I wanted to do was ask more questions.

"So want me to help you get back?"

I hesitated for just a moment before I nodded. Because even though I wasn't thrilled about what I'd be returning to, I *did* have to get back. And this was my best option for getting there. "Thank you—that would be great." He pointed in the opposite direction of the way I'd been walking. I breathed out a sigh of relief that I wouldn't be wandering these woods when it was getting dark, about to be a bear snack.

"So you must live around here too, huh?" I asked as the path narrowed and I fell into step behind Holden. The name on the back of his Yankees shirt read ROMANOFF.

"I live across the lake."

"Oh, that modern house?"

Holden made a face. "Yeah. It didn't used to be like that. It used to be more like a cabin, and it was way better. But my dad tore it down. The new house only got finished this spring. I miss the old place."

We walked in silence for a few minutes, Holden always pointing out the turns in the path we would take. The more we walked, the clearer it got that I never would have found my way out on my own.

"So what were you doing in here by yourself?" he asked as we both ducked at the same time to avoid a low branch.

"Am I not allowed to be in the woods? *You're* here by yourself."

"Fair point. It just seemed like . . . maybe there was something else going on."

"Well," I started. For whatever reason, it felt like I could trust him, even though we'd literally just met. "They wanted to throw me in the lake! I'd just gotten here, and they told me I had to jump in or they'd throw me in."

I expected him to be horrified, tell me how awful that was, give me some sympathy, but Holden just nodded. "It *is* tradition."

"Well, someone could have mentioned it. And then I would at least have worn a bathing suit!"

"So what are you going to do?"

I just looked at Holden. "About what?"

"Jumping in the lake. Are you going to do it?"

"Do you really think they'll make me?" I had been hoping that by the time I returned, the lake-throwing moment would have passed.

"I don't think it's about *making* you," he said. "It's that, according to them, the summer doesn't start until you've jumped in the lake. I guess it's like—do you want to join in? Or not?"

"I just . . ." I could feel the frustration building in my chest. "Nobody told me that I have all these cousins, and all these aunts and uncles. And I thought the summer was going to be something else. And now I'm thinking maybe it was all just a huge mistake."

I heard a theatrical *gasp* from behind us. I turned around and felt my heart plunge.

Standing in a row were Diya, Max, and Hattie. And it was clear from all their expressions that they'd just heard every word I said.

I heard a twig break and turned to see Holden running back through the woods—I could see just a flash of his Yankees shirt, and then he was gone.

"Thanks a lot," Hattie said. She looked mad, and I had a feeling she had been the gasper. "That's the thanks we get for coming to find you—"

"Was that Holden?" Diya interrupted, looking to where he'd disappeared to.

"Um, yeah," I said, not sure why he'd suddenly left without even saying goodbye.

"You saw him? You talked to him?" Max asked, his eyes wide.

"Yeah." I was starting to get scared. What if they were about to tell me that a kid named Holden died twenty years ago and I'd just been talking to a ghost? "Why?"

My cousins all looked at one another, and it was like they were having a silent conversation that I wasn't a part of. Finally, Diya just shook her head and started walking.

"This way," she said. Max and Hattie fell into line behind her. "Let's go."

We walked in silence for a while until I couldn't stand it anymore. "Look, I'm sorry if you're mad about what you heard me say. But—"

"We're not mad about that," Diya snapped.

"We're not?" Max frowned. "I kind of am."

"No, I mean we *are*. But we can be mad about more than one thing at once."

"I sure can," Hattie piped up. "I have a list of all the things I'm currently mad about. Want to see it?"

"No," Diya and Max said at the same time.

"Your loss," Hattie said with a shrug.

"How is it our loss?" Max asked.

"Maybe you're on it." Hattie raised an eyebrow. "And now you'll never know."

We stepped out of the woods, and it was suddenly brighter and warmer out, even though I could see the shadows starting to lengthen.

"Want to know about Holden?" Max asked. I nodded. I expected him to explain, but instead he started walking and gestured for me to follow. I hurried behind him, and Hattie and Diya followed behind me as he walked to the end of the dock. "So," he said. He pointed to Holden's house. "We all used to be really good friends with Holden. He'd been coming here his whole life, same as us. Gramps and his grandfather were best friends."

"It's so sad," Hattie said, shaking her head. "It's a tragesty."

"That's not a word," Diya pointed out.

"It is. It's 'tragedy' and 'travesty' combined."

"You can't just combine two words and call it a word."

"Um, I think I just did?"

"But *anyway*." Max raised his voice, talking over Diya and Hattie. "After Holden's grandfather died five years ago, Holden's dad sued Gramps, and they've been in court ever since."

"Holden's dad is the *worst*," Hattie said.

"Basically, Holden's dad is claiming that he owns our land too. He wants to build condos on all of it." She shook her head, sounding disgusted.

"They're still fighting over ours," Max continued. "But this spring Holden's dad got permission to build condos on his land."

"Right across from us," Hattie huffed, glaring across the water. "So awful."

"Okay." I wondered if there was something I was missing. "But what does this have to do with Holden?"

"Because," Diya said, "ever since that happened, Holden apparently decided he doesn't want to be our friend anymore. He hasn't spoken to us since. Not a single word." She frowned at me. Her eyes were stormy. "But apparently, he's more than willing to talk to *you*."

She turned and stalked away, and Hattie and Max followed—leaving me alone on the dock with a head full of questions.

CHAPTER 7

I stood alone at the end of the dock, wondering what happened now. There were no instructions, and nobody around to tell me what to do. It seemed like I wasn't going to be thrown into the lake, which was a good thing—but it also meant that I didn't know where to go now, or what the plan was.

My bag was still at the end of the dock, and as I crossed to get it, I fought down a panicky feeling. This was why I'd always preferred life on set—there was a *structure*. There was always someone to ask. Everyone had a place they were supposed to be, with spelled-out rules.

I hoisted my bag over my shoulder. I figured I'd go up and get my trunk where I'd left it and then . . . I wasn't sure what came after that, which only increased my panic. But it seemed like a good place to start, at any rate. Maybe when I got there, I could find someone who could tell me what I was supposed to be doing right now (as long as that wasn't jumping fully clothed into a lake).

I walked up the path, past the cabins. There was an olive-green one that had INFIRMARY painted on the door in white. I was sure this was unused—a relic from when this had been an actual camp—but then as I passed it, I could have sworn I heard, from inside, a voice that sounded British.

I walked until I reached the lodge, and its wraparound porch with Adirondack chairs on it, spaced out in imprecise intervals.

I looked where Kendra had left my trunk—but it wasn't there. Had someone put it in whatever room I'd be staying in? But if so, why hadn't anyone told me where that was? Where were the so-called adults? Why wasn't anyone making sure I was okay?

I was about to call my dad and see if he could help when I heard a screech of tires, and a second later an old, dented Volvo sputtered down the driveway, crunching over the gravel. It parked haphazardly, and then a woman got out. She slammed the door and kicked the front tire. Then she howled in pain and jumped up and down, clutching her foot. "Ratsfratza!" she yelled. "Rutabaga! Fudge! Double fudge. Ducking double fudge . . ."

The woman stopped fake-swearing and stood up, out of breath. She was wearing black pants, a white shirt, and a blazer. She pulled off the blazer, crumpled it into a little ball, threw it on the ground, and stomped on it once. Then she picked it up and looked at it with distaste.

She headed toward the lodge, stopping short when she saw me. She blinked for just a second, then smiled. "You must be Ryanna," she said. "I'm Quinn. I'm your aunt." Then she made a face. "Don't call me Aunt Quinn, though. None of the rest of them do. It would make me feel like I was eighty."

"Oh," I said. "Um, okay. Hi." She looked a lot younger than my other aunts and uncles, like maybe she was only in her twenties, with reddish-blond hair.

"You look so much like Casey used to," she said with a sad smile.

"I do?" I asked, my breath catching in my throat. After all, this was why I had come—not for any of the rest of it. I was here to learn about my mother.

"Yeah," Quinn said, still looking at me. She shook her head after a moment. "Anyway! It's nice to see you again. The last time you were, like, three, so I doubt you remember. Are you all settled in?"

"Well, I . . . kind of don't know where I'm supposed to be? Or what happened to my trunk."

"Huh. Where are the other hooligans?"

"I think they're mad because I wouldn't jump in the

lake with my clothes on." I decided to keep to myself the multiple other reasons my cousins might be mad at me.

"So you're having a bit of a day," Quinn said, giving me a smile. I gave her one back, feeling cautiously confident that *she* wasn't about to throw me into the lake. Between the car-kicking and the blazer-stomping, she seemed to have her own stuff going on. "How about I show you around? And we'll find your trunk."

I nodded, immensely relieved that I wouldn't have to try to sort this out on my own.

She nodded toward the lodge. "Let's start here."

Quinn pulled open the screen door, and we stepped into the room. It was huge and airy, the ceilings high and peaked, with wooden beams crisscrossing them. Hanging from the beams were flags and pennants. There were also painted oars tacked up all over, and I barely knew where to look as I tried to take it all in.

Faded woven rugs covered the wood floor. On one side there were two long wooden tables with benches, and on the other side was a huge stone fireplace. In front of the fireplace were three squashy-looking couches and the biggest coffee table I had ever seen, currently covered with books and a half-finished jigsaw puzzle.

"So this is the main house," Quinn explained, taking a step inside. She pointed to the two long tables. "This all used to be the mess hall, but when it stopped being a camp, we no longer needed seating for two hundred and added the couches. Mom and Dad—your grams and gramps—sleep upstairs, but everyone else is in their cabins. The kitchen is in here, and the nice bathtub, and the den. But nobody really hangs out in the den unless it's raining."

"Ah," I said, trying to act like any of this was making sense to me.

"We eat in here," she said, gesturing to the tables. This half of the room really did still look like a mess hall in a camp movie. I half expected to see British and American identical twins up to no good, or a food fight breaking out.

"Breakfast is serve yourself, and so is lunch," Quinn explained. "Except on Sunday, when Gramps does eggs and waffles. Dinner is always at seven, and we all take turns cooking it."

"We . . . do?" I'd never cooked anything more complicated than microwave popcorn, and sometimes I even managed to burn that.

"The adults," she assured me. "But we're always happy to get help."

I nodded, relieved. I could see that there was a giant chalkboard leaning against the wall by the tables. CAMP VAN CAMP was printed across the top of it, with DAILY ACTIVITIES! under that—but it was currently blank.

"Want to see the kitchen?"

"Sure," I said, and she led me through the swinging doors at one end of the mess hall. We stepped into what seemed like more of a kitchen you'd see in a restaurant than in a house. It was huge, with long silver prep tables, a massive dishwasher, and multiple refrigerators. It was one more reminder that this really had been a camp at some point, set up to handle hundreds of people.

In the middle of it, chopping vegetables and looking irritated, was my uncle with the beard, the one who was Hattie's dad.

"Hey, Benji," Quinn said, stepping closer. "We're giving Ryanna a tour."

"I would have given a tour!" I looked around to see where the voice had come from, and then I realized that it was Hattie, sitting on one of the countertops. "I didn't know that was happening."

I was relieved to hear Hattie say that. It seemed like she was my best chance at getting along with a cousin.

"Well, you're welcome to help," Quinn said.

"I thought you were going to help *me*," Uncle Benji said. He sounded stressed—there were two open cookbooks in front of him, and assorted pots and pans strewn about.

Hattie glanced over at her father, and her eyes widened. "Um, no thank you."

"Come on, Hats."

"I'm still mourning!" she said, shaking her red curls. "I'm in *grief*! I can't be expected to cook dinner."

"Uh—right," Uncle Benji said. "Sorry, honey. How was the interview?" he asked Quinn as he started chopping again.

"Ugh," she said, making a face. "Don't ask."

I wondered if the interview was the reason for the car-kicking and blazer-stomping, but since Quinn said not to ask, I wasn't sure that I should inquire.

Quinn looked at Uncle Benji, who had started muttering to himself, and took a step back toward the door. "Well, we'll leave you to it."

"Someone help me chop!" he called plaintively as we all stepped out of the kitchen, the door swinging shut on his stricken face.

A moment later, Hattie joined us. "Where to?"

Quinn thought for a moment, then pointed. "The cabins."

We walked down the path together. "That's the infirmary," Hattie pointed out.

"You can still go in and grab, like, a Band-Aid or an aspirin," Quinn explained. "But there's not a nurse in there anymore."

"Plus, Archie lives in there now," Hattie added.

"Who?" I asked. My head was swimming. There were still more Van Camps I hadn't met yet?

"He's not related to us," Hattie assured me. "He's just working with Uncle Neal for the summer."

"Who, Archie?" I looked over and saw Uncle Byron wandering up. He had a towel slung over his shoulders, and he adjusted his black-framed glasses. "Yeah, we've kind of adopted him. Neal's working on a research project all summer, and Archie is his intern." Uncle Byron turned to Quinn. "Hey, how was the interview?"

"Ugh," Quinn said. She shook her head. "No bueno." She held out the blazer to him. "Thanks for this."

Uncle Byron took it and frowned. "Why is it all dirty?"

"I *might* have had to step on it in frustration. But I'll pay for the dry cleaning."

"So! Like we said, this is the infirmary," Hattie said, maybe sensing that this would be a great time to change the subject.

"If you need a Band-Aid or something, just make sure to knock first," Quinn said. "Archie's been kind of grumpy lately."

"I don't think he's happy about being here," Hattie said.

"Why do you say that?" Byron asked.

"Because the last time we went into town, he said, 'Hattie, I'm not happy about being here.'"

"Excuse me!" The infirmary door banged open, and a guy who seemed college-aged stepped out. He looked South Asian and had a crisp British accent. "I can hear you, you know."

"Hi, Archie," Hattie said, waving cheerfully.

"Forgive me if I didn't realize accepting this internship would mean being stuck in the middle of nowhere all summer."

"You could have googled," Hattie suggested.

Maybe getting advice from a nine-year-old was too much for him, because Archie turned around and stomped back into the infirmary cabin. A second later, though, he stuck his head out again.

"Sorry, that was rude. You must be Ryanna. I'm Archie. I'm a huge fan of your dad's movies." He gave me a weak smile, glowered at everyone else, then retreated to his cabin and slammed the door again. But since it was a screen door, it just bounced open a few more times.

"Movies?" Hattie asked. She'd gone very still, and her eyes had gotten huge. "Your *dad's movies*?"

"Um, yeah he's a screenwriter—"

"What!" she screamed. Quinn and Uncle Byron both winced. Hattie turned to them, pointing an accusing finger. "And nobody *told ME*?"

"Hattie wants to be an actress," Quinn explained.

"I *am* an actress," she declared. "I'm just waiting for the world to recognize my talent." She tossed her hair over her shoulder and stalked off back toward the lodge.

"Well, I'm going for a swim," Uncle Byron said. He shook his head as he looked at the wrinkled blazer in his hand and headed down toward the lake.

Quinn turned to me. "Ryanna, it's always a good idea to respect other people's clothes. Or if that's impossible, get them dry-cleaned first."

"Right," I said with a nod. "Um, what interview is everyone talking about?" It was starting to feel weird that other people kept asking Quinn about it and I was totally in the dark.

Quinn sighed. "I'm a journalist," she said. "Well— trying to be. I got my master's this past spring but haven't been able to get a job anywhere, or even anything published. And I was interviewing with a paper today, but as soon as they heard I'd never broken a big story, it was basically over."

"Oh. I'm sorry." I didn't know much about journalism, except that my dad was always complaining about being misquoted whenever reporters from *The Hollywood Edit* called him.

"Something will turn up. Just have to keep plugging away. What do you want to see next?"

What I really wanted was to see where I'd be staying, close the door, have some peace and quiet, and maybe read one of my Miss Terry books. "Is there . . . I mean, can I see my room?"

"Sure," Quinn said. She gave me a smile that let me know she maybe understood what I was feeling. "All the kids' cabins are on this side." She pointed to the other side of the lodge. "Adult cabins are over there, so everyone can have their space."

I followed her down the path until she stopped at a large white-painted cabin. It had three steps up to it, with two chairs outside the door. There was a flashlight next to the door, and a hand-painted sign that read HUMMINGBIRD CABIN.

"This is yours," she said. Quinn pushed open the door, and I followed her inside, blinking a few times to let my eyes adjust to the dimmer light. The first thing I noticed was my trunk with *R. S.* painted on the lid, waiting for me just inside the door.

The second thing I noticed was that we weren't alone in the cabin.

There were two sets of bunk beds, one against each wall. Diya was sprawled out on the top bunk of one, reading a graphic novel.

"Welcome to the girls' cabin," Quinn said, smiling at me.

"The . . . girls' cabin?" I echoed. My stomach plunged as I looked at Diya, who lowered her book, not looking thrilled to see me. "Like . . . the two of us stay here together?"

"Three," Quinn said. She pointed to the unoccupied top bunk. "Hattie's in here too."

I nodded, fighting the feeling that I was about to start crying. I wasn't even going to get my own room? I was going to have to be in here with two other people, neither of whom liked me very much?

At least it wasn't tiny—there was a high ceiling with a Camp Van Camp flag tacked up to it, and on either side of each bunk bed was a dresser. But it was still going to be three of us in here? I'd never even had to share a room with one person, let alone *two*.

"I just didn't realize," I said, glancing at Quinn and lowering my voice, "that I would be sharing a room. I mean, cabin. I have my own room at home."

"We all do," Diya said, raising an eyebrow at me. "But that's why it's fun—we all get to be together in the summers."

I opened my mouth to reply but then closed it when I realized I didn't know what to say. Could I opt out of this? Pretend I snored or something?

"Anyway," Quinn said after the silence in the cabin had gotten uncomfortable, "I'll leave you ladies here to get acquainted. Dinner at seven." She started for the door, then turned back and smiled at me. "And don't forget what I told you about respecting other people's clothes."

Diya's eyes widened, and she whipped around to stare at me. "You told her?"

Quinn frowned. "Told me what?"

"About the Slurpee that spilled on your sweatshirt."

"Icee—" I started, but Quinn was already talking over me.

"What sweatshirt? My *white* sweatshirt?"

"I didn't tell her," I said, holding my hands up.

"Well, I clearly know *now*." Quinn pointed at Diya. "We'll talk about it later, kid."

And then she left the cabin.

I was still standing in the middle of the room, not sure what I was supposed to do. I crossed to the door and picked up my trunk, like maybe it would have some instructions on it.

"You'll have to take the bottom bunk," Diya said, her words clipped. She pointed to the one across from her. "That's Hattie's."

I looked up and realized I should have been able to tell—a slightly shaky NYC skyline had been painted, along with comedy and tragedy masks. Pictures of kid actors were taped all over. Some I recognized—including the girl who'd been in the most recent Ghost Robot movie—but there were also some that looked older, in black and white, and one girl who looked a little familiar, with tight curls and dimples.

"Talking about me?" Hattie asked as she banged the door open and stalked into the room, her cheeks still flushed.

"I was just telling Ryanna she couldn't take your bed."

"Did she try to?"

"No," I said quickly. "I just didn't know where I should go, that's all."

"Well—both the bottom bunks are empty," Hattie said. She pointed to the one underneath Diya. "But you might want to take that one." She looked at the other bottom bunk with a sigh. "That was Karma's bed."

"Okay, that one is great," I said. I really didn't want to sleep in a bed where a lizard had most likely died.

"That's your dresser," Hattie said, pointing to a small white dresser on the left side of the bunk bed. It was covered in stickers and scratches, like it had been used at camp for years and years. "And the closet is there. And—"

"I don't think," Diya interrupted from the top bunk, "that we should just be pretending that everything is fine."

Hattie frowned. "I'm not pretending anything. But even if I wasn't, you wouldn't be able to tell, because I'm such a good actress." She gave me a bright smile. "Maybe you could mention it to your dad?"

"She didn't jump in the lake! So technically her summer hasn't started yet. And I don't think we should just gloss over that."

My heart sank. Everyone glossing over that was what I'd been banking on.

"Until Ryanna jumps in the lake wearing her first-day clothes, she's not one of us. She's just a *tourist*." And with that, Diya rolled over to face the wall, ending the conversation.

Hattie shifted her weight from foot to foot, then walked back across the room to her bunk and climbed up it.

I crossed with my trunk over to what I now knew was my bunk and unlatched the trunk, the sound incredibly loud in the silent cabin.

I stood there in silence, surrounded by my cousins who were mad at me, and wondered how I was ever going to get through the summer.

CHAPTER 8

Halfway through dinner I started to formulate my escape plan.

Because it was all just way too overwhelming.

The conversation around the table was flying fast and furious. We were eating pizza—apparently Uncle Benji's cooking hadn't worked out. But there were so many people, there were *eight* pies in the middle of the table, and it looked like that might not even be enough. Dinner at our house was three people and a cat, and a dinner with twelve other people was something else entirely. I was surrounded on all sides by Van Camps talking and yelling and laughing—trying to keep up and keep everyone straight.

I glanced over and saw my cousins all leaning together and laughing about something. My face burned. They were probably laughing about *me*. Diya was probably getting them all to agree that since I hadn't jumped in the lake, I'd never be a part of their group. They were probably wishing I'd never come.

I was starting to wish that too, as I pushed my crusts aside. This was *so* not what I had expected. Diya clearly didn't want me here. Everyone was a part of this family, and I was not. I'd missed all the stories and all the history. I'd never fit in.

And so, I decided, as Uncle Benji cleared our pizza plates and Hattie jumped up to help him, I wouldn't even try.

I was going to leave.

The second I started forming this plan, I felt better. A plan meant that I had something to focus on. A plan meant going forward and fixing the problem.

And that was before I even saw the bathrooms. There were normal bathrooms inside the main lodge. But when we walked back to the Hummingbird Cabin after dinner, Hattie pointed out a small wooden building I hadn't paid any attention to, thinking it was just another cabin.

But no. *This* was the bathroom. There was no bathroom inside our cabin. To go to the bathroom—or take a shower, or brush my teeth—I'd have to walk outside to get to this. Luckily, all the showers had stalls, and there was one long row of sinks in front of a mirror that was covered with names and drawings scratched into it. "What if you have to go to the bathroom at night?" I asked Hattie.

"What do you mean?"

"Like, you have to walk outside? In the dark?"

"Um, yeah. There's always a flashlight by the door of the cabins. So you can use that."

I nodded as we walked back, but all this did was let me know I was doing the right thing. I was *not* going to stay here.

But for my plan to work, I would have to pretend that I was. I didn't want anyone to try to talk me out of it, or tell me I couldn't go. So I was just going to split, leave a note behind, and deal with any consequences later. Ask forgiveness, not permission, like Terry learned in *The Asphalt Jungle Gym*.

I brushed my teeth and got ready for bed along with Hattie and Diya—I couldn't see a way to take my toothbrush with me without being suspicious, so I just left it in the bathroom with a silent farewell. I changed into my pajamas—but put my clothes right back in my trunk, which I'd placed at the foot of my bed, and hoped nobody noticed that I hadn't unpacked at all.

Nobody seemed to—Diya and Hattie were too caught up in an argument about a white-noise machine to pay attention to me.

We got a "Lights-out!" knock on the door from Aunt Katie, and Diya reached over and hit the switch with her foot, plunging us into darkness. A second later, Hattie turned the lights back on while she got some socks out. But then she snapped the lights off again, and then it was dark and quiet.

I lay there, awake, waiting and listening. There was a part of me that felt just how easy it would have been to sink down into the pillow, with its faded blue-and-white striped pillowcase, go to sleep, and just forget the plan.

But then I forced my eyes to open. As soon as I was fairly certain everyone around me was sleeping, I eased slowly out of bed, waiting at every moment for Diya or Hattie to sit straight up and demand to know what I was doing.

When I was sure that nobody was waking up, I grabbed my trunk and crept slowly over the wooden floors. The door squeaked on its springs when I pushed it open, but nobody in Hummingbird Cabin stirred.

I stepped out and slowly pulled it shut behind me. I took out my phone. I would call my dad and either have him come get me or send a car. I'd be gone as soon as I could. But the call didn't go through—I had no service.

I stared down at my phone, tapping once on the screen, but nothing changed. This had *not* been part of the plan. I looked and saw that the trees opened up by the driveway—so probably going up to the lodge was my best shot at getting a signal.

The lodge porch lights were still on, but it didn't look like any of the inside lights were on. And even if Gramps was still awake, I doubted he'd be able to hear me outside.

I struggled up toward the lodge with my canvas bag and my trunk, holding my breath as I passed cabins along the way, just hoping that nobody would jump out and demand to know what I was doing. I used my phone's flashlight to show me the way, because it was *dark* out, in a way it never really seemed to get in LA.

When I reached the steps, I stopped and dropped my trunk with a groan. It was cute—I agreed with Ginger on that—but I couldn't help thinking that a regular suitcase would have been a lot easier to maneuver.

I paused for just a moment—waiting to see if I'd woken anyone up—but all was quiet. I turned the flashlight off on my phone and started to dial my dad's cell phone number.

"Going somewhere?"

I jumped and turned around. There was a woman sitting on the porch—one I hadn't noticed before because she was just out of the light. She was wearing jeans and a plaid shirt with a vest over it. Her hair was white and cropped short, and she looked . . . familiar somehow.

"Oh," I said, looking at my phone. "Um . . ."

"Don't let me stop you," the woman said as she got up out of the Adirondack chair she'd been sitting on—in the dark, apparently—and walked down the porch steps to join me. She gestured to my bags. "It just looks like you're leaving us."

"Well," I started. Then I realized I had no way to spin this. "Kind of?"

"We should at least meet officially before you do that," she said. She took a step forward, and I could see that her skin was very tan, and very lined, like she'd lived most of her life in the sun. Her eyes, though, were bright blue. "I'm your grandmother. You can call me Grams. And you must be Ryanna."

"Hi," I said, realizing that *of course* this was my grandmother. Who else would it have been? But something about this woman kind of made her seem like a cowboy drifter who'd wandered in from an Old West town. A word from one of my dad's scripts came into my mind—*flinty*. Serious and short, she seemed the opposite of Gramps, who'd been tall and twinkly.

"You look *so* much like my Casey did."

"I do?"

She looked at me a moment longer. "The hair's a different color. But other than that . . ." She gave me a quick smile, then shook her head. "So!" She sat down on the top porch step and patted the space next to her. "Want to tell me why you were sneaking out under cover of night?"

I sat down next to her and sighed. "It just . . . wasn't what I thought it was going to be. I didn't even know I had a million cousins—"

"Four."

"And I had thought it was just going to be me and Gramps and . . . well, you. And they said they were going to throw me in the lake if I didn't jump in, and . . ." Now that I was saying them out loud, my reasons were no longer sounding so compelling. "But anyway, I just don't think it's a good fit. So it's probably better if I go."

"Better for whom?"

"Well . . ."

"Because I worry if you leave now, your cousins and aunts and uncles might be missing out on a chance to get to know you. And me and your gramps, too. But more than that . . . I worry that *you'll* be missing out. And teaching yourself that you can always run when things get hard."

"I'm not leaving because it's hard," I said, but my voice trailed off at the end. Wasn't that actually what I was doing? "I just . . ."

"I know we can be a lot. I should have been here to help ease you in. But when there's a white-winged tern sighting, I lose all sense."

"There was a Viking chameleon funeral."

She threw back her head and laughed. "Well . . . like I

said, we can be a lot. But . . ." She leaned a little closer, like she was sharing a secret. "If you can get past that, we're also a lot of fun. I promise."

"I don't know. . . ." The thought of having to get into another car and drive for three hours wasn't sounding so appealing. But going back to my bed with its soft sheets really was.

"Tell you what," Grams said, slapping her hands down on her knees. "Why don't you sleep on it? This valley's all fogged in right now anyway—that's why it took me so long to get home. It would take a car ages to get here. And then if you feel the same way in the morning, we can figure it out."

I thought about it. I could just go back to the cabin and go to sleep and figure this all out in the morning. And plus . . . if I left, I wouldn't ever know just what had been so bad about PocoMart.

I yawned, suddenly tired, and covered my mouth with my hand. "Okay," I said around the yawn. With every passing moment I was getting more and more sleepy. But in my defense, it's hard to be super awake when you're wearing your pj's.

Grams smiled at me and gave me a short nod. "Good. And since you are staying—at least for the moment—I can give you this." She stood up, walked back toward the chair she'd been sitting in, and reached for the backpack stowed next to it. She rummaged around in it, pulled out a slightly battered paperback book, and handed it to me.

It looked older—the cover was illustrated, like a painting, showing a girl peeking around the corner of a cabin with broken windows and a KEEP OUT sign. *Cara Vanessa Cole and the Mystery of the Haunted Cabin*, the title read.

"Oh," I said, looking up at Grams. She smiled at me like I was supposed to know what this meant. "Thank you?"

"You're welcome," she said with a nod. "Now get to bed, and I'll see you in the morning."

"Okay," I said. I tucked the book under my arm and turned on the flashlight on my phone, hauling my trunk back down toward the cabin. I looked up at the lodge halfway through, expecting that my grandmother would have gone back inside, but she was still standing by the porch light, watching, like she was making sure I made it back to my cabin okay.

When I made it to the cabin porch, I dropped the trunk and looked at the book again, using my phone's flashlight. Had my dad told her that I liked mysteries? And that was why she'd given it to me? It seemed kind of random.

I opened the book and felt my breath catch in my throat.

Someone had written on the inside cover, with curly cursive handwriting, in faded green ink.

This book is the property of Casey Vivian Van Camp, 12 years old.

. . .

The morning light streamed in through the windows of Hummingbird Cabin, and I stretched and turned another page. I'd been worried that I would sleep later than everyone else in the morning—I was still on California time, after all—but when I woke up, Hattie and Diya were still asleep.

I'd immediately picked up the book. I'd started reading it last night, standing outside the cabin using the flashlight, until I got too cold. I'd never heard of this series before, but I was already a huge fan. It was a mystery all about a summer camp in New Jersey, and a teenage detective, Cara Vanessa Cole. As soon as she gets there, she immediately starts hearing rumors about a haunted cabin. But as she investigates the mystery, she finds that the rumors are all being manufactured by the suspicious camp director. I had no idea why, but I was dying to find out.

> Cara looked around the cabin and let out a breath she didn't know she'd been holding. After all that she'd been primed to see here—all the rumors and stories and mysteries around this cabin—she'd been expecting something different. Ghostly footprints across the floor. A cracked mirror, oozing blood. Skeletal hands dripping with lake water reaching out for her at every turn. But the cabin was surprisingly neat and well swept for one that

had supposedly been empty for thirty years. There were stacks of plastic file folders and what looked like bottles of chemicals in the corners.

What was going on here?

Cara looked around, her mystery sense starting to tingle. Something was very wrong . . . but it wasn't a ghost.

It was just that someone wanted people to *think* there was a ghost.

But why?

Knowing that her time was limited, she hurried around the cabin, opening the dresser drawers. They were empty—but taped to the top of the bottom drawer was a document. She unfolded it and her eyes widened. "Bingo," she breathed.

I stared at the page in front of me. My mother had drawn an arrow at the top, then straight down the margin to the bottom, like she was pointing at the whole page. In the margin was written—in the same handwriting as was on the inside cover—*TRY THIS*. What did *that* mean?

I turned back to the inside cover and ran my fingers over the writing there.

My mother's handwriting. This had been *her* book— when she was around my age. She'd cracked the spine and had dog-eared page nineteen and written *this* for whatever reason on page thirty-nine. She loved mysteries, just like me!

I reached into my bag on the floor near my bottom bunk and carefully pulled out the picture of my mother. I realized now that I knew where this picture had been taken—by the picnic table next to the dock. I looked at her bright smile, the two fingers she was holding up, her locked pink-and-purple tackle box. She'd been here. Maybe at one point she'd even stayed in this very cabin.

I closed the cover and looked around the cabin. Hattie was sleeping on her back, one arm thrown over her eyes, covers kicked half off. I couldn't see much of Diya in the bunk above me, but I could hear her steady breathing and see the fingertips of the arm that was dangling over the side of the bed.

I just lay there in bed, in the quiet, for a moment, and then I came to a decision.

I was going to stay.

Seeing my mother's name in the book had been enough to remind me of why I'd wanted to come here in the first place. I wanted more than just a book and a picture. I wanted to know all the stories, everything I could about her. I at least had to give it a try. An *actual* try.

And if I was going to stay . . . it meant that I had to do my best to be a part of things.

All at once, I knew what I had to do.

I carefully tucked the book with my mother's picture in it under my pillow and climbed out of bed. I grabbed what I needed from my trunk and got dressed as quietly as possible in the closet. For a second I was tempted to put on my bathing suit, but I knew deep down that would be cheating. So I just put on everything I'd worn yesterday, down to the same socks and sneakers.

When I stepped out of the closet, I saw that Diya was awake. She was wearing a pair of glasses and sitting up in bed, yawning.

"Hi," I said before I could lose my nerve. "So . . . I'm going to go to the dock now."

She rubbed her eyes behind her glasses—then they widened as she took in what I was wearing. "Really?"

"Uh-huh."

"Interesting." She looked at me a moment longer, then grabbed her pillow and flung it across the cabin, where it hit Hattie on the head.

"Ow!" Hattie protested, sitting up and flinging it back at her. "I'll have you know I was having a great dream. I was on set, playing myself in the biopic of my life, and—"

"Look at what Ryanna is wearing."

Hattie blinked at me and gave me a hopeful smile. "Does that mean . . . ?" she said, then paused. "What if she only has one outfit?" she asked Diya in a loud whisper.

"I have more than one outfit," I assured her. "I'm just trying to follow the rules."

"About time," Diya said, but she didn't sound mad about it—it was almost like she was impressed against her will.

"So," I said. I took a step toward the door. "I guess I'll be right back?"

"No way," Diya said. She climbed down the bunk bed ladder in two big steps. "We need witnesses."

Witnesses apparently meant Pete and Max, because five minutes later, they joined me and my girl cousins on the dock. Everyone was wearing their pajamas except Max, who was already dressed and looked much more awake than the rest of us.

"I was sleeping," Pete said around a huge yawn.

"You can go back to bed when we're done," Diya told her brother.

"Want me to sing the song?" Hattie asked eagerly.

"No," everyone else on the dock said.

"I'm okay," I assured her. "I think I remember it from yesterday." I turned to face the lake.

The water was totally still, and there was early-morning mist coming off it. I looked across to what I now knew was Holden's house. For just a second I hoped that he was awake early and looking at the lake for some reason. I wanted him to know I had taken his advice.

I looked back down at the water and tried not to think about how cold it was going to be and how much I hated getting wet with my clothes on. I'd come this far, after all. I just had to do it.

And before I could talk myself out of it, I took a running leap and jumped off the end of the dock.

I closed my eyes as I plunged into the lake. I surfaced a moment later. It wasn't quite as cold as I'd been afraid it would be, and it was deep—my feet weren't even close to hitting bottom.

I looked at the dock and saw all my cousins—even Pete, even Diya!—clapping for me. I started to swim back toward the ladder on the side of the dock just as Hattie went running, launching herself off the end of the dock in a spectacular cannonball. She surfaced next to me and grinned. "Nicely done."

I smiled back at her. "You too."

Max came next, holding his nose as he jumped into the water. Diya pushed Pete in, then followed after him.

I treaded water, not caring anymore that I was swimming with all my clothes on. My cousins all surfaced around me, and Diya gave me an approving nod.

"Now," she said, her voice definitive, "your summer can officially begin."

PART TWO
THE MAP

CHAPTER 9

S o what now?" I asked as we all trooped up to the lodge in search of food. After we'd gotten our fill of swimming, Pete had headed back to his cabin, and we'd flopped onto the dock to dry until we realized we were hungry.

"What do you mean?" Max asked.

"I mean, what's the plan?" Now that I'd decided I was staying, I wanted to make sure I had a sense of what the days would look like here.

Hattie pulled open the lodge door. "I don't understand the question."

"Like . . . what do we *do* all day?"

"Whatever we want," Diya said.

"No, I mean—"

She gave me a pitying smile. "I'll explain over breakfast."

I stepped into the lodge. Breakfast was underway. To

the side of the table on a long counter, food had been set out—boxes of cereal, a bread basket, and what looked like a steel container of oatmeal that I didn't think I would be going near. There was a giant coffeepot along with pitchers of juice and milk, stacks of bowls, silverware, and cups. It reminded me of breakfast buffets I'd seen when we'd stayed at hotels.

Gramps was sitting at one end of the table with a newspaper—the *Pocono Eagle*. Uncle Neal was typing on a laptop with one hand while eating a croissant with the other. Aunt Abby was wearing workout clothes, eating oatmeal, and looking very awake as she did a crossword in pen. This was in contrast to Uncle Dennis, who looked half asleep as he drank coffee next to Uncle Byron, who kept stealing berries off his plate while he typed something on his phone, frowning. Aunt Katie was there, chatting with Uncle Benji as they stood by the toaster at the buffet, but none of the parents seemed bothered that their kids had just come to breakfast in damp pajamas.

"Do they care we went swimming?" I asked in a whisper as I stepped behind Max in the buffet line. "Is it allowed?"

"Here's the thing," he said as he adjusted his glasses, reached for a bowl, and shook some Cinnamon Toast Crunch into it. "Our parents always say that they need a break in the summers too. And that we're old enough to be

trusted to manage our own time and make responsible decisions. So you don't really need to ask for permission—and
the days are ours to do what we want."

"Unless there's a lesson," Hattie said with a shrug.

"A lesson?" I echoed.

"Sometimes the parents decide our brains are turning
to mush, and they try to teach us something. But it doesn't
happen that often. It'll be listed if it does." She pointed at the
blank chalkboard with DAILY ACTIVITIES! printed at the top.

"And you don't *have* to go, but if you do, you get extra
dessert, so most of us do," Max explained.

"We can offer our own, too," Hattie said. "I'm currently
preparing a workshop on accents that I think will be just
smashing."

"Oh, I wish I could come, but I'm busy," said Diya as
her bagel popped out of the biggest toaster I had ever seen.

"You don't even know when it is."

"And yet," Diya said patiently, "somehow, I have a feeling I'm going to be busy."

After a moment of deliberation, I also grabbed a bagel—
plain—and spooned some berries onto my plate. I toasted
the bagel just enough to warm it, then spread some peanut
butter on it. Then I took my plate and a glass of juice and
walked over to the end of the table where my cousins were
sitting.

"Morning," Uncle Byron said, glancing up from his phone. Then he frowned. "Is it raining?"

"No," Max told his father. "We went swimming."

"Maybe wear a bathing suit next time. Just a suggestion."

Grams entered from the other end of the lodge. I saw that across from the big fireplace and squashy couches there was a staircase that led to the second floor—where, I presumed, Grams and Gramps's bedroom was. "Morning, all," she said. She paused by our table for a moment and caught my eye. She raised an eyebrow. "Ryanna? Are you . . . settling in?"

I knew what she was asking. I gave her a smile back. "All settled. After breakfast, I'll get unpacked."

She gave me a tiny wink and then headed straight for the coffee, stopping on the way to kiss Gramps on top of his white hair, which was sticking up in all directions.

I had just taken a bite of my bagel when Archie flung the door open and moped inside. I hadn't realized until then that "moped" could be a way of walking, but it was the only word that fit. He crossed right to the food table and picked up a bagel and a banana. Then he walked to the Daily Activities board and, to my surprise, wrote *3 Cricket* on it. He sighed, then turned and slumped out, letting the door slam behind him, having not said a word to anyone.

"What do we think that means?" Diya asked. "Is Archie telling us that he saw three crickets?"

"Or maybe he wants to play cricket at three?" Uncle Benji asked. He shook his head. "He needs to be more specific."

"He didn't even toast his bagel," Hattie said, eyes wide. "He *really* must be miserable."

"We just need to find him some friends his own age," Aunt Katie said.

"Who, Archie?" Uncle Neal asked as he finished his last bite of croissant. "He's having a blast here."

Hattie coughed, Uncle Byron raised his eyebrows, and Max shook his head gravely.

"He *isn't?*" Uncle Neal sounded shocked. "But Archie can't *leave*. He's the best intern I've ever had." He wiped the crumbs off his hands, then seemed to realize he'd just brushed them into his keyboard. "My laptop!" he cried.

"Why does your dad have an intern?" I asked Diya, just as Pete ambled in carrying his soccer ball.

"Soccer ball outside," Grams said immediately.

"But—" Pete started.

"You smashed two windows the last time you were kicking it around in here." She nodded toward the door. "On the porch."

"Okay." Pete dropped it outside, then headed back in, going straight for the buffet table.

"Our dad has an intern because he's a professor," Diya said. "He teaches history. My mom's a professor too."

"Math," Aunt Abby said. "Who knows a three-letter word for 'drill'? It's also a bird." She looked around at all of us expectantly.

"No idea," Gramps said cheerfully. "Good luck, though."

"Mom?" Aunt Abby turned to Grams, who was sipping her coffee. "I know you know."

"Of course I know," Grams said calmly, taking another sip. "But if I tell you, how will you learn?"

"Mom!"

"We live outside Philly," Diya went on, maybe realizing I needed more background on everyone. She explained that usually Pete was at a soccer camp until August but had decided to give it up this year and be here all summer. Uncle Dennis was a freelance architect, and Uncle Byron worked in advertising. They lived with Max in New Jersey, and Uncle Byron commuted into New York City for work. And Aunt Katie worked for an e-commerce site.

"Do you guys live in New York?" I asked, remembering the skyline painted by Hattie's bed. I looked between Hattie, Aunt Katie, and Uncle Benji.

"No," Aunt Katie said with a shudder. "Benji and I met there, but I was always determined to get out. All those buildings made me feel like I was living in someone's hair."

"Gross," Max said.

"*So* gross," Pete echoed, looking appreciative. He had a bagel in each hand and was alternating bites.

"We live in Maine," Hattie said with a groan. "*Maine!* Hours away from anyplace where I could become a professional actress."

"What do you do?" I asked Uncle Benji.

But rather than answering, everyone either looked away or down at their plates, and I heard someone mutter something that sounded like "Sweden."

"Sorry," I said. I glanced at Hattie, my cheeks getting hot. Probably, Uncle Benji was out of work. I suddenly regretted asking. It was something I'd learned to never ask my dad's friends, since according to him, writers will always *tell* you if they have a job, but if they don't, they don't like to be reminded of that fact.

"You'll notice," Gramps pointed out to me, but also to the table at large, "that none of my children have chosen professions where they have to work in the summers. I don't think this is an accident."

"Of course it isn't," Aunt Abby scoffed. "Summers here were the focus of the whole year. I wasn't going to forfeit that just because I had the misfortune of growing up."

"Not everyone has the luxury to take summers off," Uncle Byron pointed out. Gramps jumped in to explain that some of my aunts and uncles were only here on the weekends—Uncle Byron took a Sunday late-afternoon bus to New Jersey, since he had to be in the office for his advertising job on Monday, and Aunt Katie caught a flight to Maine Sunday night so she could go to work. Apparently, they both returned on Friday afternoons to spend the weekends here.

The parents started talking among themselves, and I turned back to my cousins. "So maybe we're playing cricket at three," I said, looking doubtfully at the board. "But what about the rest of the day?"

"We just do what we want," Diya said. "There's no *schedule*."

"But . . ."

"That's the whole point of summer," Max said as he scooped up a spoonful of cereal. "No structure."

I opened my mouth and then closed it again. I didn't want them to think I was uncool or dorky, but the thought of just . . . all day, stretching out, was maybe making me feel like I was going to break into hives. "So," I finally said after a pause in which everyone just ate their breakfast, "if you can do anything . . . what kinds of things *do* you do? Besides, um, lizard funerals."

Hattie shook her head gravely at me. "Too soon."

"Sorry."

"We go swimming," Max said, turning to me. "Canoeing or kayaking, too. There's the arts and crafts cabin, and we go exploring in the woods, or ride our bikes. . . ."

"Just not to PocoMart," I said, and Diya narrowed her eyes at me. I held up my hands. "I'm just trying to figure out the rules."

"Not to PocoMart," Hattie confirmed.

"And . . . why is PocoMart bad?"

Diya glanced down the table—none of the adults were paying attention. It looked as if maybe Uncle Dennis had fallen asleep sitting up, and Uncle Byron was taking advantage of this and freely helping himself to Uncle Dennis's breakfast.

She leaned in, and we all did too. "It has to do with Holden's dad."

"He owns PocoMart," Max said, dropping his volume to match Diya's. "He bought it last year, and once our parents found out, they said we couldn't go. Because of the ongoing lawsuit. They don't want us to do anything that would be seen as supporting him."

Diya finished the last bite of her bagel and pushed her plate away. "Done," she said. "I'm going to change out of this and into my actual bathing suit."

"Oh," I said, glad to grab on to some semblance of a plan. "Are we swimming?"

"Probably eventually," she said with a shrug.

"Wait, did Ryanna ever get a tour?" Max asked as he clattered his spoon into his empty cereal bowl.

"Yesterday," I said with a nod. "Well—kind of."

Max shook his head. "We need to give you the real tour, then."

"Yes," Diya said. She arched an eyebrow and leaned across the table to me. "Let's start with the haunted cabin."

I just stared at her. "The what, now?"

CHAPTER 10

We split up, going back to our respective cabins—the girls to the Hummingbird Cabin, and Max to the Swift Cabin he shared with Pete.

I wasn't sure what to wear—since we *didn't have a schedule*—so when I saw that Diya and Hattie were changing into bathing suits, and then putting shorts and T-shirts on over them, I did the same. But while I was rummaging through my trunk, Hattie decided she wanted to "help me unpack"—aka look through all my clothes. She seemed to have expected more from someone who lived in LA, and even though I kept trying to tell her our part of Los Angeles was quiet and suburban, she didn't seem inclined to believe me. But she was impressed with the nice dress Ginger had made me bring and hung it up reverently in the closet while Diya sighed impatiently.

I grabbed my flip-flops as we headed out of the

Hummingbird Cabin, but both Diya and Hattie were barefoot. There was so much gravel around—on the driveway, on all the walking paths. How did it not hurt their feet?

I was worried that Max would be upset that we'd taken longer to get there than we'd told him, but when we arrived, he was sitting cross-legged, a little ways away from the cabin, sketching in a pocket-sized notebook.

I didn't feel like I knew him well enough to ask what he was drawing. But Diya took one glance at the notebook and groaned. "Already?"

"Of course," he said, like it should have been obvious. "I've been working on this all year. Now I'm just formalizing details."

"Sandcastle plans," Hattie explained to me. "Max and his dad get super into them, and there's always one day every summer when we all get conscripted to help them."

"It's *epic*," Max insisted, pushing his glasses up. "Admit it, you had a good time last year."

"I didn't!" Diya shook her head. "I was in charge of hauling buckets of water."

"That was only because you were insisting on adding your own design elements," Max explained patiently. "We couldn't have you adding porticos to an Art Deco structure."

"His dad is an architect," Diya said, rolling her eyes.

"Um, when does this happen?" I asked.

Max shrugged. "It all depends. Conditions have to be right. And we're never sure when exactly it is. It's just good to finalize design plans." He stood up and nodded toward the cabin in front of us. "Are we really doing this?" There was a note of fear in his voice.

"Yeah," Hattie said, now also sounding unsure. "Maybe we tell Ryanna about the cabin from, like, farther away. Or on the dock!"

I stared at it. It was on the edge of the cabins on the adults' side. I could see it was maybe a little more run-down than some of the others, with weeds growing around the foundation, like it had been sitting empty for a long time. But it looked normal—painted gray and with a few green summer leaves lying on the porch.

"We can do it here," Diya said, even though she also sounded a little nervous. She gestured to it. "This," she said, her voice low and spooky, "is the Goldfinch Cabin."

"Okay," I said, looking at it. "What's the big deal?"

"The big deal," Hattie said with a dramatic flourish, "is that ever since a fated day in the nineties, this cabin has been haunted. Haunted by a girl who, in a thunderstorm one August night . . . *disappeared*."

I just blinked for a second. "Well—what happened to her?"

"Nobody knows," Max said, matching Hattie's spooky tone. "Her body was never found."

"Her *body*?"

"Rumor has it," Diya said, "that she went walking along the lake, and *something* pulled her in."

"And so she haunts her cabin," Hattie continued. "And the place she wishes she'd never left. The place she longs to return. You know she's there because she leaves wet footprints across the floor."

"Wet footprints?" I stared at my cousins. This was sounding familiar—this was exactly what had happened in my mom's Cara Vanessa Cole book about the haunted cabin. Was this just a coincidence? Did all camps have the same kind of ghost stories? "There's no such thing as ghosts."

"You sure about that?" Diya asked.

"And there's certainly no such thing as a ghost that haunts a cabin at a summer camp. In fact, in this book I'm reading—"

"You don't know what you're talking about, Ryanna," Diya interrupted me. "Like, practically every horror movie is a ghost haunting a summer camp. It didn't come from nowhere."

"Well, surely all the people who lived here afterward would have reported ghostly footprints going across the floor," I said.

Max shook his head. "This cabin has been closed since then. Nobody goes in here *ever*. I bet people haven't been in here since then. Not even the grown-ups."

I scoffed. "The *grown-ups* don't believe in this. Come on."

"They do!" Hattie insisted. "None of them go in here either."

I looked at my cousins skeptically. I could only assume this was some kind of hazing ritual—some big joke. "No way."

"Way," Max insisted.

I looked around and saw Uncle Benji a few cabins down. "Um," I called, "could we ask you a question?"

He stood up and ambled over to us. "What's going on?" he asked, looking around at us, then at the cabin. "What are you doing here?"

"We were just having a discussion." I gestured to my cousins. "They think this cabin is haunted."

"Oh yeah. That rumor was going around when we were kids here too."

"So it's not haunted?"

Uncle Benji laughed. "Of course not." I shot all my cousins a look.

"Okay, then," Max said, "if it's not haunted, why don't you go in?"

Uncle Benji paused, then took another step back. "Uh—no."

"You said you didn't think it was haunted!" I reminded him.

"I *don't*," Uncle Benji insisted. He cast an uncertain look at the door and took another step back. "I just don't want to go in there."

"Why not?" Diya asked, folding her arms and giving me a look of satisfaction.

"For reasons that are my own!" Uncle Benji turned red and stomped back to his cabin.

"Bye, Dad!" Hattie called after him. "That was fun."

"So," Diya said to me, a challenge in her voice. "If you're not scared of the cabin—"

"I'm not—"

"And you're not afraid of ghosts—"

"There's no such thing—"

"Then you would be willing to go in. With the lights off. And stay there for five minutes."

I looked at the door, wishing I felt as confident about this as I had just a few seconds before. There hadn't been an actual ghost in the Cara Vanessa Cole book, either, but that didn't mean it hadn't scared me a little until I realized that. "Um . . . sure," I said, knowing I couldn't back down now.

"Great," Diya said.

Max gasped. "Don't do it, Ryanna! You have so much to live for!"

"Yeah, maybe . . . rethink this?" Hattie suggested.

"There's nothing to be afraid of!" I said, even though my voice shook slightly. "I'll do it."

I walked up to the door, holding my head high. I reached for the doorknob, secretly hoping that it would be locked—but it turned easily in my hand.

"It was nice knowing you!" Diya called after me.

I gave her a look that was much more confident than I felt, and stepped inside the cabin.

"Close the door!" Diya yelled.

I reached for the door with shaky hands and pulled it shut.

It was really dark inside—I started to turn on the lights, but then remembered that being in the dark was part of the deal. My eyes adjusted, and I could see that the layout was the same as our cabin—two bunk beds on either side, dressers next to them, a closet with a scratched mirror. All at once I felt a chill—the thought of looking in that mirror was suddenly really scary.

It was quiet in there, and I realized I hadn't moved even a step. Would I be able to claim I really wasn't afraid if I didn't even venture inside?

"There's no such thing as ghosts. There's no such thing as ghosts," I said to myself, annoyed to hear that my voice was trembly. I took a step inside—and froze when I heard a creak in the floor. "Hello?" I called. My heart pounded. "They're doing this to mess with you," I muttered.

I could see there was a thick layer of dust on the floor and cobwebs in the corners. I made myself take another step inside. The floorboards creaked and groaned under my feet. All the hairs on the back of my neck were standing up.

But it was five minutes. I could do this.

I tried not to think about ghosts or footprints or haunted mirrors. Instead I focused on how this haunted cabin story was so close to the one in my mother's book. Why were these stories so similar?

I just didn't understand it. Had my mother drawn that arrow in the margin because it reminded her about the story of her camp? But then what did *TRY THIS* mean? Or . . .

Something clicked in my mind. I remembered how Cara had discovered that the rumor about the haunted cabin had actually been started and spread by the camp director. He was trying to keep everyone away because that's where he was counterfeiting money. And he would have gotten away with it too, if Cara Vanessa Cole, and her mystery-solving prowess, hadn't shown up.

I closed my eyes for just a second, thinking hard. So maybe this *wasn't* a coincidence after all. Maybe . . . My mind was whirring, my thoughts going faster and faster. Maybe my mother had been the one who started the rumor? And she'd gotten the idea from the book!

"You doing okay in there, Ryanna?" Max called, sounding scared.

"Yeah," I called back, distracted, no longer scared in the

slightest. I looked around, trying to think. What had been on that page? It was where Cara finds the recipe for how to counterfeit money taped to the top of the bottom drawer.

"It's not possible," I said to myself as I walked over to the chest of drawers by the side of the bunk. Feeling silly even though there was nobody watching me, I opened them and felt around inside—just dust and some loose pennies. "Stupid idea," I muttered, even as I walked over to the other drawer. There was nothing in either of the top two, but as soon as I touched under the bottom drawer, I felt it.

It was a folded piece of paper, and I took it out with shaky hands, not quite able to believe what was happening. It was like I'd stepped through the pages of the book I'd just been reading.

I unfolded the paper and saw it was a drawing, a sketched-out map. The writing on it was definitely my mother's—it was the same as her writing in the book. And she'd written the words across the top in confident capital letters—*TREASURE MAP*.

I stared at it. My mother had left a treasure map in a cabin that nobody had been inside in over twenty years? What did it lead to? Was it actually real?

I felt the goose bumps on my arms rise. It was as though my mother and I were having a conversation. Like she'd reached out through the past to talk to me now, years after she'd gone away. It shouldn't have been possible—but somehow it was.

There was a pounding on the door that made me jump. "Ryanna!" It was Max, and he sounded like he was at the end of his rope. "Are you okay? Did they get you? I think they got her! Someone, break down the door!"

"It's fine," I called. I closed the dresser drawer and hurried over to the door. I pulled it open to see everyone standing on the threshold, looking terrified. "It's all right," I said, trying not to laugh.

"Was it terrifying?" Hattie asked, her eyes wide.

"Was there a ghost?" Diya echoed.

"Well . . ." I held out the paper to them. "There kind of was."

I looked down at the map, trying to take in every detail. We'd weighted it down with

some stones, and we had gathered around it on the dock. (I'd also run back to the Hummingbird Cabin to get my phone and had taken a picture of it. I wasn't taking any chances—this was a treasure map of my mother's that I'd *found*. Right now it was the most precious thing I owned.)

The map was smaller than a regular piece of paper, with a jagged bottom, like it had been ripped. *TREASURE MAP* was written at the top and underlined twice—you could practically feel my mother's excitement in writing it.

The drawing was of a lopsided half circle. Little trees were drawn around the top, and at the bottom seemed to be water. Among the trees there was what looked like a clearing, a large rock, and an *X* next to it. Written in small letters under the *X* was *Once you have tasted the taste of sky*—which didn't mean anything to me.

And at the very bottom were the words *PROTECT THE THINGS*, which also didn't mean anything to me. What things? What was my mother trying to tell me?

"Okay, explain this," Diya said.

"Which part?" I asked, leaning down to look at it.

Diya tapped on the clearing. "Here. This is in our woods. But the rest of it doesn't make any sense. Where's the camp? Where's the dock?"

"This is real?" I asked, leaning closer to it. I'd just assumed this was an invented treasure map to an imagined place—Narnia or Middle Earth or Green Gables. "This is *here*?"

"I mean, it's not to scale at all," Max said, shaking his head. "But I think so. It's almost like half of it is missing."

"What do you think it's for?" I asked, leaning in to look at it closer. Was there actually something my mother had hidden long ago? Something that *I* could actually find?

"Well, it says *Treasure Map*," Hattie helpfully pointed out. "So . . . treasure, I would assume."

Diya gasped so loudly, everyone turned to look at her— including Pete, who'd been passing by on the lake, on a float shaped like a slice of pizza. "Jeez," he said, raising his sunglasses to frown at his sister. "You okay?" Diya waved him off, and Pete shrugged and went back to his phone, which was in some kind of plastic protective device.

"What?" Hattie asked, her eyes wide.

"Okay," Diya said, her voice sounding shaky. "You know how my dad is always talking about history and I'm always ignoring him?"

I didn't, but all my cousins nodded, so I nodded too. "So this one time he was talking about the history of this area, and how there were these train robbers back in the 1800s, and how one of their hideouts was around here. And who knows, he might have been tossing that in there to make sure I was actually listening. But maybe . . ."

"Maybe your mom found some treasure," Max breathed, staring at the map. "And buried it in the woods!"

I looked around the circle. My heart was beating hard. Two days ago I'd been living my life in California. Now I was sitting on a dock in Pennsylvania with cousins I hadn't known existed, looking at a treasure map my mother had written. "You think there's really something here?" I asked. "It's not just . . . a joke?"

Diya jumped to her feet. "Only one way to find out."

Hattie and Max scrambled to their feet as well, and after a moment I stood up too. "So you guys would want to . . . do this with me?"

I hadn't wanted to assume. But they all looked impatient for me to join them, not put-upon or annoyed that I was tagging along.

Hattie shot me a look that said *duh*. "Of *course*!"

Diya nodded. "No time like the present."

Max gave me a smile. "Let's carpe this diem."

"Huzzah!" Hattie cried; her shaky English accent was back. She pointed toward the woods. "To adventure!"

I bent down and picked up the paper carefully, and tucked it in my shorts pocket. Then I looked around at the circle of my cousins and smiled. "Let's do it."

CHAPTER 11

We walked into the woods with our treasure-hunting supplies. These included several gardening trowels, a bucket shaped like a sandcastle, three plastic shovels, and a slightly rusty compass. We'd picked it all up from the equipment shed—which was actually much larger than a shed. It was a huge building with equipment for every kind of sport you could imagine—skates and nets and rackets and balls and archery arrows and targets. I had been torn between wanting to look around and take it all in, and needing to try to find my mother's treasure as quickly as possible.

Once we had gotten equipped, Diya led the way into the woods. We passed what must have been Aunt Abby and Uncle Neal's cabin—Aunt Abby was reading a book on the porch. "Where are you off to?" she asked, looking up.

"Going on a treasure hunt," Diya said easily to her

mother. "If we're successful, we might not be back in time for lunch."

I waited for my aunt to tell us to put the things back, that we weren't allowed to go do this on our own, that she—or someone—was coming with us. Or at least to ask a follow-up question. But Aunt Abby only nodded and went back to her book. "Just make sure you have sunblock on," she said, already turning a page. "Good luck."

"Thanks!" my cousins chorused back at her, and then started walking again.

"She doesn't care that we're doing this?" I asked, hurrying to catch up with Max. "We don't have to ask if we can?"

"They prefer that we don't," Diya assured me.

We walked into the woods, the path soon narrowing so that we walked single file. As we got farther from the camp and deeper in, it started to get darker and cooler.

"Okay," Max said when we'd been walking for about ten minutes, looking down at his compass. He stopped and pointed. We were back at the clearing I'd accidentally encountered—the one that had caused me to realize I'd gone the wrong direction.

I thought about how I might still be lost in the woods if not for Holden. But why had he suddenly stopped being friends with my cousins? I was having trouble squaring this with the helpful guy who'd volunteered to lead me out of the woods. It was yet another mystery to try to solve. After a very unmysterious eleven years, I was suddenly racking them up.

We walked into the clearing, and I saw in real life what had been drawn on the map—a large rock with a flat top, and a huge tree, its branches arcing down. I looked from my mother's drawing to the scene in front of me. My arms were covered in goose bumps. She'd drawn something that was *real*. I was standing in front of it. So maybe the treasure was real too.

"Can I see that?" Diya asked. I handed it over, about to ask her to be careful. She still had two parents, after all— she didn't know what it meant to only have one, and to have everything they left become rare and special and precious. But she took it gently from me, like she somehow understood this without me having to tell her. "Okay," she said, striding up toward the tree and looking around. "This map isn't exact *at all*, but it looks like the spot is right under the tree."

We all joined her—and I felt my hopes deflate when I saw that the ground was covered in knotty tree roots. How were we supposed to dig there? How had anything been *buried* there?

"What did it say again?" Hattie asked, pushing up her sunglasses—pink, sparkly—and leaning over to look.

"*Protect the things,*" Max recited with a definitive nod.

"No, the other thing." Hattie squinted at the map. "'Once you have tasted the taste of sky,'" she read, then shook her head. "What is *that* supposed to mean?"

I had no idea. "Maybe it'll make sense once we find the treasure?"

We all looked down at the ground again, then at one another. I wondered if everyone was thinking the same thing I was—that this was *not* going to be easy. But I took a shovel from Diya anyway, and we started to dig.

"UGHHHH," Hattie groaned an hour later, tossing her shovel aside. "I give up. I quit. My blisters have blisters."

I set my shovel down and shook out my hand, feeling much the same way. We'd all been trying to dig, but it hadn't been easy. The ground was as hard as a rock—plus, it was also *filled* with rocks. We hadn't found anything except some worms and bugs that did *not* seem happy about being disturbed. And the hardest part was that it was so difficult to dig among the tree roots. We kept looking at the map, trying to figure out if we were reading it wrong, or if there was anywhere else we should be trying to dig, but the *X* under the branches of the tree was pretty clear. I was trying to hide my disappointment, but I was feeling really let down. When you find a treasure map by chance, it seems like you *should* be able to find the treasure.

"This is hard," Diya said, brushing her hand across her forehead and leaving a smear of dirt behind.

"Well, yeah," Max said, still unsuccessfully trying to dig in a small space between two tree roots—his shovel barely fit. "If it was *easy* to find buried treasure, everyone would do it."

"I don't think we're going to find it," Hattie said, and Max stopped trying to dig.

"Well, not with that attitude, we won't!"

"No," Diya said, nodding. "I agree. It's impossible to dig here, and there are four of us. I don't think Aunt Casey could have done it on her own and then covered it up so that we couldn't find where it happened. I don't think it's here."

"You think someone else got to it?" I asked. Diya hesitated. "What?"

"Maybe . . . it's just a map," she said with a shrug. "Maybe she just hid it as a prank on one of the rest of them, but it never got found."

"I don't know," Max said.

"Yeah," I agreed, wiping the dirt off my hands and then looking at the map once more. It was so *specific*. Would someone go to this much trouble just to mess with their brothers or sisters? "I just really think . . . there's something there."

"Well," Diya said as she stood up and dropped her trowel into the bucket, "I just think we need more information. And we're not going to do any good thinking on an empty stomach." As if on cue, I heard the faint sound of a bugle being played.

"What is that?" I asked, standing up too.

Max grinned, dropping his shovel in the bucket with Diya's. "That's lunch."

We put everything back in the equipment shed and then headed up to the lodge for lunch. It seemed kind of like breakfast—people were coming and going, some sitting down and eating, some taking food with them. Quinn was eating a sandwich on the porch, but she waved at us as we came in. And like breakfast, it was buffet-style, and choose your own, with salad and sandwich fixings. Everyone ignored the salad, despite Aunt Abby talking up how great it was. I walked over to the sandwich station with my cousins and looked past the veggies and cold cuts, not quite able to believe what I was seeing. Jars of peanut butter, lots of different flavored jellies and jams, and the kind that had peanut butter *and* jelly in the same jar. Ginger, in her quest against refined sugar, had switched us over to organic peanut butter. It was the kind you had to keep in the fridge and stir. So I was eagerly reaching for the kind of peanut butter that actually tasted good, when I saw it.

A jar of marshmallow fluff.

I picked it up carefully, like it might disappear at any moment, and looked around at my cousins, who were toasting bread and assembling their own sandwiches—Pete was carefully laying piles of deli meat and cheese on his. "Can we have this?" I asked, trying to keep the excitement out of my voice. Ginger never would have let this cross our threshold, and it was something even my dad had refused to buy in the pre-Ginger years.

"Sure," Hattie said with a shrug. "Have whatever you want."

So I made myself a peanut-butter-and-fluff sandwich, sure at any moment that an adult was going to swoop in and ask me what I thought I was doing and hand me an apple. But nobody seemed particularly invested in what we were eating—except Aunt Abby, advocating for salad—and I was able to enjoy the best sandwich of my life in peace.

When we were done, I followed my cousins' lead—putting our dishes into the machine in the kitchen they called Hobart, and then heading back out into the sunshine.

"What do you think?" Diya asked as we stopped just outside the lodge. She frowned down at her hands. "I'm not sure I'm up to digging right now."

"Me neither," Hattie said immediately.

"Yeah," I agreed, looking down at my own hands, which were still faintly red.

"But we're not *giving up*," Diya said. "We're just going to regroup and attack with more information. Maybe there's a clue on the map we're missing."

"You mean . . . you want to keep doing this?" It had been so hard, and we hadn't found anything—I'd been worrying I would be on my own if I wanted to keep looking for my mother's treasure.

"Of course," Max said. "How often do we find a treasure map? But I could also use a digging break. Should we swim?"

Diya and Hattie nodded, and it was like someone had yelled *Break!* because Hattie and Diya started walking in one direction, and Max started walking in the other. "Meet you on the dock," Diya called to him. I stood between them, not sure what I should do now, when Diya turned back to me, shielding her eyes with one hand. "Come on, Ryanna!" she called, and I smiled and hurried to catch up with them.

Hattie showed me where I could claim a beach towel—it turned out the laundry room was a building next to the infirmary that I hadn't paid attention to before. In addition to the washers and dryers, there were lots of extra sheets and towels, and an enormous stack of brightly colored beach towels.

I grabbed a blue-and-white striped one, and we swung by the bathroom, where there was a gigantic pump bottle of sunscreen—there was one in our cabin too, along with multiple bottles of bug spray. After we put some on, we headed out to the dock.

It turned out that actually swimming in the lake—on purpose, with a bathing suit—was way more fun than jumping into it with clothes on. The lake was cool but not cold, and if you waded in from the beach, you could go out pretty far before the bottom dropped out. In the center of the lake—by the floating dock in the middle—it was so deep that I had to work hard to swim down far enough to touch the sandy bottom.

I learned that there were three prime floats in real contention—a swan, a unicorn, and the slice of pizza. When we first arrived, Uncle Neal was coming out of the water with the unicorn, and Uncle Benji and Aunt Katie were sprawled on the beach on towels, while Uncle Dennis sat in a beach chair nearby, hat over his face, taking a nap. But the lake was empty except for us, which felt magical. The lake was so big that, while you could see Holden's house across the water, it would take you a while to swim there. And it was just the four of us in it—swimming around, trading floats, jumping between the floats, getting tired and drying off on the dock or beach, and then jumping back in. Pete came and joined us for a bit—he was partial to the float shaped like the slice of pizza—but didn't stay that long.

Diya explained, with a roll of her eyes, that her brother was much too cool to hang out with the younger kids for more than a few minutes at a time.

"I don't know why he even came this summer," she said, floating on her back and squinting up at the sky. "My theory is that his soccer camp didn't want him back, and he's too embarrassed to tell us."

Over the course of the afternoon, I learned that the floating dock was always home in races and games, but you had to be on it, not holding on to the buoy, which was attached to the dock on a rusted chain. There was a rule that if any thunder was heard, we had to get out of the water until twenty minutes passed between sounds of thunder. And if any lightning was spotted, we had to get out of the water, full stop, and go up to the lodge.

We'd wound up back on the beach after a game of sharks and minnows had ended in a photo finish and an argument had broken out that left Diya swimming off angrily and Hattie bursting into tears. I'd looked nervously at Max—what did this mean? What happened now?—but a few moments later, Diya came back and spread her towel out on the sand, and Hattie ran out of the water to sit next to her, and it seemed like that was that. No hard feelings, no grudges held.

"Um, good afternoon?" I shaded my eyes and turned to

see Archie standing next to the dock, looking annoyed. He had a bat over one shoulder—but not a baseball bat; it was almost flat at the end.

"Hi, Archie," Max said with a wave. "What are you doing here?"

"Oh wait," Hattie said, tilting her head to the side. "Is this about what you wrote on the board? Grasshopper?"

"Cricket," Archie said, sounding weary.

"We weren't sure if you were offering to teach us," Max pointed out. "We thought maybe you were just telling us how many crickets you've seen."

"I was offering to teach," Archie said with a deep sigh. "I'm regretting that now."

"We want to learn!" Hattie said, scrambling to her feet. "It's a game of gentlemen and kings!"

"Meet on the south lawn in ten minutes if you want to learn," Archie said with a shrug. "Or not." He walked away, that weird wooden bat over his shoulder.

Max glanced around at us. "What do you think?"

Diya shrugged. "I mean, why not?"

"Great!" I pushed myself to my feet and wiped the sand off my hands. Then I turned back to my cousins. "Wait, what's the south lawn?"

CHAPTER 12

The south lawn turned out to be a big grassy field. It was to the side of the lodge, past all the adults' cabins. There were three faded archery targets at one end, and two posts holding up a slumping volleyball net. But we were in the middle of a wide-open space that had been carved out from the trees.

"This is where we always start capture the flag," Diya told me as we hustled to join everyone. I could see that Pete was already there, along with Quinn and Uncle Neal.

"Capture the flag?" I echoed. I'd seen it played in camp movies but had never actually done it myself.

Hattie nodded, her eyes shining. "We do it once a summer. Last year we played adults against kids, and it was so fun because—"

"Ahem!" Archie looked at us significantly, and we sat on the field next to Pete and quieted down. "So," he continued as he paced back and forth, bat over his shoulder, "welcome. I'm about to give you an education into the world's finest game."

"So how do you win?" Pete asked, sitting up straight. Even though it was a cricket lesson, I could see he'd brought his soccer ball. It was the most engaged I'd seen him—maybe because sports were finally involved.

"All in due course," Archie said, shaking his head. "Before we get into things like points and scoring, we need to investigate the fundamentals. Really start with the basics. Because when you understand cricket, you understand . . . the meaning of life." He paused dramatically and looked at us expectantly, like he was anticipating a bigger reaction.

"Wow," Quinn said a moment later. "Ooh. Wow."

"That's patronizing," Archie said with a small sniff. He pulled out a ball from his pocket and held it out. "Who can tell me what this is?"

"Um, a *ball*," Diya said. She wasn't rolling her eyes, but it sounded like she wanted to.

"No," Archie said, his voice serious. "It's *destiny*."

"So can we play?" Pete asked, sounding impatient.

"First we have to understand the history of the game. We have to respect it. We have to honor it. . . ."

"Uh. Is this going to take long?" Diya asked. "I thought we were going to play cricket and still have time to do other stuff."

"Oh, no no no." Archie shook his head. "Cricket is not a quick game. Sometimes games last for days."

"Days?" Pete grinned. "That's awesome. Everyone, shut up so we can learn."

Diya shot me a look, rolling her eyes and then leaning back on her hands. I gave her a sympathetic one back, but inside I was thrilled. She'd given me a look that had included me! Like I was part of the group, understander of grimaces.

Archie was talking about where the name "cricket" came from, and I felt my attention wandering. I looked around and saw, to my surprise, my grandmother in a tree.

Well, not really in a tree—at the other end of the field, there was a tree that had a small raised platform built around it. She was standing on that, binoculars lifted to her eyes and fixed on something in the distance.

"I'll be right back," I whispered to Hattie. I wasn't sure what the rules were about leaving a lesson once it had started, but I didn't think I'd get into trouble or anything.

Hattie nodded. She was braiding grass she'd plucked, and it seemed like absolutely nobody—except Pete—was paying attention to anything Archie was saying.

I waited until Archie turned his back to demonstrate something, and then I took off, running full-out. I jumped the volleyball net—it helped that it was sagging pretty low—and kept running until I reached the base of the tree my grandmother was in.

"Hi," I said, looking up at her.

She held up one finger, but not in a rude way—just like she was letting me know she couldn't talk right then. A moment later she lowered her binoculars and smiled down at me. "Hi, yourself," she said. "So you jumped in the lake with your clothes on?"

I nodded and tried to sound blasé. "It was no big deal."

She smiled, then turned her attention back to the distance. "Glad to hear it."

"What are you looking at?"

"There's a hawk in a tree across the lake," she said, squinting. She looked down at me again and raised an eyebrow. "Want to see?"

"Uh-huh." There were two steps up to the raised platform, and I climbed them in one leap.

"Okay," she said, moving aside to make room for me. "Let me just find him." She lifted the binoculars again, and I took a breath to tell her what I'd run over here to say.

"Thank you for the book," I said. "I'm halfway done with it already. I can't believe it was my mom's—and from when she was around my age!"

Grams lowered her binoculars with a nod. "I thought you might like it."

"And I love mysteries too!" I blurted out. "So we have that in common!"

She smiled at me. "I'm happy to hear it."

I wondered if, since we were here, I should take this moment and ask her what had happened between her and Gramps and my dad. Why was this the first time I was meeting everyone? Why hadn't I been in touch with them before? I took a breath—

"There!" Grams handed the binoculars to me—they were surprisingly heavy—and pointed across the lake. "Sometimes you just have to wait for the right moment."

I nodded and looked through the binoculars, thinking that maybe that applied to me asking her these questions. Maybe now wasn't the right moment—but sometime in the future, it would be. I had just spotted the hawk when I heard a scream from the field.

I lowered the binoculars and looked over. Mayhem had broken out. Diya had taken Archie's cricket bat and was hitting the ball to Pete, who fielded it and then started running toward Quinn, who was motioning to him like an air traffic controller. It looked like they had turned the cricket lesson into some kind of baseball-tag combo. Archie was standing in the middle of the chaos, yelling, "This is insubordination! Return my bat at once! This is *not cricket*!"

I looked over at Grams, who shook her head. "Want to go back there?"

"Um . . ." I watched as Archie tried to chase Pete, who tossed the ball to Hattie, who tossed it to Uncle Neal, who caught it, immediately dropped it, and started violently swearing. "I think I'm okay here."

"Good call. And in that case . . ." She slung the binoculars around her neck. "Why don't I meet you at your cabin in ten minutes? There's something I want you to have."

"Sure," I said immediately. I wanted to know what it was—but somehow didn't think I could ask without being incredibly rude.

"Great," she said with a nod. "See you in a jiff." I watched her as she headed back toward the lodge.

Since I had a few minutes—my cabin was pretty close to the field—I stood on the platform for just a minute more, trying to process the day and take it all in. It felt like a *lot* had happened. Had days been this busy back in California? Somehow I doubted it. I started to leave—when something carved into the railing of the platform caught my eye.

It was a quote. In neat, professional-looking script was written: *Once you have tasted the taste of sky, you will forever look up. —Leonardo da Vinci*

I gasped. The map! My mother's treasure map had had the beginning of this quote written on it. It had been written right under the *X*. But what did it mean? Did it mean that we actually needed to be looking over here and not in the meadow?

I stared at it for a moment longer, trying to figure it out, then realized I had to go and meet my grandmother. I gave the cricket lesson—which had basically descended into anarchy—a wide berth. And even though I was running full-out, by the time I reached the Hummingbird Cabin, my grandmother was already there with a large canvas tote at her feet.

"Sorry," I said, breathless.

She waved this off. "Never apologize."

"But. Um. What if you do something wrong—"

"Here." She lifted up the canvas bag and set it at my feet. "I didn't want to overwhelm you yesterday. And I wasn't sure if you would like them. But since you seemed to appreciate them . . ."

I looked into the bag and gasped with joy. It was packed with books, all paperbacks. There were the Baby-Sitters Club— the books, not the graphic novels—and something called the Saddle Club. But mostly they seemed to be more Cara Vanessa Cole mysteries—I hadn't realized that it was a series. "Are these . . . ?" I asked, my heart pounding with excitement.

"Your mother's," Grams confirmed with a nod. "I've been saving them—she adored these books when she was your age. You never saw her without one."

I stared down into the bag, happily overwhelmed by how

many there were. It would take me all summer to read these. "Thank you."

"Enjoy," she said. "And if you'd like, I have some more of Casey's things in the attic from when she was near your age. Seems right you should have them."

I nodded so hard, my braid bounced on my shoulder. "Yes! I mean—yes, please. If you don't mind."

"Not at all." Grams smiled at me, then started to head toward the lodge.

I sat down in the chair outside the cabin and carefully picked up one from the top, the eighth book in the series— *Cara Vanessa Cole and the Vanishing Pointe*. It looked like in this one, Cara Vanessa Cole was going to solve a mystery at a museum—she was peeking around a corner as two suspicious-looking people surrounded a statue of a dancer. I couldn't wait to dive in. But before I even read one page, I opened up the front cover, holding my breath, hoping it would be there—and it was.

This book is the property of CVC, 12 years old.

I was sorting the books by series, and then within the series by number, when Max ran up.

"Hey," he said, out of breath. "Archie stormed off in a huff. He told us we were all pillocks and Billy-no-mates. Nobody knows what that means, but we think it's bad. Anyway, we decided we want to play an actual game, not just fake cricket to bug Archie. We voted on kickball—want to play?" He took a gasp of air when he finished saying this.

"Yes," I said, jumping to my feet. "Just give me a second." I carefully brought all the books inside the cabin and laid them on my bed—I'd have to figure out a shelving system at some point. And then I took the map and tucked it into the haunted cabin book, along with my mother's picture. I'd have to tell my cousins about the quote—maybe it would mean something to them.

Feeling like there was a lot going on—but in a good way—I hurried back out to join Max.

We ran over to the south lawn together, and I saw that bases had been set up—real bases, the kind we had for PE at school. Presumably these had come from the equipment shed. Just thinking about the glimpse I'd seen there made me want to really explore it and see all they had.

We ended up with two large teams playing kickball as it very slowly started to get dark out. I was on a team with Max, Pete, Aunt Abby, Uncle Benji, Quinn, and Aunt Katie.

The other team was Gramps, Diya, Uncle Neal, Hattie, Max, Uncle Dennis, and Uncle Byron.

Pete was our captain and declared us the Bonecrushers, whereas Hattie decided that her team would be called the Rainbow Unicorn Narwhal Crew.

But despite the difference in names, the teams were well matched—and after an hour of kickball, we came off the field to kick with the score all tied up at 3–3. I walked over to sit on the sidelines as Aunt Abby and Pete limbered up and everyone else flopped onto the grass. Aunt Abby was up first, and Diya was pitching. Diya called out, her voice taunting, "Good luck getting past me! You couldn't hit the side of a brick wall."

"No trash-talking your mother," Uncle Neal called absently.

Diya turned to frown at him just as I heard the *thwack* of a strong kick and saw the ball go flying.

"That's what I'm talking about!" Pete yelled as Uncle Dennis and Hattie chased down the ball and Aunt Abby rounded the bases, her arms raised in victory.

I leaned back on my hands to take it all in, as all around me my relatives jumped up and down and cheered, or booed, or trash-talked. And when it was my turn to kick, everyone on my team (and even Gramps, I noticed, though he was on the other team) yelled, "Go, Ryanna!"

I pushed myself to my feet and walked to the plate, smiling, feeling glad that I was there—and knowing for sure that staying had been the right decision.

Even though we lost the game, 8–5.

CHAPTER 13

I woke up the next morning with a start, my eyes flying open.

I looked at the underside of the bunk above me as I yawned, trying to decipher the decades-old graffiti that had been carved into the wood.

Summer '88
Anna <3 Ryan
MAGPIE CABIN
CHAMPIONSSSS!!!!!
Blue Jay Cabin SUX
i hate it here i want to GO HOME
best summer ever

I stared at the carvings for a moment, and they reminded me that I had my own carving to figure out—the da Vinci quote that was both on my mother's map and on the bird-watching platform. What was the connection?

I climbed out of my bunk and looked around—Hattie and Diya were still fast asleep, which was maybe not surprising. According to the crooked clock on the wall—the hands were oars—it was just a little after seven.

I wasn't sure when breakfast started—I had a feeling that Quinn had told me during my short-lived tour, but that was all fuzzy now—but my stomach rumbled loudly enough that I decided I'd go investigate.

One step outside had let me know that it was cold this early, so I turned around and tiptoed over to the closet, pulled on a hooded sweatshirt over my sleep tank and shorts, and then headed up to the lodge.

I paused for just a moment as I looked out at the lake, which was sparkling in the early-morning sunlight. It didn't seem like anyone else was up but the birds—and they were certainly making their presence known.

I pulled open the door to the lodge and looked around. The buffet where the food had been was empty, and my stomach growled again. Maybe I was too early? I had just turned to head back to my cabin when the swinging door of the kitchen flew open and my grandfather emerged, carrying a bowl of cut fruit.

"Ryanna!" He smiled at me like I was just the person

he'd hoped to see, way too early on a Sunday morning. "Good morning! Are you an early bird like me?"

"Well," I said. I shifted my weight from foot to foot. I didn't want to lie—and back in California, my dad and Ginger were always yelling at me to wake up and get a move on in the mornings. "I guess I am on the East Coast."

He threw back his head and laughed. "Happy to hear it."

Gramps had his glasses perched on top of his head and was wearing actual clothes—a faded blue sweatshirt and jeans. I looked down at myself, suddenly wondering if it was okay that I'd shown up in what were basically my pajamas.

"Well, I was just getting breakfast together," Gramps said as he set the fruit bowl down on the buffet table. "Want to help me?"

"Sure," I said, and he smiled at me.

"Great," he said, clapping his hands together. He squinted and looked around. "Just as soon as I find my glasses . . ."

"Um," I said. I gestured to his shock of white hair, which was standing up in a million directions. "They're on your head."

Gramps patted his head and then plucked his glasses off, gazing at them with a look of wonder. "So they are! Amazing." He held the kitchen door open for me, and I stepped inside, Gramps following behind me. "I *do* tend to be a little forgetful," he said cheerfully. I had noticed by now that *cheerfully* was how he did most things. "Your mother was always after me about it."

I felt a thrill at the way he'd just so casually said *your mother*, like it was the most natural thing in the world. "She was?"

Gramps nodded, putting his glasses on and crossing to one of the industrial silver refrigerators. "She had an amazing memory—she never forgot anything, or where she put anything. She was always yelling at me when I'd misplace things. She said I couldn't be trusted." He twinkled at me as he brought over a gallon of milk to the center prep table.

"What are you making?"

"Waffles!" he opened up the other refrigerator and emerged with a carton of eggs. "On Sundays we always do a bigger breakfast. Your aunt Katie and uncle Byron both head out later, and it's nice to give them a send-off."

"Can I help?"

He nodded. "I would love that. But what would be *most* helpful right now is to get the coffee a-brewin'. Do you know how to make coffee?"

"Kind of. We have one of those pod machines at home." I looked at the coffee maker—the biggest one I'd ever seen. "Does it use pods?"

Gramps shuddered. "Never speak of pods in this house. Well, I'll teach you. It's a skill everyone should learn."

He showed me how to measure out the rounded table-spoons of coffee grounds, and then where to add the water to the giant coffee machine. I watched it, listening to it brew as Gramps made his waffle batter—even though he seemed to constantly be misplacing things he'd set down only a moment before. When the coffee stopped making hissing, bubbling sounds, Gramps raised an eyebrow. "I think the coffee's done."

"How can you tell?"

"I've done this a latte."

I groaned appreciatively. I took a breath to tell him that my dad—who loved puns—would have appreciated that. But then I hesitated. I didn't want him to get upset if I brought my dad up.

Gramps took down a chipped Pocono Coffee Shop mug from the cabinet, poured himself a cup of my coffee, and added cream. Then he took a sip.

"Well?" I asked, crossing my fingers it had turned out okay. It was such a big coffeepot that if we'd messed it up, we were going to have to throw out a *lot* of coffee.

"Delicious!" He took another long sip, then raised his mug to me. "The job is yours if you want it."

"The job?"

"You can make coffee every morning! You can be the camp barista. Especially since you also seem to like to get up early and get the day started."

I was a little worried that Gramps was just being nice and telling me that my coffee was good—it seemed like something he would do. But then Aunt Abby came in from running her morning 5K and pronounced it great, and Uncle Dennis shuffled in, looking half asleep, and drank two cups in rapid succession. And by the time everyone had woken up and gathered in the mess hall, enough adults had had my coffee that I didn't have to worry.

And nobody had to pretend about the waffles—they were *great*.

Once we'd all gotten our waffles and had eaten at least one, I'd told my cousins what I'd seen on the bird-watching platform, hoping they'd have some insight into what it meant.

"What exactly did it say?" Max asked.

"Once you have tasted the taste of sky, you will forever look up," I answered Max. "It's by Leonardo."

Hattie paused, a bite of waffle halfway to her mouth. "The actor?"

"No," Diya said with a long-suffering sigh. "Leonardo *da Vinci*. The artist and inventor."

"And architect," Max supplied.

"Oh," Hattie said, sounding entirely less interested now. "I guess that's cool too."

"But I don't understand the connection," I said, spearing my own bite of waffle and dragging it through the whipped cream. "Why does it have a quote from the bird-watching platform if the map shows the meadow over by the north field?"

"Maybe . . . we were digging in the wrong place?" Hattie suggested hesitantly.

Diya shook her head. "No. Aunt Casey knew this place. She drew the meadow; she meant the meadow. It's obvious."

"What about Aunt Casey?" Pete asked, walking past us, a fresh stack of waffles on his plate.

"Go *away*." Diya glowered at him.

"You said her name," Pete said, glowering back at his sister.

"Yeah," I said as I looked at Pete, confused by this. "But why does it matter if we're talking about my mom?"

"She was Pete's godmother," Max explained, and my eyebrows flew up.

I stared at him. "She was?"

Pete nodded. "Aunt Casey was the best."

"Wait," I said, sitting up straighter. "You remember her?"

"I was seven when you guys stayed here the whole summer," he pointed out. "Of course I remember her."

"Okay, bye now," Diya said, turning her back on him. Pete rolled his eyes.

"Diya!" Hattie cried. "Maybe he knows something."

"He doesn't know anything," Diya assured her. "About anything."

"Wait," I called, because Pete was starting to walk away. Maybe he had information about the treasure map! I didn't want to let the chance go by. "Did my mom ever talk to you about a map? Or . . . a tree?"

Pete raised his eyebrows. "What kind of map?"

"Does it matter?" Diya snapped. She gave me a look that said *told you*.

Pete shook his head. "We mostly talked about *Teen Titans Go!* It was her favorite show."

That was a surprise. "It was?"

He nodded. "We always watched it together."

"Because you wanted to watch it," Diya said slowly. "It's not like Aunt Casey liked it."

"She did so!" Pete insisted, even as I could see that he was looking embarrassed. He shook his head and stomped out of the lodge.

"That was helpful," Diya said with an eye roll.

"Okay, we won't ask Pete," Max said. "But it can't be a coincidence, right? The quote being the same? It's like we have a clue but no idea what it means."

"I know," I said. I put my head in my hands and closed my eyes, trying to think. Whenever Terry Turner was stumped by one of her cases and needed to figure something out, she went to a quiet, dark room, preferably with her dogs, Jessica Fetcher and Wagatha Christie, until she understood what her clues meant. But I didn't have a quiet room—all I had was a noisy mess hall and a repeating quote that didn't make any sense.

"Once you have tasted the taste of sky," I muttered to myself, "you will forever look . . ." I raised my head and gasped.

"What?" Diya asked, blinking at me. "You okay?"

"I think I figured it out," I said, my mind whirring.

"Were we looking in the wrong place?" Hattie asked.

"Yes," I said. "But also no." My cousins all gave me looks that basically said *Huh?* and I laughed. "I'll show you," I said as I stood and picked up my plate. I pushed through the swinging door into the kitchen, dropped my plate into Hobart, and ran back into the mess hall before the door had even stopped swinging. My cousins were all still sitting at the table, looking confused, and I laughed as I headed for the door. "Come on!"

"No *way*," Diya said. She sounded impressed in spite of herself. We were back in the meadow, at the same spot we'd spent so much time fruitlessly digging in. But we weren't digging now.

"How did you figure it out?" Max asked, also sounding impressed.

"It was right there in the quote. Once you have tasted the taste of sky—"

"You will forever *look up*," Hattie finished.

Looking up was what we were all doing. We were standing underneath the tree—which was how we could see that high up and dangling from one of the branches was a bright purple object. My mother's map had been correct after all. When we'd seen the *X*, we'd all assumed it meant we had to dig, but we'd been wrong. The treasure had been right here—we'd just been looking in the wrong direction.

As I gazed up at the purple thing twisting slowly in the breeze, I felt an excited flutter in my chest. This wasn't just something I wanted to be true because I was looking for a connection to my mom. It *was* true. There was a map, it had led us here, and now we were moments away from finding her treasure.

"So what now?" Diya asked, and I lowered my head to look at her.

"We get the treasure," I said, like it should have been obvious. Because wasn't it?

"Well, yeah. But *how*?"

We all looked up again, and I understood what she

was saying. Suddenly the purple thing—whatever it was—looked awfully high.

"It's very impressive," Hattie said. "That's not an easy tree to climb."

The branches of the tree formed a canopy, but they all started pretty far up the trunk. How were we supposed to climb it?

"How did she even get it up there?" Max asked.

"Hmm," Diya said. She started to walk around the trunk of the tree, hands on her hips. She'd made it almost all the way around back to us when she yelled, "Aha!"

"Aha what?" Hattie yelled back, just as a rope swung through the branches.

"There was a *rope*?" Max asked, shaking his head. "Ryanna, your mom was *very* efficient."

"Seriously," Hattie said. The rope came to a twisting stop, and I saw it had been tied up high, to one of the thickest branches within the tree. I had no idea how my mother had managed it—or if it had been here before, and that's why she chose to hide the treasure here—but I was still impressed.

"It was tucked around the trunk," Diya said, coming to join us. "There was a nail in the tree it was coiled around."

"So one of us is going to have to climb the rope." My stomach clenched as I said it. I had not thought that I would be confronted with my PE failures until next year's gym class, let alone in a meadow in Pennsylvania. "Uh-oh."

"What's the problem?" Max asked.

I took a breath and, even though my cheeks were burning, told them all about gym class and how everyone had laughed at me while I'd just clung to the rope, spinning around but somehow not able to get up more than one handhold before slipping back down again. "So I'm not sure I should be the one to do this," I said as I looked at the rope, and then at the purple mystery object hanging alongside it.

"No, it *needs* to be you," Hattie declared. "You have to face your fears!"

"I already went into a haunted cabin!"

"But you weren't afraid of that," Diya said, raising an eyebrow at me.

"And plus, it wasn't actually haunted," Max added.

"I'm not going to be able to do it," I muttered. I wiped my hands on my shorts. My palms were already starting to get sweaty, which didn't seem ideal right before I was about to climb a rope.

"Well, not with that attitude you won't." Diya shook her head. "But you have to at least try, right?"

I looked up at the rope and swallowed hard but nodded. This was my mother's map, after all. I was the one who'd figured out the clue. I *did* have to at least try. If my mother had somehow managed to get this all the way up there, the least I could do was attempt it.

I wiped my hands off again and took a step toward it just as Max yelped, "Wait!"

We all turned to look at him. "What?" Diya sounded baffled.

"I just suddenly realized this rope is probably really old," Max said. "What if Ryanna's climbing up it, and it, I don't know, *frays* or something, and she comes crashing to the ground? She could break an arm!"

"I'm not going to break an arm," I said, even as I felt a little nervous swoop in my stomach. I had just assumed that if there was a problem, it would be my ability to climb the rope, not the rope falling apart.

"Well, let's be logical," Hattie said, squinting up at it. "Ryanna, how old do you think Aunt Casey was when she made the map?"

"Maybe a little older than me," I said. "Twelve?"

"Okay," Max said. "So this map is like . . . thirty years old?"

"Maybe twenty-five," I said, trying to do the math.

"I would think a rope would still be good after that long," Hattie said with the confidence of someone who wasn't going to have to climb it.

"But that's also assuming the rope was new when she put it up," Max pointed out.

Diya shrugged. "One way to find out." She ran forward and grabbed the rope, hanging off it, and pulling with her arms. "I think it's fine," she said. She jumped down and brushed off her hands, then gave me a *here you go* gesture.

I let out a shaky breath as I walked toward the rope. I tried to block out the memory of everyone's laughter, bouncing off the gym walls and making it sound like it was coming from every direction. I knew my cousins wouldn't laugh at me if I failed. So I had to at least try.

I grabbed it above my head and pulled myself on, gripping it with my other hand and twisting my foot around to provide support, the way we'd learned in PE. I looked up above me—the purple object seemed impossibly high.

"Don't think about it!" Diya yelled. "Just one hand over the other. You can do it."

And maybe if it had been Hattie or Max, I wouldn't have believed them in the same way. But something about the way Diya said it—*you can do it*—felt more like a promise than an encouragement. "I can do it," I muttered to myself. I reached my hand up and, to my shock, pulled myself up.

"Keep going," Diya yelled, and I gripped the rope with my other hand. "You can't stop moving or you'll get tired."

"Go, go, go!" Hattie yelled.

"Safely!" Max added.

I nodded and tried to do what Diya said, just worked on putting one hand above the other, not stopping to look down or really think about what I was doing. And somehow it was working—in what felt like not all that much time, I was eye-level with the purple mystery object. I could see now that it was a bandanna with something inside. It was knotted at the top and tied with string onto the branch. I pulled at the string, and it untied and fell straight down.

"Heads up!" I yelled as I looked down to where the bandanna was falling—and immediately gripped the rope harder. The world below me wobbled and spun as I realized just how high up I really was.

"We've got it," Max said, holding up the purple bandanna, and I silently prayed that the treasure inside it—whatever it was—wasn't breakable.

"Come on down," Hattie called.

"Uh-huh," I said, still staring down at the ground, which was distressingly far away. Now that I was up here, how was I supposed to get down? We'd had big thick mats underneath the ropes we'd climbed in PE—not that I'd gotten high enough to need them—and most people had just jumped down.

"Keep your foot wrapped around," Diya called up to me. "And hold your hands loosely on the rope, and let yourself slide—*slowly!*—down."

"Okay," I said. This didn't sound great to me, but my arms were starting to get really tired, and I was really wanting to not be up in the air anymore—not to mention the fact that my mother's treasure was down there, and I wanted to get to it ASAP. I opened my hand and let myself fall a few feet before I gripped the rope again and winced. "Gah!"

"What?" Max yelled, sounding worried.

"Rope burn," I said through gritted teeth. "It's fine." I lowered myself down, a few feet at a time, until the ground looked close enough for me to jump. I landed hard and stumbled forward, catching myself on my hands.

"You did it!" Hattie said, jumping up and down.

I smiled at her, but my focus was on the purple bandanna in Max's hand.

He gave it to me, and I untied the double knot at the top. I opened it up—and saw that inside there was a small suede pouch with a flap, like a tiny envelope.

"Open it!" Max said.

I opened the flap—and saw a glint of something inside. I turned it over, and a silver necklace tumbled out, along with a folded piece of notebook paper.

The necklace had two charms strung on it—a heart and a small silver key.

"Ooh," Hattie said, reaching for it. "Shiny." Diya slapped her hand down. "What?"

"It's from Ryanna's mom." Diya shook her head. "*Obviously*, Ryanna gets it."

"But—" Hattie protested. Diya turned to face her. She sounded more serious than I'd ever heard her.

"Henrietta," she said, full-naming Hattie. Max drew in a shocked breath. "You have Aunt Katie. And you're going to have birthday and Hanukkah presents from her for years. Ryanna doesn't have Aunt Casey anymore, and it's like she just got a present from her. And you want to take it away?"

Hattie's blue eyes filled with tears. She threw her arms around me. "I'm so sorry!" she wailed.

"It's really okay." I patted her back a few times.

"How awful of me, Ryanna! Truly terrible! I'm so ashamed. Can you ever forgive me?"

Diya widened her eyes at me, and I understood what she meant. With Hattie back to being overly dramatic, things were going to be fine. "Of course."

Hattie broke away and nodded down at the necklace in my hand. "I can help you put it on."

I lifted my hair up and bent my knees so that Hattie could do the clasp, and then I turned to face my cousins, sliding the charms back and forth on the chain. I'd only had this necklace for a minute, but it was already my favorite thing. I never wanted to take it off.

"Looks good," Max said approvingly.

"So it's just a necklace?" Hattie asked. "Then why did the map say *protect the things*?"

I shrugged. "Maybe she meant it about protecting *her* things. Like her jewelry."

Hattie nodded slowly. "I guess that makes sense."

"What does the paper say?" Diya asked.

I unfolded it and smiled when I saw my mother's handwriting—familiar to me now.

> Congratulations! You one!
> CVC 12

Max frowned. "She spelled 'won' wrong."

"Maybe she was in a hurry."

"What's that mean?" Hattie asked, touching the initials.

"That's her name and age. She put it inside all her books, too." I looked around at all my cousins and shook my head. "I just can't believe we found her treasure."

Suddenly it felt harder for me to catch my breath. I'd thought maybe I'd get stories and pictures about my mom, but *this*? This was something I hadn't even known to dream about. It was more than I ever could have imagined. Like Diya said, somehow, against all odds, my mother had given me a present. And the only reason I'd found it was because I liked mysteries—like her. Because I'd been able to figure out the clues. The ones she'd left, not knowing it would be me—her daughter—who found them one day. It was even better than getting a present. It was like I'd *earned* a present. Something of hers that had meant so much, she'd hidden it in a tree to protect it.

And now I had something of hers to keep for always.

"Well done, team," Diya said with a nod. She clapped her hands together. "Now. Lake? Races? I call pizza float!"

CHAPTER 14

We spent the rest of the afternoon—breaking only for lunch—in a series of high-stakes float races. We were all on the dock with the floats, about to jump in for the tie-breaking race, when thunder rumbled somewhere in the distance. All my cousins groaned, and Max checked his watch. "T-minus twenty minutes," he said with a sigh.

"Hey!" Quinn called from the end of the dock. "You all heard that, right?" We all nodded. "No swimming for twenty."

"Nineteen and five seconds," Max corrected.

"Well, while you're waiting," she said, walking a few steps onto the dock, "you might want to get some sticks. We were thinking we'd go up the hill after dinner."

Max gasped happily, Hattie clapped her hands together, and Diya said, *"Yesssss,"* while pumping her fist. Quinn smiled at all of us and walked away, and I turned to my cousins, baffled.

"What does *go up the hill* mean?"

"It means," Hattie said, practically jumping up and down, "we get to introduce you to one of our best traditions."

"Which is?"

Diya grinned. "S'mores."

It kept thundering off and on all afternoon—so much so that we finally just gave up on trying to swim. We got snacks, said goodbye to Aunt Katie and Uncle Byron, who were leaving for the week, and then turned our attention to finding the perfect s'more sticks.

We all doused ourselves in bug spray—I'd learned the hard way that mosquitoes tended to be plentiful in the woods—and then started hunting for fallen branches and twigs. My cousins informed me that when we had s'mores— which was at least once a week, sometimes twice if we were lucky—it was always our job to provide enough s'more sticks for everyone.

"There's an art to it," Max said as he picked up a branch and examined it critically. "You can't have a tiny little twig. But you don't want a huge branch, either."

"Thin but not too thin," Hattie added, picking up a stick, then shaking her head and tossing it over her shoulder.

"If we don't get enough sticks for everyone, we don't get s'mores," Diya said, her face grave.

"I mean, that's what they say," Hattie said, picking up a stick and rolling it between her palms. "We've never put it to the test, but I'd prefer not to find out if they mean it."

"Same," Max said fervently.

"Me too," I agreed, picking up what looked like a promising contender. I figured my cousins didn't have to know I'd never done real campfire s'mores before, especially since this seemed like a well-established tradition with them.

By the time we'd found enough sticks for all of us, plus some backups, it was almost time for dinner. And even though it was good—Uncle Dennis grilled burgers and veggie burgers—I wolfed down my food as fast as possible, just wanting to get to dessert.

After everyone had eaten, Diya and I cleared the plates, and Quinn loaded them into Hobart. When we pushed out of the swinging kitchen doors, I saw that all my cousins—even Pete—were standing up by the door, everyone looking at Grams.

"What do you think?" she asked with a grin. "Does it seem like a nice night for a fire?"

As if that was the cue they were waiting for, all my cousins bolted for the door, and I followed after them.

"No running with sticks!" I heard Aunt Abby call as I jumped down the three steps of the lodge at once. We all gathered up the sticks we'd found—Pete helped us carry them—and I followed everyone out past the lodge, past the south lawn and the field, and up a small hill at the very edge of the woods that I'd never paid much attention to before. When we got to the top, I saw that there was a ring of mismatched Adirondack chairs and benches all facing a big circle in the center marked with stones.

This was where one of the adults would build a fire (apparently Grams was the best at it, but Uncle Benji was pretty good too) and we would make s'mores.

After waiting for what felt like *hours*, even though according to Max, it was only ten minutes, the adults arrived with the s'more supplies, and we could begin.

Gramps laid all the components on one of the benches—a giant box of graham crackers, and bags of jumbo marshmallows, and mini chocolate bars—while Grams got the fire going.

When the fire was impressively large and crackling, we were finally able to start. I hung back at first, watching my cousins to see what they did, but soon figured out my technique: get a marshmallow on the stick, but not too close to the end—you didn't want it dropping off and landing in the fire and having to start all over again. Diya preferred to rotate her stick in the flames, whereas Max would pull it out when things were looking too crispy, then put it back in again. Pete liked his marshmallow almost black, but Hattie preferred hers practically still raw.

I discovered I liked mine somewhere in the middle— lightly browned on the outside and gooey on the inside, so that when you placed it over the chocolate and sandwiched between the two pieces of graham crackers, the chocolate melted and the graham crackers stuck together.

Once I was happy with my marshmallow doneness, I took my completed s'more back to my chair by the fire and looked around for just a moment before I took a bite. Hattie was next to me, almost done with hers. Pete had somehow made a triple-decker one that looked too big to even eat. Grams was reminding everyone about fire safety, and Gramps had a chocolate smudge on his cheek.

I took a bite of my very first campfire s'more and grinned. It was, by far, the best I'd ever tasted.

"Good?" Diya asked me, her mouth full. I nodded, my mouth equally full, and finished it in two bites.

I leaned back in my chair and slid the charms on my new necklace back and forth. My *mom's* necklace. Maybe she had once sat in the very seat I was sitting in.

"Did my mom like s'mores?" I asked, turning to the relative closest to me, Aunt Abby, who smiled.

"Loved them," she said. "She used to do an open-faced thing, didn't she, Dennis?"

Uncle Dennis smiled and looked up from where he was assembling his own s'more. "She liked to flatten down the marshmallow and then top it again with double chocolate, but no graham cracker."

"I remember that," Grams said. "It was always a mess! Chocolate stains on everything . . ." Her voice hitched slightly, and she trailed off. She shook her head. "I'm sure you don't want to hear about this."

"I *do*," I said immediately, leaning forward. "I want to know everything I can. I feel like I really don't know a lot about my mom when she was a kid, or my age, or a teenager. . . ." I saw my grandparents exchange a look. "My dad talks about her," I said, a defensive note coming into my voice. "It's just . . ." I stopped, not sure how to put this into words. How it sometimes felt like I was only getting *facts* about her. How all the pictures we'd had out on display had migrated up to my room when we moved into our new house—the ones that had been downstairs were replaced with pictures of my dad and Ginger. How sometimes I didn't even know *what* I wanted to know. I just wanted more than what I had.

"I think Ryanna learning more about Casey sounds like a great idea," Uncle Neal said, giving me a smile. "Especially since I didn't know her as well as I'd have wanted to either."

"I know!" Hattie clapped her hands together. "What if every time we come here, everyone has to bring a fact or a story about her? We can call it *S'more about Aunt Casey!*"

Grams groaned but Gramps looked appreciative. "Nicely done," he said to Hattie. "Your Uncle Byron would have appreciated that."

"He would," Uncle Dennis said, shaking his head. "Nobody tell him, or he'll use it in an ad campaign."

Aunt Abby leaned over and squeezed my shoulder. "I think that sounds like an excellent idea."

"Me too," I said, smiling wide.

And while we all started prepping our second s'mores, Uncle Benji told me a story about how he and my mom had snuck out when they were teenagers to go to a concert—a story that, judging from my grandparents' reactions, they were hearing about for the first time.

As the laughter died down and I brushed the last crumbs off my hands, I drew my knees up to my chest and pulled my sweatshirt over them, feeling happy and full, with just the right amount of sugar buzz.

I looked up at the sky and stared in surprise. It wasn't totally dark out yet, but almost, and the stars here were brighter and more plentiful than I'd ever seen them in California. They took over the sky, whole constellations I never got to see back home.

I was about to say something about the stars when something in the grass caught my eye. "What was that?"

"What's what?" Max asked me, carefully carrying his third s'more back from the fire and taking his seat.

"I thought I saw . . ." I looked around, and a second later I saw it again. In the grass a few feet from me—and dotting the air—were lights, winking on and off in the fading twilight. I pointed. "There!"

Max followed where I was looking. "The fireflies? What about them?"

"Fireflies," I said, almost to myself. I'd seen them in movies, and read about them in books, but had never seen any myself in real life. "We don't have them back home."

Max stared at me. "You don't?"

"They're . . ." I couldn't stop looking at the fireflies—trying to follow them as they flitted through the air. I'd think I'd lose one, only to see the light finally blink on again. And the lights kept showing up in the grass, blinking on and off at intervals, a tiny little light show beneath and all around me. It was the most magical thing I'd ever seen—and everyone else was just acting like this was totally normal. "They're *wonderful.*"

"Yeah, they're good," Max said, taking a bite of his s'more. "We're used to them, I guess."

I nodded, still not able to tear my eyes away from the grass. How was I ever supposed to go back to regular summer nights in California, now that I knew what fireflies were really like? Knowing that they existed in theory was nothing like actually getting to experience them in person. For just a second I was jealous of my cousins, who'd grown up with them, who just took them for granted.

But a moment later I felt a surge of joy. I might not have grown up with fireflies, seeing them every summer—but that meant I could appreciate them more now. I could see the magic in them more clearly since they hadn't always been around.

The fire smell was carried on the breeze, and my cousins were laughing next to me as the sparks from the fire rose, up and up, like they were determined to join the stars above. I took it all in—everyone in the campfire circle, the sky and the stars and the fireflies. I twisted my new necklace around my fingers and just breathed it in for a moment, the magic and woodsmoke.

And then I jumped up—more than ready for another s'more.

PART THREE
THE CREW

CHAPTER 15

FROM THE DESK OF RYANNA STUART

Hi, Dad!

Sorry about when I called the other day.
I guess I got the time zone wrong? I
didn't mean to wake you up. (But you knew
that you should have your phone on Do Not
Disturb when you're sleeping, right? Otherwise
I'm worried people will be waking you up all
night. Are you getting your seven hours?)

How's Budapest? How's the movie? I
was sorry to hear that one of the actors
quit and stormed off the set. Hopefully
you'll find someone new! And maybe they'll

be better? Who cares if that other actor had all those Oscars? Those awards are mostly political, like you're always saying.

Things are good here! We're—

HI MR. RYANNA'S DAD, IT'S HATTIE I'M RYANNA'S COUSIN I'M AN ACTOR DO YOU NEED A KID IN YOUR MOVIE? I'M 9 BUT MY AGE RANGE IS 8–11 LET ME KNOW I CAN SEND MY HEADSHOT—

Um. Sorry about that. Hattie saw me writing to you and stole the letter. And I'd start it over, but this is my nice stationery, and I'm almost out.

Anyway, things are good here! Did you know Mom liked mysteries when she was my age? Did she like them even after she was grown up?

Everyone is swimming in the lake and yelling for me to join them.

Talk soon (and I promise not in the
middle of the night!).

Don't forget to drink water! And let me
know if you need more vitamins!

Xoxo,
Ryanna

Ginger

> Hi kid! How are you?

Me

> Hi Ginger! Sorry I didn't see this until now
> I don't keep my phone w me very much

Ginger

> That's a good thing! Keep it up

Me

> Are you feeling better?

Ginger

> ??

Me

> The flu you had!

Ginger

> Oh. Right! I am feeling better.
> Not 100% myself

But I'm sure I will, eventually!

Are you having fun?

Me

I really am 😊

From: David Stuart
To: Ryanna Stuart
Subject: Checking in

Hi, kid!

Thanks so much for writing. Are you getting along with everyone? Are you having fun?

If anything ever gets to be too much, you know we can arrange for you to talk to Dr. Wendy, right?

Thanks for reminding me about the water and vitamins—but shouldn't that be my job? 😉

The shoot is going . . . okay. I'm really ready to do something different after this, I think. More grounded. No more zombie superhero monsters.

I miss you! Remember, I'm back in August if you want to leave a little early.

Love,

Your dad

• • •

After two weeks, I felt like I had life at Camp Van Camp pretty much figured out.

Every day started with breakfast in the lodge. I always was the first one up—I found my eyes snapping open every morning like clockwork. I'd learned to just put on my bathing suit first thing, because I knew there would be swimming—usually multiple times—at *some* point during the day.

I'd sneak out of our cabin without waking my cousins and go up to the mess hall, where it was always just me and Gramps for a bit.

Making coffee had officially become my job, and it was something I was feeling more and more confident about. I loved that no matter what else the day might bring, I knew I had this one scheduled moment, to ground me and make me feel like things weren't totally chaotic.

I'd get the coffee brewing, then help my grandfather get everything ready for breakfast. For whatever reason, we waited until other people came down to start eating—but I liked having this time, just the two of us, without pressure to say anything but somehow finding it easier to talk as we set out the bagels and butter and honey and jam and fruit. We would either play music—Gramps loved Wylie Sanders and the Nighthawks; I preferred Taylor Swift—or Gramps would tell stories about back when this had been a camp. He'd tell me all about his best friend, Robert—Holden's grandfather—who'd run the camp across the lake. I'd tell him about my life in California, and the plot of my current Cara Vanessa Cole mystery. And all too soon, people would straggle in from their cabins, some always half asleep, like Uncle Dennis, some very energetic, like Aunt Abby, who liked to work out every morning before breakfast.

Once my cousins arrived, we would have breakfast—bagels or cereal or toast (never oatmeal, because yuck). Every day was different—like I'd been told, there was no schedule and no place we were required to be (other than back in the mess hall for dinner at seven). But the nice thing about that was that I could help make the schedule—we were very democratic when we decided what we felt like doing. So when I had something I really wanted to do, we could do it. And there were a *lot* of options.

There was lake stuff—swimming, or kayaking, or float races, or diving contests, or stand-up paddleboarding. Or we'd go to the equipment shed and get what we needed to play a game. Beyond the standard games that we had equipment for, we had spent three days creating our own sport, ActionBall!, that was a combination of kickball-baseball-quidditch. It involved Archie's cricket bat, so we had to steal it while he was busy working with Uncle Neal.

There was also the arts and crafts cabin. (We weren't allowed to use the kiln or the pottery wheel without supervision, but everything else was fair game.) For days that were overcast or thundery, there was the bookcase in the lodge that was stuffed with board games and puzzles and decks of cards. There was helping Max plan his epic sandcastle (since Uncle Dennis was an architect, he and Max would spread out plans over breakfast and talk about sand moisture density until Diya yelled at them for wrecking her appetite) and clearing an area of the beach for him so that he could work on it. But even when we made plans, there was no rule that we had to stick to them.

Some days I just felt like reading on the beach or the dock. I was now four books into the Cara Vanessa Cole mystery series. I liked them even better than my Miss Terry books. And the fact that these had been my mother's, with her name or initials and age written on every inside cover, made them even better.

And sometimes when I was reading, I would get little hints about her. I'd linger over every page that had a corner turned down, or a crease, or what might have been a chocolate smudge. Because my *mother* had dog-eared page forty-one, and left a receipt from Claire's marking her page. And whenever that happened, I got an excited shiver knowing that during another summer, in this same place, years ago, she'd been reading the same page as me, probably also changing her mind about the involvement of R. Ed Herring, the suspicious museum guard.

Sometimes my cousins would join me and we'd all sprawl on the dock or the beach with our books—Pete read mostly comics and graphic novels; Hattie read actors' biographies; Max was very into a complicated fantasy series that he'd tried to explain to me multiple times and I still wasn't sure I fully grasped; and Diya liked science fiction.

So between reading and float races and excursions into the woods and ActionBall!, the days were just packed.

I hadn't seen Holden again since our meeting in the woods. Occasionally we'd see a figure over on his dock, on his side of the lake, but nobody said anything about it—though I noticed whenever it seemed like there was someone on the Andersens' dock, nobody suggested races out to the floating dock or kayaking around the lake. Sometimes my cousins would start a story that he was part of—a memory from a summer past—and then would stop talking abruptly when he came up, always leaving the story unfinished.

Hattie had given her accent lesson. (None of us got better at doing a British accent—including Hattie—but Gramps was now walking around calling everyone "guv'nor.") We'd had one more lesson from an adult—Quinn had shown us how to make friendship bracelets. We found a ton of embroidery string and beads in the craft cabin, and since that lesson, we all usually had string with us, working on bracelets, getting competitive with trying to learn new patterns. (The day Hattie figured out how to do backward chevrons and then refused to teach us until Diya threatened to stab her unicorn float was a particularly dramatic one.)

After the lesson, I'd usually find myself joining Grams for her bird-watching. We didn't talk all that much, but it was nice just to hang out, searching the sky and trees for whatever it was we were looking for that day. I still hadn't found the right moment to ask about what happened with my dad—and plus, I figured, I still had over a month. I knew the right moment would come up eventually.

One day while we were tracking a hawk who was swooping in circles above us, I'd asked her if she knew why my mother had given me my name. I'd asked all my other aunts and uncles, but everyone had just said a variation of the same thing—that at some point when she was around my age, my mom had started telling everyone it was her favorite name. But nobody knew the origin of it—not even Aunt Abby, who had a really great memory (something Diya and Pete frequently complained about).

"Your name?" Grams had echoed, lowering the binoculars.

I nodded. "Nobody else seems to know where it came

from. And I asked . . . my dad. . . ." I hesitated after saying it, the way I always did on the rare occasions I brought him up around my grandparents. Grams just nodded slightly, and I continued. "And he said he didn't know either. Just that by the time he met my mom, she was already telling him that's what her daughter was going to be named someday."

Grams smiled. "That sounds like my Casey. She knew her own mind. But sometimes not everything is a mystery. She might have just liked the name."

I nodded. I knew that this could be true—and I would have believed it if my name were Olivia or Jade or Emily, something more common. But nobody had even *heard* of my name. So where had it come from? I was about to ask this when I saw a flash of wings out of the corner of my eye and pointed up. "Hawk!"

Somehow it felt like I'd been there a lot longer than I actually had. I could already understand the camp customs and jokes and routines, and even though my dad had mentioned I could leave early if I wanted to, I wasn't in any hurry to leave—after all, we had dessert after dinner *every night.*

And my favorite of all were the s'mores nights. We'd gone up the hill twice more since I'd first seen the fireflies. But even better than the s'mores were the stories I was getting about my mom. I'd learned lots of facts about her. (She had loved pineapple pizza; she had watched *Anastasia* enough that she could recite the whole movie by heart; when she was little, she'd wanted to be a marine biologist.) I would sit there with my s'more and listen as my grandparents and aunts and uncles—and sometimes Pete—spun the stories out for me. And with every anecdote about Halloween costumes and class play disasters and her yearlong mini golf obsession, it was like she was becoming more and more real to me every day.

So between everything—the float races and my cousins and the time with my grandparents and the lessons and the stories and the s'mores—after two weeks, I felt like I finally understood how things worked at Camp Van Camp. I knew the routines and the cast of characters. I was sure there wasn't going to be a whole lot anymore that was going to surprise me.

But then I walked into the mess hall on Monday morning and saw that someone had written on the Daily Activities board.

HELP WITH PLANNING A MURDER—BENJI! ☺
MEET BY PICNIC TABLE BY THE LAKE, 3:00
P.M. PAPER/PENS PROVIDED. BRING IDEAS!

"Gramps?" I called, getting worried. He came through the swinging kitchen door holding a plate of bagels.

"Hmm? How's the coffee coming, guv'nor?"

"I'm on it," I said, walking over to the huge coffee maker. "Um . . . I wasn't sure about what was written on the board for today."

"Oh yeah?" He squinted at it. "I didn't take a gander yet." He patted the top of his head, looking for his reading glasses.

"Lanyard," I said, and Gramps looked down and saw that they were attached to a lanyard around his neck. I'd gotten used to just reminding Gramps of where his glasses were at all times, since he really didn't seem to be able to keep track of them.

"There they are," he said with a smile as he put them on. "Never get old, Ryanna."

"Don't intend to."

"Excellent." He took a step closer to the board, and I expected some kind of reaction—horror, or at least alarm. But when he turned around, he just looked normal. "What?"

"I had some questions about . . . the whole *murder thing*."

"Oh, that's just Benji."

"What do you mean, 'that's just Benji'?"

"It's for his job."

"And what . . . is his job?" I was just now realizing that I still didn't know, and remembering how weird everyone had acted on that first night when I'd asked. Maybe because he was a contract killer!

"He writes crime novels," Gramps said, smiling when he saw my expression. He raised an eyebrow and headed back into the kitchen. "Disappointed?"

"No," I said honestly. I was frankly relieved that my uncle wasn't a murderer-for-hire. But now that I could think more clearly, it seemed unlikely. Did they really get to take whole summers off and live by a lake? And they probably didn't live in Maine during the rest of the year either.

I tried to think as I finally started making the coffee, measuring out the scoops now without having to walk myself through every step. My dad *loved* crime novels. He always said that he wanted to adapt one, maybe even direct it—and I knew he was getting tired of writing his superhero and robot ghost movies. But because of that, I was familiar with a lot of the writers' names—the books were all over our house.

And if we'd had anything in our house with *Van Camp* on it, I would have noticed it immediately, because I knew it was my mother's last name—she'd never changed her name even after she and my dad got married; she was always Casey Van Camp. So I definitely would have noticed them, either in our house or in the bookstore.

But as I headed back into the kitchen to get water for

the coffee, I figured that maybe Uncle Benji wasn't a very good writer, and that was why his books weren't around. No wonder he needed our help figuring out his murder.

The rest of the morning and afternoon was taken up with a game we invented called Water Is Lava. It was basically the floor-is-lava game, except with water. The water was lava, and we'd constructed an obstacle course with the floating dock, stand-up paddleboards, and kayaks that you had to try to climb over, all without falling into the water. And then once you did fall into the water—because it was hard not to—you lost points and had to do a dare.

I was totally caught up in the game—balancing on the pizza float—and it wasn't until I heard someone yell, "Hey! Aren't you going to help me with my murder?" that I remembered there was something on the schedule.

I looked over to see Uncle Benji standing at the edge of the dock, looking plaintive, and Diya took the opportunity to push me into the water and declare victory for her team.

We were still arguing about whether this was fair as we swam over and then joined everyone else for the murder talk at the picnic table. Max opted out—he said he had to work on his sandcastle preparations.

I'd never seen the picnic table—the one from my mother's picture—so packed before. We never used it to eat. The lodge was so close, after all, it had never made any sense to carry food down here and then carry empty plates back up again.

But it was full now. In addition to me, Hattie, and Diya, Uncle Benji was there with his laptop, Quinn was there with a notebook, and Archie was there, looking despondent as usual. Diya, Hattie, and I took seats on the side of the picnic table opposite the adults. There was a stack of pens and legal pads, and Hattie immediately took one and started signing her name on it over and over.

"For when I'm famous," she explained. "You need to have a great, memorable signature. Your fans expect it."

I saw that there was a thick hardback novel on the table next to Uncle Benji—and I recognized it as the one my dad had been reading on the plane. "I know that book," I said, picking it up and feeling the heft in my hands. I looked at the gray-and-black cover featuring a black bird against a white snowscape. The title, *The Stockholm Syndrome*, was printed in big letters, but most of the cover was taken up with the author's name—Sven Svensson. "My dad was reading it on the plane."

"He was?" Uncle Benji asked, sitting up straighter. "Did he like it? What did he think of the ending? How did he feel about the pacing?"

"Um." I handed the book back to him. "I'm not sure. Why do you care?"

Hattie stopped signing her name and pointed to her father with a flourish. "He wrote it!"

"I thought someone named Sven wrote it."

"He's Sven! It's a total secret." Then she gasped and clapped her hand over her mouth.

Diya sighed. "Is this why we shouldn't tell Hattie secrets anymore?"

"I'm great at keeping secrets," Hattie bristled. "I didn't tell anyone about how I broke the glass tiger in our living room."

"You what, now?" Uncle Benji asked, his face getting red. "The one your mother and I got on our honeymoon?"

"Yes, but it's actually okay," Hattie explained, "because Mom told me she broke it years ago and replaced it without telling you, so it wasn't the original." After she'd said this, her eyes opened wide. "I mean . . ."

"What!" Uncle Benji yelled.

"Forget I said it," Hattie said quickly. "I was just . . . improvising. For acting. And . . . scene!" She gave an exaggerated bow.

"Nice try, kid."

Diya shook her head. "Nobody tell Hattie any secrets."

"I've got no secrets to tell," Archie said with a deep sigh. "Because nothing happens here and I'm moldering away in Pennsylvania."

"You sure you want to be here?" Diya asked, looking at him skeptically. "You could do . . . anything else right now."

"There is *nothing* to do here and no point to life."

"Well, this will be fun," Quinn muttered.

"No, it's good," Uncle Benji said, starting to type. "It's a very Swedish energy. Real *winter in Malmö* kind of attitude. Keep it up."

"Wait, I'm confused," I said, looking back at the thick hardbound book. "Why are you Sven Svensson?"

Uncle Benji took a deep breath and explained that ten years ago, he was trying to sell a crime novel—but nobody wanted it. "It was the height of the Swedish thriller, though," he explained while Archie put his head down on the picnic table with a loud sigh. "So I thought, what do I have to lose? I moved the setting to Sweden, submitted it under a pen name . . . and it sold."

"Bestseller," Hattie said proudly, smiling at her dad.

"Yeah," Uncle Benji said with a grimace. "But that became part of the problem. Nobody could know my real identity, and I had to keep on being Sven. And I'd love to have one of the books made into a movie, but even that's too dangerous. I can't take any meetings because I don't want people to find out."

"So he's basically lying," Diya summed up.

"I'm not sure using a pen name is necessarily *lying*,"

Uncle Benji protested, but he was steadily turning redder. "But anyway, that's not why you're here. You're here because I'm stuck on the newest book. My detective character needs to solve a murder. But the readers have been complaining that they're too easy to solve."

"I thought they were also complaining you keep getting the geography of Stockholm wrong," Hattie interjected.

"Well, that too. So! Any thoughts? Whatever you got— no bad ideas, I swear."

I thought hard. I'd read a ton of mysteries—but neither Terry Turner nor Cara Vanessa Cole had ever had to deal with actual death. More like missing dogs and items stolen from toy stores and people cheating on their homework.

"Well, what about an icicle?" Diya asked. "It's the perfect weapon because when it melts, it disappears."

Quinn raised an eyebrow at her. "How do you know that?"

Diya shrugged. "Everyone knows that."

"Can you have a character die of boredom?" Archie asked, not bothering to lift his head from the table. "Just, like, waste away because there's nobody their own age to hang out with?"

"I'm not sure," Uncle Benji said.

Archie lifted his head. "I thought you said no bad ideas."

"You did say that," I confirmed. Uncle Benji sighed but typed it into his computer.

"Wait," I said, looking over at Max, who had made a

gigantic pile of sand and was running it through his fingers and making notes in his notebook. "What about a sandcastle?"

Diya shook her head. "I don't think you could use a *sandcastle* as a murder weapon."

"You might be able to," Quinn mused. "If it was big enough." She looked over at Max, and then we all did.

Max stopped and looked at us. "What?" he called, sounding nervous. "What is it?"

"Nothing!" we all called back.

"What about lava?" Diya asked after a moment, her gaze fixed on the lake where we'd had our obstacle course.

"Lava?" Archie said skeptically, but Uncle Benji nodded.

"Lava could be interesting," he said, typing on his computer.

"Do they even have volcanos in Sweden?" Archie asked.

"I feel like your detective is allowed to go on vacation sometimes, right?" I pointed out. Archie groaned.

"And," Diya said, clearly warming to her theme, "lava is hot enough that it can completely melt someone's skeleton, so they could get rid of the evidence! No body, no crime!"

"That's very helpful," Uncle Benji said, typing faster now. "Lava . . . sandcastles . . . maybe this is a holiday book. And Bjorn Bystrom goes on vacation and has to solve a case when he thinks he is just there to relax. Or! Maybe!

Someone knew he'd be there, and targeted him. . . ." Uncle Benji trailed off, typing furiously.

"Just thank me in the acknowledgments," Diya said airily.

"See, this is the nice thing about fiction," Quinn said as Hattie started practicing her signature again. "You don't have to uncover a major scandal or make a discovery in order to get hired."

Uncle Benji shot her a sympathetic look. "Still no job?"

Quinn shook her head. "Nope. If I could find some really good story and report on it, I know that would change things. . . ."

"Well, good luck finding that around here." Archie sighed as he got up and slumped away.

"I think Neal needs to vet his interns more carefully next time," Uncle Benji said, shaking his head. He looked across the table and smiled at us. "But thanks so much for your help! Ice cream for dessert to thank you, how about that?"

"Great," I said, smiling at him. "Thanks."

"Let's go," Diya said, jumping up and yanking my hair to take me with her.

"Ow!" I said, even as I followed. Hattie had jumped up too, and she and Diya were running over toward the beach, where Max was.

"Max," Hattie called, "Dad said ice cream for dessert!"

Max's eyes lit up. "Really?"

"Really!" Diya practically yelled.

"Am I missing something?" I asked as I looked between my cousins. I'd realized that Hattie lived in a land of hyperbole—everything was always the best or the worst, the most amazing day or the most tragic, with no middle ground. But generally Diya and Max had more perspective about things.

"When we say *ice cream*, we don't just mean eating dessert here after dinner," Diya explained.

"Oh," I said. I looked around at my cousins. "Then what does it mean?"

Max grinned. "It means we're going to Sweet Baby Jane's."

CHAPTER 16

Sweet Baby Jane's turned out to be an ice cream parlor. Right after the dinner dishes had been loaded into Hobart, my cousins had run out the lodge door, all of them screaming, "Not middle!"

They ran to the driveway and slapped their hands on one of the four cars parked there, then started arguing about who had gotten there first. I hadn't known this was a thing we had to do, but I resolved to make sure to do it next time. Diya and Pete got into a shoving match over who had gotten to their SUV first, with the plates that read SOLV4X. Aunt Abby had declared that because they were fighting, Diya would get middle on the way over and Pete would get it on the way back. Hattie had successfully claimed a not-middle seat in the station wagon—it turned out to be her family's car. And Max had called it on the truck, which was Grams and Gramps's. Quinn's beat-up Volvo stayed behind—we could fit into three cars, just barely, but we fit. It helped that Uncle Neal stayed behind to attend a virtual department planning meeting. Grams took his shotgun seat in the SUV, and Uncle Neal left Aunt Abby with his order and stern warnings that she not eat his ice cream on the drive back home—from the way he said this, it seemed like that had happened before.

I ended up in the truck. Gramps was driving, Quinn shotgun, and me and Max on either side of Archie, who'd ended up in the middle but claimed he didn't mind because there was no point to anything.

"Three cars just to go get ice cream," Gramps said, shaking his head. He pulled down the driveway, and we started to head into town. "This is why we used to have the camp bus."

I stared out the window in the fading twilight—it was almost dark but not quite yet—and I realized with a start that this was the first time I'd left the grounds since I'd arrived.

It was funny to realize how Camp Van Camp had become my whole world, and how everything else had disappeared. But maybe that was the whole point of actual camp too—that you got to live in the camp bubble and forget about your "real" life back home.

We parked on the main street—which was helpfully called Main Street—and headed toward the ice cream parlor.

It was a warm night—which I was still getting used to.

Back in California, even in the summers, as soon as the sun went down, it got cold. As we reached the ice cream parlor with its blue awning, I could see there was a crowd spilling out the door—it seemed like everyone else in Lake Phoenix had decided it was a good night for ice cream as well.

"Okay," Gramps said, clapping his hands together. "Van Camps, circle up. There's not enough room for all of us in there, so figure out what you want, and we'll go in and order it."

"Also, Diya's banned, remember?" Pete asked, grinning at his sister. She whacked him in the arm.

"Yes, let that be a lesson," Gramps said to our group. "Don't ask for so many tastes of flavors that you are banned from the premises."

"They shouldn't have so many flavors if they want you to be able to make an informed choice!"

"Ryanna," Grams said, nodding toward the door, "since you've never been here before, go in and see what you want."

"I've never been here before either," Archie said petulantly. Then in an undertone he muttered, "Everyone forgets about Archie."

"Okay, Archie, you go too," Grams said. "Everyone else, make your choices quick or you don't get ice cream!"

I pulled open the door of the ice cream parlor and was immediately hit with a blast of air-conditioning. The store was crowded, and I had to maneuver around people to try to get a clear view of the menu—which *was* really big, the list of flavors going on and on, so maybe Diya had a point.

I had lost Archie somewhere in the crowd and was just trying to pick something fast. As I stared at the endless flavors, it occurred to me that maybe I should have asked my cousins what they liked to order here. Because I didn't want to choose *wrong*. Who knew when we'd be back here again? How many murders would Uncle Benji need help with this summer?

I looked out through the front window and saw everyone crowding around Uncle Benji, who was typing people's orders into his phone. Maybe I could dash back outside, ask for recommendations—

"Ryanna?"

I turned around and saw Holden. He had a chocolate dip in a cone that was also chocolate-dipped. Since I'd seen him last, it looked like he'd gotten some sun—his dark red hair was lighter, and there was a sunburn across his nose. "Oh, hi." I glanced outside toward my cousins. Had Holden seen them? Or had he just ignored them, like he'd apparently been doing all summer?

"I'm glad I ran into you," he said. He looked around, then took a step over to the one spot in the store where there wasn't a crowd—near the water dispenser with little paper cups. I followed. "I need to talk to you about something."

"Um. Okay. About what?"

Holden took a big breath—then took a bite of his ice cream, like he needed the frozen courage. "I know everyone is mad at me," he said, glancing outside quickly. "I know they think I'm ignoring them."

"You *are* ignoring them." I remembered him fleeing through the woods, after all.

"But there's a reason," Holden said as a family approached the watercooler. We took a step away. "It's complicated. It's because of this thing, but now I think I have a way to fix it! But I wasn't sure they'd even hear me out because of the way I treated them, which is understandable—"

I held up my hands. "Stop. Breathe. What are you talking about?"

"Ryanna?" I looked over to see Uncle Benji come inside and take his spot in line. "Just let me know when you know what you want, okay?"

I gave him a thumbs-up. I'd forgotten I was supposed to be making ice cream decisions. "Sure thing!"

"Okay, so I'm just going to say it," Holden said. He looked more pale than he had a moment ago. His freckles were standing out on his cheeks. "So my dad and your grandpa were in court fighting over the land—"

"I know about that. And your dad got permission to build condos on his side."

Holden shook his head. His face was grave. "Not just his side."

"What are you talking about?"

"Holden?" Across the ice cream parlor, a tall blond girl was getting napkins from a dispenser with one hand while holding a triple-decker scoop in the other. "You okay?"

"Um." Holden looked down at his cone, which was dripping all over his hand and onto the floor.

"I've got you," she called.

"That's my au pair, Ella. She stays with me when my dad's out of town."

"Oh." I knew there were lots of other things I needed to ask about. But what if we had this in common? "Is, um . . . Is your mom . . . ?"

"She's back in Connecticut. I live with her during the year, and spend summers with my dad."

I nodded. It sounded like his parents were divorced or separated, which was much more normal. And while I was glad Holden's mom was still around, I couldn't help but be a little disappointed for me. I hadn't met anyone my age who'd also lost their mom. It made it really weird and lonely—like I was fluent in a language but had nobody to speak it with.

"Ryanna?" Uncle Benji called, and I saw he was moving up in the line. "Do you know yet?"

I looked from Holden to the board. I wasn't sure I was up

to this level of multitasking. "Almost!" Even though I knew it was impossible, it somehow seemed like even more ice cream choices had been added since the last time I looked at it.

"Okay," Holden said, stepping closer and lowering his voice. I saw Ella start to walk toward us. It was like a clock had just started ticking. "My dad won the lawsuit. The judge says *all* the land—his *and* yours—belongs to him. He's going to start construction in September."

"No—I heard it was just your side—"

"It's not," he said grimly. "Camp Van Camp is going to be torn down at the end of the summer."

It felt for a second like the world tilted. I reached out for the countertop to steady myself. "He's going to tear it down?" My voice came out in a hoarse whisper.

Holden nodded.

"But do they know about this? Grams and Gramps? The aunts and uncles?"

"They do," Holden said. He glanced behind him and started talking faster. "But at the beginning of the summer, I realized that the cousins didn't. Their parents hadn't told them. And I didn't want to be the one to tell them. But then I couldn't hang out with them, knowing this and not saying anything—it would have felt like I was lying."

"So why are you telling me?"

"Because I think I can fix it."

"How?"

"I'll explain everything. Can you get everyone together to meet with me tomorrow?"

"Ryanna?" Uncle Benji called, sounding panicked. I noticed there was only one group ahead of him—a couple with their arms around each other.

"Coming!" I called, looking up at the board again. The choices swam in front of my eyes. I was supposed to pick an ice cream flavor under these circumstances?

"Just get the cousins on the floating dock by nine tomorrow," Holden said, now talking fast. "I'll take care of everything after that. I think I've got a way to fix it all."

"Ready?" I looked over and saw that his au pair—Ella—was standing behind him. She smiled at me. "Hello."

"Hi," I said. I glanced over and saw Uncle Benji waving at me to hurry up. "I—"

"What's taking so long?" Archie snapped as he strode up to me. "Benjamin is almost at the front of the line, and he needs—" He stopped short. He was staring at Ella, who was calmly eating her ice cream cone. "Sorry," Archie said, blinking hard. "I wasn't . . . I mean . . . hello."

"I thought you were in a hurry," Holden pointed out.

"Hmm?" Archie asked. He frowned at me, like he wasn't sure we'd met before. "I just . . . ice cream?"

"You're in the right place for it," Ella said.

"Yes," he said, nodding vigorously. "You're so right. Just . . . couldn't be righter. I'm Archie."

She smiled at him. "Ella."

"Ryanna!" I looked over to see Uncle Benji now at the register, and I knew I was out of time.

"I have to go," I said, mostly to Holden—it looked like Archie wasn't about to move unless someone physically moved him.

"Tomorrow?" he asked, his voice barely above a whisper. "Nine?"

I nodded even though my head was spinning. The camp was going to be torn down? And I was the only one of my cousins who knew about it?

I hustled across the ice cream shop to stand next to Uncle Benji. "Sorry about that," I said. I looked at the board again, but I no longer had any appetite for ice cream. "Uh, vanilla."

"It took you that long to come up with *vanilla*?" Uncle Benji spluttered as the girl behind the counter punched it into the register.

"Okay," she said. "That'll be . . . eighty-five dollars."

Uncle Benji's eyes widened, and he took out his credit card. "This is turning into an expensive murder."

The girl behind the counter stared at us, alarmed. "Next!"

• • •

We ate our ice cream sitting on the benches and picnic tables to the side of the store. The fireflies were winking on and off in the grass, and my vanilla soft serve was creamy and sweet, but it was like I couldn't take in any of it.

I looked at my aunts and uncles and grandparents, all laughing and trying each other's flavors. How could they be keeping all this from us? Had Holden gotten it wrong?

All at once I remembered a line from the letter my grand-parents had sent. They wanted me to see the camp *while I still could*. And that was the proof I needed that Holden was telling the truth.

I didn't feel up to talking much—but that worked out because everyone else was either focused on eating their ice cream or in a happy post–ice cream daze. It was quiet on the car ride home—except for Archie, who was humming some kind of power ballad under his breath.

"D'you know," he said, wonder in his tone. I saw, to my surprise, that he was smiling. I had never seen him do it before. I honestly hadn't realized he had so many teeth. "I never understood how wonderful this town is until now. It's peaceful . . . and quaint . . . and full of unexpected beauty."

"Did you get a personality transplant in addition to your ice cream?" Quinn asked.

"I beg your pardon," Archie retorted.

Quinn laughed, and they started bickering good-naturedly, but I tuned them out. And when Gramps put on his turn signal to take us home, I felt my chest tighten as I looked at the lodge.

If Holden was telling the truth—and I believed he was—we were in the very last summer of Camp Van Camp.

CHAPTER 17

R yanna. You okay?" my grandfather asked.

"Hmm?" I replied, looking up from where I was standing by the coffee maker. My thoughts were spinning. I had barely been able to sleep last night, and I'd woken up filled with dread. Questions were rolling around in my head, and it was hard to focus. "What?"

"It's just that you've been standing like that for ten minutes," he said, gesturing to me. "And we still have no coffee."

I looked down and saw I was holding the bag of coffee grounds, but my hand with the spoon was hovering in midair above it. "Ah," I said. "Right." I started to scoop the coffee into the basket filter.

"Looks like you've got something on your mind."

"Yeah," I admitted as I poured in the water and pressed the button on the machine to brew the coffee.

"Anything I can do to help?"

"Well . . ." I looked at Gramps and took a shaky breath. "So I ran into Holden at the ice cream parlor last night. . . ." I told my grandfather everything Holden had said, ending with my promise to have my cousins out on the dock at nine.

By the time I'd finished, the coffee was made and we were sitting across from each other at the table.

Gramps took off his glasses and polished them, then put them back on with a sigh. He suddenly looked older than he had a few minutes ago. "I knew we hadn't seen Holden around much this summer, but I had thought that was Rick's—his father's—doing. I hadn't realized why he'd been avoiding us. Poor thing."

"So it is true?"

"It's a long story." Gramps took a sip of coffee and looked at me across the table. "Bob Andersen, Holden's grandfather, was my best friend in the world. He was my best man at my wedding to your grams. Just a great guy." Gramps smiled, his eyes getting faraway. "His family had owned this whole plot of land forever, and in the seventies . . ."

My eyes went wide. "In the olden days?"

Gramps winced. "I'm choosing not to acknowledge that. But back in the seventies, he sold our half of the lake to me. We didn't even go through lawyers—just wrote out a deed on a piece of paper, we both signed it, and I gave him a check. And then I built the camp here with your grams, and then there were two camps across the lake from each other, and it was great."

"What happened?"

"Well, Bob closed his camp in the eighties, and we closed ours in the nineties," Gramps said. "And we just enjoyed spending time in our houses without having to run a business. And Bob and I would kayak out to meet each other in the middle of the lake and catch up. Our families were close—your mom even dated Rick for a while."

"What! My mom dated Holden's *dad*?"

Gramps laughed. "You don't have to sound so disgusted. They were teenagers, it wasn't too serious. But honestly, I wasn't so upset when it ended. Even when he was a kid, Ricky was . . . not my favorite," he finally finished, his tone diplomatic.

"So what happened?"

"Well, five years ago, Bob died," Gramps said. His eyes looked sadder than I'd ever seen them. "And I didn't have my friend anymore. I couldn't kayak out to the middle of the lake and go fishing, or just chat about my day with my oldest pal. And that was hard enough. But then Rick demanded proof that we were allowed to be here at all."

"Wait, I thought you said that you and Bob signed a paper. And that you paid him!"

"Well, you know me and holding on to things," he said with a sigh. "I couldn't find it anywhere. And I was even pretty sure I'd put it in my office for safekeeping. But honestly, Ryanna, I hadn't thought I'd need it. I never thought Rick would try to kick us out."

"But that's not fair!"

Gramps nodded. But when he spoke, his voice wasn't angry—it was just sad. "I know. But Rick said that since I couldn't produce the paper Bob and I signed, we were on this land illegally, and he owned it all."

"But you paid for it! The two of you signed a paper!"

"I know. And we hired lawyers, and so did Rick, and we took it to court. But without that document, we didn't have a case. At least he gave us till the end of the summer before he tears it all down." He shrugged. "We've had a good run here. Lots of good memories—made even better by you being here. Just think, if you hadn't come, how would the coffee get made?"

"Gramps."

"We'd all be walking around here half asleep! Wishing we had someone to provide us with caffeine!"

"Why didn't you tell us?"

Gramps turned his mug in his hands. "We all decided we wanted you kids to have one last summer. We didn't want everything to be overshadowed."

I nodded—then got up the courage to ask what had been going around and around in my head since last night. "Was that why you finally wrote to me—since it's the last summer? Was that the reason?"

Gramps took a breath, then nodded. After a moment, he said, like he was choosing all his words carefully, "Your grams and I wanted to make sure you came here so you could remember it. This place is your history, after all. And we knew it was what your mom would have wanted."

I nodded. I could sense that there was something my grandfather wasn't telling me, but I didn't know how to ask what that was. "If we could find the paper," I said slowly, trying to put things together, "we could stop Holden's dad?"

"We could, yes. But when I tell you we've looked everywhere, we've looked *everywhere*."

"And you didn't have it in an email?"

"We didn't even *have* email in the seventies."

I gasped and he laughed, just as Aunt Abby came in through the door, fresh from her morning triathlon. "Morning, all!" she said cheerfully as she helped herself to some coffee. Then she looked at us, and her smile faltered. "What's going on here?"

Gramps stood up from the table. "Let's gather the troops. We need to have a tribunal."

• • •

I hadn't been sure what a tribunal was, but it seemed to mean a meeting with everyone in the lodge, crammed onto the squashy couches or sitting on the floor.

My cousins looked either annoyed or perplexed, but I could see the adults exchanging glances and Pete frowning hard, his arms crossed tight across his chest.

"What is this about?" Diya asked around a yawn. "I'm starving."

"Won't take long," Gramps said. He and Grams were sitting in two chairs pulled close to each other, and she reached over and squeezed his hand. He took a big breath. "We need to tell you all something."

By the time Gramps had finished—with Grams chiming in—Hattie was crying. Max was twisting his hands together, and Diya's face had flushed a dull red, and she was glaring at the woven throw rug.

"So you lied to us," Diya said. Her voice was shaking. "None of us knew—"

"I knew," Pete said. We all stared at him.

"What!" Diya seemed even more outraged about this.

"We thought your brother was old enough," Uncle Neal said, "to make an informed decision about how he wanted to spend his summer."

"So that's why you didn't go to soccer camp," Max said. Pete nodded.

"I can't believe you lied," Hattie said. She turned to her dad. Uncle Benji was holding up his phone, where he'd FaceTimed Aunt Katie in.

"We shouldn't have," Quinn said. "But I think we all wanted to pretend it wasn't happening."

A heavy silence fell over the lodge. I looked around—I couldn't quite believe it. Everything about this place felt fixed and permanent. And in two months it would all be *gone*?

"Okay," Diya said, slapping her hand onto the floor. "What's the plan? We have to do something."

"What do you mean?" Aunt Abby asked, her voice sharp. "Kids, there's nothing to be done here. If there was a solution, we would have found it years ago."

"But," Hattie said, shaking her curls—somehow even they looked deflated this morning—"maybe there's something that you just haven't thought of? And—"

"No," Uncle Benji said firmly. "Henrietta, I need you to stay out of this. It's way above your pay grade. It's way above mine."

"Listen to your dad," Aunt Katie said from the phone. "I think you kids should just let this go. You should all concentrate on having fun."

The tribunal broke up after that. Everyone was subdued and sad—even the grown-ups who were trying to put a positive spin on it.

We all ended up sitting on the front steps of the lodge, my cousins still looking shell-shocked.

"I can't believe this," Hattie said, her voice wobbling. "What are we supposed to do in the summers now? Am I just supposed to stay in *Maine*?"

"So Holden told you all this?" Max asked.

I nodded. "Last night at the ice cream parlor."

"He should have just *told* us instead of avoiding us all summer," Max said.

Diya whirled around to face me. "Wait a sec, why did he tell *you*? He doesn't even know you!"

I suddenly realized that there was a part to this I'd forgotten to tell my cousins—the tiny beam of light at the end of the tunnel. "He told me because he says he has a plan." My words were coming out fast. "He thinks he has a way to fix it."

My cousins all exchanged looks—Diya skeptical, Max wary, Hattie hopeful.

"What plan?" Diya asked.

"If we meet him on the floating dock at nine," I said, pushing myself to my feet, "we can find out."

CHAPTER 18

B y the time we made it out to the dock—Hattie and
Max shared a kayak; I took a stand-up paddleboard;
Diya swam—Holden was standing there, waiting
for us.

I saw that there was a one-person kayak tied to the ladder, the oar resting inside it. Holden gave me a quick smile,
then adjusted his Yankees cap a few times, moving the brim
up and down. He looked nervous.

We secured our watercraft and climbed onto the dock,
my cousins staying on the opposite end from him.

"So what is this about?" Diya asked, narrowing her eyes.

"I should start off by saying sorry," Holden said. He
took a shaky breath. "I didn't know how to be friends with
you and not talk to you about what was happening. So I
just . . . stopped."

"Why didn't you just tell us?" Max asked.

Holden shrugged. "I figured that if your parents weren't letting you know . . . there was a reason. And I didn't want to go against that."

"Well, don't just disappear next time," Hattie admonished.

"*Next* time?" Diya asked.

"I mean, you didn't have to speak the words. You could have written us a letter! Or used semaphore flags! Or—"

"Or you could have told us the truth," Diya interrupted. "That's what a *friend* would have done."

Holden's shoulders slumped. "I know. But since it's my dad who's causing all this . . ." His voice trailed off and he shrugged unhappily.

"So what's the plan?" I prompted after a moment of awkward silence. "You said you had a way to fix this?"

"Right," Diya said. She pulled her braid forward, squeezed the water out of it, then tossed it over her shoulder again and folded her arms. "Talk."

"We have to stop the construction," Holden said, looking around at all of us. "We have to stop what my dad is doing, and I think I know how."

"Really?" Hattie asked, her voice going high and excited. "That's great!"

"I don't believe you," Diya said, shaking her head.

"I'm telling the truth. I've been trying to figure it out for weeks now—because we have to do it before it's too late."

"You *want* to stop your dad?" Max asked, frowning.

"Of course I do!"

"But you would go against him?" Hattie asked, her eyes wide. "And his whole . . ." She made a vague gesture with her hands, like she was searching for the right word. Finally she finished. "Thing?"

"I mean, he's not going to be happy about it," Holden said, swallowing hard. "But he's doing the wrong thing, and I know it. And he does too, probably. Deep down." All of my cousins gave him *Really?* looks, and Holden smiled. "*Very* deep down."

"Okay," Diya said. "So *if* I believe that you're going to be on our side and try to stop your dad, what's the plan? How do we do it?"

Holden nodded at his house across the lake, then looked back at all of us. "If you come with me, I can show you."

"Whoa," I said as I stepped inside Holden's house and looked around. Everything was huge and white and modern. It was the opposite of our overstuffed, cozy, slightly worn lodge.

I'd been to houses in LA that were similar—places where none of the couches looked comfy and I was always afraid of spilling something or breaking something.

"Are all the houses going to be like this?" Max asked, his

eyes wide as we walked into the house. "The ones your dad is building?"

"That's the plan," Holden said grimly. "Ours is supposed to be the show house, so people can 'see the vision.'"

"It's *horrible*," Diya said. "This house used to be great! Don't you remember? And it's all *gone* now. This is a tragesty!"

"She used my word," Hattie whispered to me.

"I hate it too," Holden assured her. "So here's what I'm thinking. First thing, we'll—" He stopped short and Diya did too, causing a mini pileup.

"What?" I asked, then saw what they were all looking at. "Oh." Archie was sitting at the island of the big all-white kitchen next to Holden's au pair, Ella, looking shocked to see us.

"What are you doing here?" he asked.

"What are *you* doing here?" Hattie replied.

"I'm just, um, visiting a friend," Archie said, sounding flustered. "Is that not allowed?"

"Well, we're doing the same thing," Diya retorted, then paused. "But 'friend' might be too strong. We're visiting a former friend who then kept relevant information from us and has been relegated to acquaintance with potential, at the moment."

Holden considered this, then nodded. "I'll take it."

"Want a snack?" Ella asked. She didn't seem fazed by any of this.

"I'm okay," Holden said. He nodded his head down the hall. "We're just going to go this way. Maybe don't come? Not that we're doing anything wrong!"

"We're going to hang out in Holden's room," Hattie said smoothly, giving an angelic smile. "Thanks so much for the snack offer, though!"

Holden hurried down the hall, and we all followed behind him. "What was that?" Diya hissed.

"I know," Holden said, shaking his head. "I'm terrible at lying!"

"Well, you're going to have to get better at it," Hattie said. "It's why I'm *great* at it, because lying is just like acting. Like right back there, for instance, my character was a girl with nothing to hide, and my objective was to make sure your babysitter didn't suspect us."

"She's an au pair," Holden said.

"What's the difference?" Max asked.

"I think my dad thinks 'au pair' sounds fancier."

"Is Archie dating your babysitter?" Max asked, glancing behind him. "I mean, au pair?"

Holden shrugged as he reached a closed door. "Maybe? Ella sure was talking about him a lot last night when we came back from ice cream. She likes his accent."

Diya shuddered. "Gross."

"So this is my dad's office. This is where all the information about the construction is."

"Whoa," I said again as we stepped inside. It was a big office, also all in white. There was a desk with a computer on it, and neatly stacked papers. But mostly I was looking at the wall behind the desk. There were floor-to-ceiling shelves on it, and they were filled with ships in bottles.

Miss Terry had solved a case, in *The Nautical Riddle*, where it turned out one of the clues had been hidden in a ship in a bottle. But I wasn't sure I'd ever seen one in real life—let alone a whole wall of them.

"Yeah," Holden said as he followed my eye. "They're my dad's hobby. They're called impossible bottles. It's what he does to relax. He's been doing them since he was a little kid. When he was younger, he used to build them with whatever was around, but now he orders these fancy kits. . . ."

"They're really something," Max said.

"But isn't it also kind of sad?" Diya tipped her head to the side. "Like, all those ships that aren't going anywhere. Just stuck inside and never able to sail."

"That's so profound," Hattie gushed.

"I really didn't mean for it to be," she said. She turned to Holden. "Okay, we're here. So how are we going to stop this?"

"I was thinking that we'd find the information in here,"

he said as he crossed around behind his dad's computer. "And maybe we could call and cancel one of the permits and then construction couldn't go through!" He looked at us expectantly. Diya and Max frowned, and Hattie shook her head.

"Sorry, but that plan isn't going to work," Hattie said, speaking slowly and a little pityingly. "They're not going to think any of us sound like your dad. And how do we know the permit people aren't going to reach out to your dad to confirm it?"

"Hattie's right," Diya said slowly, like she was figuring this out as she spoke. "We need to do something where it would stop this and throw a wrench into the plans—so much so that it would be really hard to get it going again."

"Or impossible," Max said. "Like some reason why construction wouldn't go forward and your dad would have to give up."

"So what can we do?" I asked. "How do you shut down a construction project?"

Hattie clapped her hands together. "Ooh, what if there was a dead body?"

Max frowned. "Are you suggesting murder? Because that's not anything I can be involved in. I think maybe you've been spending too much time helping your dad with his books."

"Not *murder*," Hattie said, rolling her eyes. "But if it's a crime scene, don't they have to stop everything? And put up the tape and nobody's allowed to go in or out because they might disturb the evidence?"

"But we don't have a dead body," Holden said, then looked nervously at Diya. "Right?"

"Of course not. The closest thing we have is Karma, who's on the bottom of the lake."

Hattie flinched. "Too soon!"

"What if we just put up some crime scene tape?" Max asked, snapping his fingers. "Then we could get the benefits of having a crime scene without the, you know, dead body of it all."

"I think that might lead to a lot of questions," Diya said. "But good thinking. I like the direction we're going."

I walked behind the desk to take a closer look at the ships while I tried to think of things that could get a construction project shut down. A bunch of my dad's movies had gotten shut down right before filming, but that usually had to do with salary disputes or third-act issues with the script or actors failing their insurance physical, none of which seemed like it was going to be helpful for us.

I looked up at the wall of ships in bottles and noticed that most of them had little plaques underneath them with the date they'd been made. From what I could see, it looked like the ones at the top were the oldest, and the ones right at my eyeline and lower down were the newer ones. You could tell once you knew—the ones at the very top looked a little less polished and professional, which made sense if Holden's dad had been making them when he was a kid. It looked like one of the sails even had writing on it. . . .

"Ryanna!"

I jumped and stumbled back into the desk, bracing my hand on it to steady myself and accidentally moving the mouse. The computer screen came to life. "What?"

"Just asking if you had any thoughts," Diya said. "Meeting with Holden about this was your idea, after all."

"Well," I said, stalling. "I . . ."

I looked at the computer screen, which had woken up. The screen saver was an artist's rendering of what things would look like when our camp was torn down. There were condos that looked like Holden's house, each with their own docks. I felt my heart pound as I stared at it, these terrible houses where right now we had the mess hall and the infirmary and the hill where we made s'mores. And all of it was just going to *disappear*?

"Wait," I said, realizing something. "Your dad's computer doesn't have a password?"

"I guess not. Why?"

"Well," I said. "The whole problem with calling as Holden's

dad was that they would know we weren't him, right?"

"Yeah," Diya said. "So?"

"So . . . if we write an email from his account . . . they'll think it *was* him. Right?"

Everyone just stared at me for a moment. Max shifted his feet uncomfortably. "I don't know," he said. "That seems like crossing a line, right? Isn't mail fraud a thing?"

"That's actual mail," Diya said. She tilted her head to the side, like she was studying me. "I didn't think you had it in you, Ryanna."

I wasn't sure if that was a compliment or not. "Thanks?"

"I don't know if we should do this," Max said. He started to edge toward the door, like he was distancing himself from all of us. "It seems like a bad idea."

"I think the bad idea is letting Holden's dad bulldoze our camp and build ugly condos on it!" Diya said.

Hattie nodded. "She has a point for once."

"For *once*?"

Max shook his head. "But we could get in, like, actual trouble for this."

"Nothing ventured, nothing gained," Hattie said.

I frowned. "Isn't that from a musical?"

"Things can be from a musical and still be true!"

"None of you will get in trouble," Holden said. "I'll take the blame."

"Oh." Max suddenly looked much less worried. "Okay, then."

"So we're doing this?" Diya asked. We all nodded and she grinned. "Excellent. Let's shut this down."

Holden searched his dad's emails until he found the name of a company he recognized—the contractor who was going to be doing a lot of the work. "Okay," he said, opening up an email. "Now we just need . . . to write it."

We were all standing behind Holden, who was sitting on the desk chair, leaning forward to look at the computer monitor. Hattie glanced around at us. "Now this is feeling weird. Like, what if someone was going around writing emails under my name? I wouldn't like it."

"But you're also not trying to raze a family home to the ground," Diya pointed out.

"That is true."

"It's like your dad said, right, Hattie?" I asked. "When he was talking about writing under a pen name. It's like we're doing the same thing. Just temporarily pretending to be someone else."

"Okay," Holden said, flexing his fingers over the keys. "Let's do it."

Twenty minutes later, we were pretty happy with what we'd come up with, and Holden rolled the chair back proudly.

Dear Mr. Contractor,

Hello and greetings, also salutations. Sorry to inform you, with regrets, that I would like to cancel the construction project we have been speaking of, and about.

I have changed my mind, and also I realized the land wasn't mine to build on. So I better go off and think about how I ended up in this mess!

Because of that, please don't contact me about this. I need some time with my thoughts. And feelings.

If I've already paid you, you can just keep the money. Call it a bonus.

Thank you and goodbye forever,

Rick Andersen
Adult

"It's really good," Hattie said. She held up her hand, and Max gave her a high five. "Should I be a writer instead of an actress?"

"It works," Diya said, reading it over again. "Send it."

Holden looked at me and I nodded, and a second later

the *whoosh* sound let us know that the email had been sent. I let out a breath and looked around at my cousins. "Do we think that did it?"

"Well, we'll wait and see," Max said. "Holden, you'll have to let us know if your dad says anything, or if he's constantly trying to get in touch with his contractor or something. That's how we'll know it's working."

"Are you still here?" Archie asked from the doorway.

Holden rolled his chair back from the desk, I turned to look at the ships in bottles, and Hattie picked up the book nearest to her. She opened it upside down and pretended to read, muttering, "Interesting, interesting."

"We were going to head out," Diya said. She folded her arms. "But *you've* been here awhile too. Is my dad paying you to flirt with a babysitter?"

"Au pair," Holden, Max, and Hattie said at the same time.

"Your father isn't paying me at all," Archie said with a sigh. "It's an internship for credit. You'll understand someday."

Diya shuddered. "God, I hope not."

"Anyway, if you're leaving, could I get a ride? I assume one of you came in a boat?"

"How did you get here?" Max asked.

"I walked," Archie said defensively. "I don't know how to

drive on the wrong side of the road. Your American system makes no sense. And it's longer than you think to walk all the way around."

"I took a kayak," Max said. "You can have my spot."

"Thanks," Archie said. He nodded—but didn't actually leave the doorway.

I looked at Holden. "So! You'll let us know what's happening with the . . . project?"

Holden nodded. "For sure. As soon as I hear. Or . . . don't hear."

"Great," Hattie said with a little hop. "I have a good feeling about the, um, project."

Diya nodded at him as she left. "Holden," she said, her tone still cool.

I gave him a smile as I headed out. "Bye."

He smiled back. "Bye, Ryanna." Then he mouthed the words *And thank you.*

"Okay, I know you all are up to something," Archie said as we walked out the door and into the morning sunshine, "but I actually don't want to know anything about it, because then I can claim full deniability if I'm asked."

Diya nodded. "Probably smart."

We went about the rest of the day as usual. Max and Uncle Dennis were finalizing sandcastle plans—they'd decided to do the building all in one day but were waiting for the perfect conditions, whatever those were. We had make-your-own sandwiches for lunch, and after lunch, in what she claimed was a fun way for us to learn math, Aunt Abby taught us blackjack. But the whole time I was going through all of it—reading on the dock or making myself a BLT or learning you always hit on ten—my mind was back with Holden and what we'd done. Had it worked? Were we on our way to stopping this? Or had his dad found out? Was Holden in trouble? Would the rest of us get in trouble too?

After Max had beaten us all, the blackjack lesson broke up, and I'd gone bird-watching with Grams. But my thoughts were all over the place, and even seeing a black-capped chickadee didn't help. I wandered back out to the beach, where I could see Max pacing around the area he'd planned for the sandcastle, and Hattie reading as she floated on the stand-up paddleboard, and Diya practicing dives off the dock. Quinn and Uncle Benji were sprawled out on the beach, reading, and Max kept glancing over at them nervously, like they were encroaching on his turf.

I walked onto the dock and sat on the end, letting my bare feet skim the water. "Want to race?" I asked Diya when she surfaced from her most recent swan dive. But before she could answer, I noticed Holden standing on the floating dock, waving at us.

"Look," I said to my cousins. "Max!" He looked up from where he was drawing a literal line in the sand and saw where I was pointing.

"Let's go," Diya said. Max hustled over from the beach, splashing into the water, and I dove into the lake and started swimming out. Hattie got back on the stand-up paddleboard, and it looked like she was towing Diya, who was holding on to the bottom fin.

We all reached the floating dock around the same time, Max pushing himself up out of the water, then helping Hattie up, and Diya and I using the ladders on either side, pushing the bobbing buoy out of our way as we did so.

"Well?" I asked as we all stood there dripping. It was just starting to get colder out—it wasn't *cold* yet, but we were at the point in the day where it was warmer to be in the water than out of it.

"Did we do it?" Hattie asked, smiling hopefully.

Holden shook his head. "Sorry," he said with a deep sigh. "The contractor called my dad after he got the email, and then he called me. I tried to pretend it was just a prank, and I think he bought it. But he was *really* mad. I don't care about that, but I wasn't able to stop it. And his computer has a password on it now."

I nodded as I let out a long breath. Somewhere, deep down, I'd known that was too easy—that we weren't going to undo all this with just one email.

"Anyway," Holden said, turning to go, "sorry it didn't work out."

I looked at Max, about to say something, but it was Diya who spoke, surprising me. "That's okay," she said. "We're just getting started. We'll figure out a new plan."

Holden turned back to us and then smiled slowly—it was like the sun coming out; it changed his whole expression. "*We'll* figure it out?" he asked, his voice hopeful.

"Sure," she said, then glanced over at me. "You know, we never did get to race."

I smiled, feeling like I knew where she was going with this. "Want to race now?" The words were barely out of my mouth before Diya yelled, "Go!" She pushed Holden into the water, then dove in herself.

"First one to our dock and then back to this one wins!" she yelled. I jumped in behind her and saw Max do a cannonball and Hattie flop onto the stand-up paddleboard and start paddling with her hands.

I swam as fast as I could, even though Max was swimming from side to side, trying to block me. Diya was so busy trash-talking all of us, she missed Holden slipping past her. Hattie had now gotten off the paddleboard but was yelling about how having to tow it was slowing her down, and I was laughing every time I came up for air.

And by the time we made it back to the floating dock, and Holden was celebrating his victory, and Diya was arguing for a rematch, and Hattie was talking about how she needed extra equipment points, I knew that the estrangement had officially ended—and that Holden was back.

CHAPTER 19

I can't believe you found a treasure map," Holden said, his eyes wide.

I grinned. "We did." I'd told him the story over breakfast that morning. As soon as I'd finished, he'd asked if he could see it. So we were now en route to the Hummingbird Cabin so I could show him.

Since Holden had come back into the group, there had been no more drama about it. It suddenly just felt like he'd always been there, slotting in easily with us. He'd usually swim or kayak over to our side of the lake at some point in the morning and then sometimes not leave until night.

I had been worried that some of my aunts and uncles might hold his stupid dad against him. And the first morning he'd stood in the doorway of the mess hall, looking unsure, I'd noticed a few raised eyebrows from the adults. But Gramps had welcomed him in with a bellowing *hello,* and after that everyone just seemed to accept his presence, like he'd never been gone.

In addition to swimming and kickball games and float races, we spent a good portion of every day brainstorming ways to stop Holden's dad. But we hadn't been able to put any plans into action since the email failure. Hattie was convinced she could somehow hypnotize Holden's dad into forgetting he wanted to tear down our camp. And even though we had been trying to dissuade her from this, she was deep into a how-to hypnosis book, trying to learn the technique.

"That's so awesome, Ryanna," Holden enthused as we made it to the gravel path and headed toward the cabin. I was still wearing my flip-flops—my feet hadn't toughened up enough to be able to walk on the gravel like my cousins did, but it *was* getting easier, and I didn't need them quite as much. I figured once I could run around the gravel and not feel anything—like everyone else—it would mean I was truly one of them. Holden frowned. "Ryanna."

I stopped and looked at him. "Holden."

"No. I just meant—I've never met anyone with that name before. Where does it come from?"

I started walking again. I should have known I'd have this conversation with him at some point—I had it with everyone I met, practically. "My mom always said she was going to name her daughter that someday. But nobody seems to know where she got it from." I could hear the frustration in my voice. I'd now asked everyone—even Gramps—but nobody had any answers for me. It just seemed like it was going to be a forever-unanswered question—even though it was about something as basic and important as my *name*. "What about Holden?"

"What about it?"

"What does it mean?"

He shrugged. "It was the name of the main character from my dad's favorite book. He says I can't read it until I'm in high school, though. He wants me to *understand the nuances*."

"Did I tell you what my Gramps told me? Our parents *dated*."

Holden's eyes went wide. "What?!"

"Yeah, apparently when they were teenagers. Maybe the next time your dad is back, you could ask him? If my mom ever said anything to him about my name?"

I knew it was a long shot—and I also had no idea when Holden's dad would even be around. I'd only glimpsed him once, when we'd been hanging out by Holden's dock. We'd seen his sports car pull up through all the gaps where the trees had been recently cut down. He'd had one of those cars where the doors rose up like birds' wings, and when Diya saw him get out of it, she made a face and said we'd head back to our side of the lake.

"I can ask," Holden said. He still looked appalled by this information.

We stepped inside the Hummingbird Cabin, and I walked immediately to where I'd lined up all my mother's books on the dresser. I was keeping my important things— the picture of her, the map—tucked inside the very first Cara Vanessa Cole book Grams had given me.

I pulled the map out and opened it carefully. Holden leaned over to look. "So cool," he said. He tapped the bottom of the map, with its jagged edge. "What does *protect the things* mean?"

I shrugged. Occasionally I wondered this myself, a tiny thought buzzing around my brain like a mosquito. "I think it must have meant this." I pulled my necklace out from under my tank top and held it toward him so he could see it. "This was what was inside."

"Does the key go to anything?"

"Not that I've found." It was tiny and looked mostly decorative—it was much too small to open any of the doors at the camp.

The screen door swung open, and Hattie bounced in, stopping short when she saw us. "Are we hanging out in here?"

"I was just showing Holden the treasure map."

"Diya was looking for you two. She wants to play ActionBall! before it gets too hot."

"ActionBall!?" Holden asked.

"We'll walk you through it," I assured him.

"Well, it's really awesome," Holden said, handing it back to me. "I wish I could find a treasure map."

"And this was with it when we found the treasure," I said. I pulled out the second paper and smoothed it out before I showed it to him, letting my fingers linger over my mother's writing.

Congratulations! You one!
CVC 12

Holden looked down at the paper for a long moment, then picked up the treasure map as well. He frowned, his eyebrows drawing together.

"What?"

"She spelled 'won' wrong," Holden said slowly.

"Maybe she was in a hurry, okay?"

"But she spelled 'congratulations' right. And that's a much harder word."

I took the paper from him, staring down at it. I'd always taken it at face value—I'd never even assumed there was more to it than a congratulatory note. "What are you saying?"

"Maybe it's another clue!"

I was tempted for a second to just dismiss this as Holden looking for a treasure map where none existed—he'd just said, after all, that he wished he could find one. But then I thought about my mom, and the birthday string tradition she'd started. And what my dad had said when he dropped me off—that she'd always loved a treasure hunt.

The door banged open again, and Diya walked in. "What's going on here? Are we playing ActionBall! or not?"

"In a second," I said. My heart was beating hard as I looked at the paper.

"CVC twelve," I muttered to myself. I'd just assumed it meant Casey Van Camp. But as I turned the book over, my eyes widened as I realized another possibility. "Cara Vanessa Cole. Twelve."

"What is she talking about?" Diya asked.

My hand was shaking as I reached for the twelfth book in the series—*Cara Vanessa Cole and the Drawing Room Mystery.* I flipped through it. My pulse was racing. And sure enough—halfway through the book, a folded piece of paper fell out.

"What is it?" Hattie asked in a whisper.

I picked it up and unfolded it, then turned around so everyone could see. "It's another map."

"Wow." Hattie shook her head as she slid the two pieces of the map together, the jagged edge lining up perfectly. "It's like a puzzle."

We'd grabbed Max and then all decamped to the picnic table by the dock, the spot where my mother's picture had been taken. And the second map actually made the first map make more sense—it was part of a *bigger* map.

You could see the lake on this one, and the dock, even though the camp buildings were still missing. The words along the bottom made more sense now too—on the first map, it had just said *PROTECT THE THINGS*. But this map continued the sentence, lining up perfectly—*THAT MATTER MOST.*

And best of all, there was another *X*—this one next to the floating dock. Meaning that the treasure hunt was continuing—that we hadn't even found the final treasure yet.

My mom had more to tell me.

"So this is underwater, right?" Holden tapped on the *X*. He hadn't stopped smiling since the second part of the map had fallen out of the book. He seemed thrilled to be part of an actual treasure hunt.

"There's nowhere to hide anything above the lake," Max agreed with a nod. "So we won't be making that same mistake again."

"Aunt Casey hid something underwater? And it's been there for twenty-five years?" Diya frowned.

"You think it will still be there, right?" A cold fear gripped my stomach. I knew a lake wasn't like the ocean—it wasn't like there was anywhere for this to *go*—it's not like it could get swept out to sea. But still—what if something had happened to it? What if a fish had eaten it?

Max nodded so enthusiastically, his glasses almost fell off. "Things can be preserved underwater for centuries. Did I tell you about the documentary I saw about the *Titanic*?"

"Yes," Diya and Hattie groaned in unison.

"I can't hear any more about the plates they found in the china cabinet," Diya said wearily.

"They were still lined up perfectly!" Max blurted out, like he couldn't help himself. "We'd thought the pattern was lost to history!"

"What do you think it is?" Hattie asked me. "Another necklace?"

"I have no idea."

"This seems like a lot of work to hide another necklace," Max pointed out.

"But if it *is* a necklace," Hattie said, her voice faux-casual, "maybe I could have this one?"

Diya shot her a look. "Hattie."

"What?"

"Protect the things that matter most," Max said, running his hand over the words. "What does that mean?"

"I mean, it's good advice," Holden said with a shrug.

I gasped, suddenly struck by a gigantic revelation. What if this wasn't leading us to another necklace? What if the treasure at the end of this treasure map . . . was the *camp*?

I stared at the paper. My heart was hammering. *Protect*

the things that matter most. That's what she'd written. And what would have mattered more to her than this place?

"What?" Holden looked concerned. "You okay?"

I looked around at everyone. "What if the treasure is bigger than we think it is? Do you know about the piece of paper?" I started to explain about the deed for the land that had been made in the olden days, before there was email, but Diya cut me off.

"Of *course* we know about it. There was a day two years ago where we turned the whole house upside down looking for it."

"That was the day I found that cool rock!" Max enthused. Diya just looked at him, and he turned his grin into a frown. "But, I mean, also sad. Because we didn't find the paper."

"Well, I think we're going to find it!" I took a big excited breath. "I think it's what the map is leading to."

I saw Diya and Hattie exchange a look. "What?"

"I'm not saying it *isn't* the deed," Diya said, even though she still sounded skeptical. "But it might just be more jewelry."

"Yay!" Hattie exclaimed.

"I think it's the deed," I said stubbornly.

"You really think your mom would have hidden something so important?" Holden asked.

"I don't know," I admitted. "But I think she might have."

"Well, we can look for this," Diya said. "But I don't think we should depend on it to save the camp."

"But—"

"I for one am getting much better at hypnotizing people." Hattie sat up straighter. "So we could be ready to implement Operation Pocket Watch any day now."

Diya raised an eyebrow. "Who have you successfully hypnotized?"

"A true magician never reveals her secrets."

Max turned to Holden. "Any luck on cracking your dad's computer password?"

Holden shook his head. "And I've tried everything. His name, my name, my birthday . . ."

"Maybe he doesn't know your birthday?" Diya suggested. "Maybe try some other dates in case he's getting it wrong?"

"Can we continue this conversation on the dock?" I asked as I stood up. Suddenly all I wanted to do was find whatever this map was leading to.

"You want to start looking right now?" Max asked.

"Of course!" I swung my legs off the bench and started running toward the dock. "I'm sure we'll find it in no time at all!"

"Anything?" Diya asked me as I surfaced. She was lying on the floating dock, a paperback copy of *The Fellowship of the Ring* in front of her. It was so old and battered, the spine cracked and re-cracked, that it lay open flat.

"Nope," I said. I held on to the ladder, pulled my goggles off my head, and threw them onto the dock.

It had been three days since we'd discovered the second map, and we hadn't found anything under the floating dock. I'd been so sure that whatever it was would be right there waiting for me that this had come as a shock. We weren't making the same mistake we'd made with the tree. This *had* to be in the water. So where was it?

Holden surfaced next to me and shook his head. "Nothing." He pushed himself up out of the water to sit on the dock. "Where are you?" he asked Diya, leaning over to look at her book.

"Council of Elrond," she said, moving it away from him. "Don't tell me what happens!"

"You've seen the movies," Max pointed out from the other side of the dock.

"But I haven't *read* it," Diya said, sounding annoyed. She marked her page by folding down a corner (I winced) and shut the book.

"Anything?" Hattie asked as she floated past on Harold the unicorn. (We'd decided to call him Harold last week. We'd also decided to name the swan float Odette and to call the slice of pizza float Slice of Pizza.) I shook my head and climbed up to sit on the ladder. It was late in the day and starting to get colder out—we'd spent most of the day on the water.

My cousins had been helping off and on, but when we hadn't found anything right away, they'd lost interest—preferring to brainstorm plans for how to shut down the construction than search underwater. Only Holden had been helping me consistently, not getting distracted by sandcastle plans or hobbits or pizza floats.

But despite all that, we still weren't any closer to finding it.

"I'll take a turn searching tomorrow," Diya said. She closed the book and looked around. "But in the meantime, we need to work on plan B for how to stop Holden's evil dad."

"Hey now," Holden protested.

"Who has other ideas for how to stop Holden's dad, who is probably good way down deep inside?" Max asked. Diya snorted.

"I tried to get Quinn to do something," Hattie said, swimming back over, towing Slice of Pizza. "But she just kept talking about *ethics* or whatever." A few days ago over breakfast, Hattie had pitched Quinn on writing an exposé about the situation, telling her it was just the story she needed to get a job. But Quinn had explained that until there were hard facts, it would be out of bounds for a journalist to write a story that she had a personal stake in—it would just seem like she had a grudge.

"I had a thought," Max said slowly, and we all turned to look at him. "What if we found an endangered species?

Then they couldn't do construction, right? Because the land would be protected?"

"An endangered species?" Diya asked skeptically.

"Ooh!" Hattie said, clapping her hands together. "Like a unicorn!"

"Well . . . I guess, technically," Max said. "But I was thinking more like something real and less . . . fantastical."

"Like what?" Holden asked.

"I don't know," Max said with a shrug. "I hadn't gotten that far yet."

"It might work," I said a little grudgingly as I scratched a mosquito bite on my elbow. Last year my dad and Ginger and I had gotten really into this nature documentary series, watching it every night on our couch, passing a bowl of popcorn between us, Cumberbatch curled up on my feet. There had been a whole episode about endangered species. I tried to push down some of the frustration I could feel rising in my chest. If my cousins would just *help* me find the deed, we wouldn't have to find an endangered species!

"I think I read that scientists are discovering new species all the time," Holden said.

"Yeah, like in the Amazon," Diya pointed out. "I'm not sure about northeastern Pennsylvania."

"Maybe because nobody's looking!" Hattie said. "We just need to find a frog or something."

"Or . . . ," Max started, then cleared his throat. "If we don't technically find an endangered-species frog in the next few weeks . . . maybe we . . . invent one?"

Holden frowned. "How do you invent a frog?"

"No, we just . . . like, photoshop some spots on a normal frog or something. Just so that they have to investigate and construction has to stop."

"I'm not sure that's going to work," I said.

"I think it's worth trying!"

"Is it, though?" Diya murmured under her breath.

Across the water, I could hear the sound of the dinner bugle. I'd found out that it was just a recording that some long-ago camper had done, and one of the adults played it over the old PA system to let us know when it was time for meals. I sighed as I wrapped my goggles around my wrist. I would just try again tomorrow, that was all.

We all got to our feet, and Diya untied her kayak from where it had been attached to the blue-and-white buoy.

"Staying for dinner?" I asked Holden. He didn't join us for dinner every night, but he was probably with us three times a week, to the point where an extra place was usually just set for him as a matter of course. "I think we're having burgers and fries and corn on the cob, and some fake burger thing made of beets and kale."

"You had me at beets and kale," he said with a grin.

I smiled too—I had a feeling Holden would be willing to study the map with me during dinner and see if there was something we were missing. He pointed toward his house. "I'll just get some dry clothes and paddle over!" He dove into the water and started swimming toward his side of the lake.

"Anyone want a ride?" Diya asked. Hattie shook her head and started trying to paddle herself in on Slice of Pizza but mostly turned in circles.

"I'm okay," I said, jumping in and grabbing the crust of Hattie's float. "I'll give Hattie a tow."

"I'll take a ride," Max said. He got into the kayak, and they pushed off across the water. "See you up there!"

I treaded water for just a moment and looked back at the dock. *Protect the things that matter most,* the map had said. There was *something* that had been hidden—but where? What was I missing?

"We going?" Hattie asked, leaning forward to look at me.

"Yeah," I said. I gave the dock one more look, like it was going to give me an answer. But then after a moment, I turned and started swimming toward our shore.

"What do you think?" Max asked, proudly holding out my phone. I squinted at the screen, then passed it to Diya, who shook her head and passed it to Hattie. We were all on our bikes outside PocoMart. Technically we weren't breaking any rules—we'd given our money to Holden, who'd been the only one to go in and get us some snacks.

After three more days of searching the lake and still not finding anything, we'd paused the investigation. It had been incredibly frustrating, diving down again and again, only to come up with nothing. Which had made me think that whatever my mother had left had been hidden under sand or washed away—or we were somehow reading the map wrong.

Either way, we'd decided to take a few days off from looking to see if we'd come up with any new ideas, and in the meantime focus on other ways to stop Holden's dad. When our brainstorming had hit a dead end, we'd all decided we would think better with some snacks.

I'd been worried I wouldn't be able to come, since I didn't have a bike, but Gramps had waved this away and taken me into the garage. I hadn't been there before. There weren't any cars in it—all the cars were in the driveway. Instead, there were rows of bikes, extra helmets, deflated floats, pumps, and a workbench.

"Pick one that fits you," he'd said, gesturing to the bikes, which ranged from toddler bikes to adult-sized mountain bikes. "We've accumulated a lot over the years, so there should be something that works. And then we'll make sure there's air in the tires." I'd found a purple one with a matching basket, Gramps had filled the tires for me, and I was all set. I'd wheeled it out across the driveway, running to catch up with my cousins, and it wasn't until I met them that I realized that I was barefoot—and that I hadn't noticed the gravel at all.

Now Hattie passed the phone back to me, and I enlarged the image. "I'm not sure . . . it's going to work."

Max's face fell. "Really?"

I looked down at the screen—it was a picture of a frog that had been pretty obviously photoshopped to have orange spots and long, curving horns. "I'm just not sure the EPA is going to come and investigate based on this," I said.

"I think they will," Max said, even though I could hear the doubt creeping into his voice. "Like if someone showed you a picture of a platypus, and you'd never heard of it, you'd think it was photoshopped too!"

"Maybe," Diya said doubtfully. "But I don't think the— what are you calling it?"

"Northeastern Dotty-Frog."

"Right. I don't think the Northeastern Dotty-Frog is going to fool anyone."

"Well, I already sent it," Max said, now starting to sound worried. "So I guess we'll see? Can you get in trouble for that? Lying to the government about inventing a frog?"

Holden came out of PocoMart, arms full of snacks. "Ryanna," he said, tossing me a bag of Ruffles, and then a bag of sour gummy worms. "Diya," he said, handing over her pretzels and Snickers. "Max . . ."

Max took his Junior Mints and bottle of Sprite. "They don't think the frog is going to work."

"The Dotty-Frog?" Holden asked. I passed Hattie her Cheetos and Reese's Pieces. Hattie had been very into orange food lately; we were all just going with it. "I think it's great."

"You think that it's *fool the EPA* great?" Diya asked as she opened her pretzels. "*Stop your dad from bulldozing our camp* great?"

"Um."

"Oh *no*," Max said, staring at the picture in horror. "What have I done?"

"Okay," Grams said, shoving a box aside and coughing at the dust that came flying up from it. "Gosh, this place is a mess. Who's running things around here?" She shot me a look, and I laughed.

We were in the attic of the garage, which was filled to the brim. It was stuffed with boxes, old furniture, lamps that listed to the side, and rolled-up posters and signs from the camp days.

I'd headed over to our regular bird-watching spot

that afternoon, but Grams had just shaken her head and beckoned me to come with her. And when I realized that we were here to find the box of my mother's things she'd told me about, I'd gotten really excited. And even though it was *hot* in the attic, and dusty, and I'd already seen more spiders scurrying around than I wanted to count (okay, fine, I did count—it was five), I was ready to spend the rest of the day there, as long as it took until we found it.

I felt like I was storing it all up—all the information and facts and stories about my mom. I still couldn't get over how much there was—like the giant photo albums in the lodge that I could look through, seeing all kinds of pictures I'd never seen before—my mother as a chubby baby, as a toddler with a fierce scowl, doing a flip into the lake at thirteen. In her prom dress, in her high school graduation gown, on the set of *Bug Juice*.

There were a bunch of her from when she was around my age, always lying under the picnic table and grinning at the camera. It was the same place she was in the picture my grandparents had sent in the letter asking me to come. I'd asked Aunt Abby about that, and she just laughed. "God knows," she said, smiling fondly as she looked at the pictures. "Casey used to love that spot. She'd say she got all her best ideas under there."

"Aha!" Grams said, and I navigated around a maze of

boxes—one was just labeled CAREFUL LIVE ANIMALS, which seemed kind of worrying—to reach her.

She slid the box over to me, and I could see it said CASEY'S STUFF on the side, scrawled in black marker. "I can have this?" I asked. I wanted to dig into this box immediately, but I somehow also wanted to do it when I was in the cabin by myself, not feeling like I had to react in any certain way.

Grams smiled at me. "Of course," she said. "And if we find anything else when we pack this all up . . ." Her voice trailed off as she looked around at the maze of boxes and things. The sheer *amount* of it was like proof of all the years they'd been here, and everything that had happened—and Holden's stupid dad wanted to tear it all down and build stupid condos instead. "Anyway. That's neither here nor there. Let's not worry about that just yet."

"I wish I remembered more of when I was here before," I said. I shook my head, hating that it was a memory I didn't have. "When I spent the summer here with my mom."

Grams looked up at me sharply, with the flinty look I sometimes saw in her eyes. "Yes," she said, and it suddenly sounded like she was choosing her words carefully. "Casey brought you up here for the whole summer practically. It was lovely. Especially since—even though we didn't know it—that would be her last summer." Grams's voice wobbled just the tiniest bit. She brushed her hand across one of the box tops, then lifted it and made a face when she saw it was covered in dust.

"Was . . . ?" I started. I didn't know why it suddenly felt like I was asking questions that I shouldn't be asking, like there was a sign saying DO NOT ENTER. "Was my dad here too?"

"A bit," Grams said, not meeting my eye. She brushed her hands off and started straightening the boxes around her. "Hasn't he ever . . . talked to you about this?"

"No," I said immediately. "What did you and my dad fight about?" I said the words all in a rush. If I stopped to think, I'd lose my nerve. "Why didn't you ever reach out before now?"

I saw Grams swallow, then blink hard a couple of times before she looked up at me again. "We decided that it would be best. We had a big fight after your mother's death. Things were said . . ." Grams trailed off, looking like she was lost in a memory. "And none of us was in a position to even be having big conversations then. We were all distraught. And taking things out on one another . . ." She stopped and took a breath. "But I regret it. Truly. You should have been here all along, Ryanna."

I nodded, feeling a lump in my throat. Was it that simple? A fight and words that couldn't be taken back? And then silence that just grew and grew?

But Grams's eyes were wet, and this was shocking enough that I didn't feel like I could ask the follow-up questions I wanted. Because maybe it *was* that simple.

"But in lieu of being able to rewrite history," Grams said, nodding at my box, "this feels like the least I can do."

I carried it, half running, back to the Hummingbird Cabin. I knew my cousins were at the lake. So for right now, I relished the silence and peace of our cabin. I sat down on my bunk and opened the box.

It was packed almost to the top—neatly folded T-shirts and sweatshirts and a pair of jeans with glittery beads going down the sides. There was something called a Tamagotchi, and neon-colored scrunchies.

I lifted up the sweatshirt on top—it said BENNETON on it—and breathed in.

For just a moment, I imagined that I could still smell my mom in it—that there was still a part of her there.

And when I put it on, it fit me perfectly.

CHAPTER 20

S o what's the plan for today?" my dad asked me over the phone. I was walking up and down the dock, pretending it was a balance beam, trying to keep my feet in a perfectly straight line. "Fireworks?"

"Later, I think," I said. It was the Fourth of July. The day had dawned hot and sunny, and the coffee I'd brewed that morning had been judged my best pot yet—I'd started adding a dash of nutmeg, in addition to grinding the beans myself. My dad and I had scheduled this call ahead of time—he said he'd wanted some reminder of the fact that it was the Fourth, since they obviously didn't celebrate it in Hungary. Apparently they had something in August called the Day of New Bread, but my dad wasn't going to be there for it, and he was still unclear if this involved fireworks, or if it just involved . . . bread.

So I'd skipped out on the midafternoon kickball game

to talk to my dad. I'd had a call planned later with Ginger, too—but my dad said she wasn't feeling great and might have to reschedule.

And while I really did want to chat with my dad and catch up with him, I was only half engaged in the conversation— my mind kept drifting over to the field and wondering who was winning, and if Max was going to let himself get drawn into a trap at second base again without me to yell at him to stay put.

With no new ideas on where to find the second clue, and no great insights on how to stop Holden's dad, we'd all decided to take the Fourth off from brainstorming and searching and just enjoy the day, which my cousins had wasted no time in doing.

"I bet you're gonna be ready to go home soon, huh, kid?" my dad asked, his connection scratchy. I stared at the phone. Go *home*? Back to California? California seemed like a whole other lifetime ago.

"Well, not yet, right?" I felt myself start to panic a little. I couldn't leave yet! It was only the Fourth of July! That was only halfway through the summer. "Why are you talking about it so soon?"

"Remember I said I have those meetings? If you're ready to go, I can get you early, and you can hang out with Nana in the city."

"I . . . um . . . When are they again?"

"End of the month," my dad said, and I started to breathe easier. That was still over three weeks from now.

I shook my head, even though I knew he couldn't see me. "I'm not ready to go yet. So you can just do your meetings and get me later like we planned, and then we can see Nana after that, okay?"

"Okay," my dad said slowly. "But if you want . . ."

"I'm good here! Really. You can take your time, okay? Happy Bread Day!"

But when we'd hung up and I'd raced over to the kickball game, I hadn't been able to shake off the conversation. Even when my cousins and Holden and I had ridden bikes over to Sweet Baby Jane's for ice cream (everyone agreed to only get red, white, or blue ice cream; I tried something called Birthday Monster, and it was *delicious*), the conversation with my dad was still buzzing around in my mind.

Of course I had known that I wasn't just going to stay here forever. That there was an expiration date on every summer. I knew that at some point, Hattie and her parents would go back to Maine, and Holden would go back to Connecticut. Diya and Pete would go back to Philly, and Max would go home to New Jersey. I'd understood this *in theory*.

But recently it had started to feel like maybe we would just keep doing this. That this was my life now—making coffee in the mornings and hanging out with my cousins and brainstorming ways to stop Holden's dad and learning about my mom and trying to find her treasure. My life in California had become hazy and distant, and I hadn't minded. But now, with one conversation, it had all been brought back.

After dinner, once it was dark enough, we all piled onto the dock to watch the Lake Phoenix fireworks, and then after the last one had filled up the sky, we'd headed up the hill to make s'mores.

And as I sat by the fire, I tried not to think about the days ticking down, when I still had no ideas for how to stop the camp from being bulldozed. We hadn't found the clue on the floating dock, I didn't know what my dad and grandparents had fought about, and I *still* didn't know where my name had come from—Holden had asked his dad, and he hadn't known either. There was too much to do here to even think about leaving anytime soon. So for right now, I just concentrated on my marshmallow, and getting it perfectly toasted.

"I think it's overdone," Hattie said, frowning at my marshmallow. I shook my head. I knew better than to listen to her—Hattie liked her marshmallows practically raw.

"It's going to be perfect," I said, carefully turning the stick in the flame. I'd found the secret was to keep it moving, never letting any one spot get too done.

"It looks good to me." Max sighed wistfully. Uncle Byron and Uncle Dennis gave him a look. He was on dessert restriction for a week, ever since he'd gotten a strongly worded email from the EPA about frog fraud. (It was the reason we'd ridden to ice cream by ourselves and felt that none of the adults necessarily needed to know about it.)

"No s'mores for the guy making up frogs," Uncle Dennis said, shaking his head. "What was that even about, kid?"

"Oh, I just . . . thought it would be cool to discover something," he said, looking away from his dads, down at the ground.

"Maybe don't involve federal agencies next time," Uncle Byron suggested as Uncle Dennis leaned over and wiped a smudge of chocolate off his cheek.

"Good note."

"I have a Casey Fourth of July story," Quinn said as she rotated her s'more, looking for the perfect bite. "When she was eight—"

Aunt Abby scoffed. "You mean before you were born?"

"I'm allowed to tell stories too," Quinn said stubbornly. "They don't have to be firsthand accounts!"

"Not at all," Gramps agreed.

"I think I know what this one is," Uncle Benji said, taking a giant bite of a triple-decker s'more. Ever since our murder-plotting session, he'd been busy writing his new

Sven book, *Death Takes No Holiday*, and had skipped the last few s'mores nights to work, so it seemed like he was making up for lost time.

"It's my favorite Casey story." Quinn smiled at me, and I leaned forward to listen. "So it was the Fourth of July, and Grams had banned all the kids from buying fireworks—"

"You bought your own fireworks?" Pete interrupted, looking stunned. He turned to glare at Aunt Abby and Uncle Neal. "I was never allowed to do that!"

"They weren't either," Grams said, shaking her head. "This banana brain used to sell them outside the gas station to kids—Roman candles, bottle rockets. Stuff they had no business having if they wanted to keep all their fingers."

"Anyway," Quinn said, raising her voice, "everyone had bought their own, of course, and Casey had volunteered to hide them. But when she went to get them . . ."

"They were soaking wet!" Uncle Benji finished, laughing now. "We couldn't understand it. When we asked her what had happened, she would only say that her hiding place had leaked."

"She never would tell us where it was," Uncle Dennis said, laughing too.

I drew in a sharp breath. My mother had had a hiding spot. A hiding spot where what she'd hidden had gotten wet.

All of a sudden, I knew what the map was leading to.

"Here," I said, handing my marshmallow to Max, who brightened.

"Really?"

"No," Uncle Byron and Uncle Dennis said, taking it from him.

"I have to . . . I'm just going to . . . ," I started. Everyone stared at me. I'd assumed a better excuse would come to me once I'd started the sentence, but when that didn't happen, I just turned and hurried down the hill.

"Ryanna?" I heard someone yell behind me, but I didn't even stop. Now that I thought I knew—now that I was fairly certain I had the answer—I didn't want to wait, not even long enough to explain. I just had to know if I was right.

I ran straight down to the dock, which was lit by the moon, huge and almost full above the lake. I didn't stop running, just threw myself off the end of it and started to swim. I didn't care that I was in my clothes—I just swam as fast as I could.

The moon was bright enough that I could see everything perfectly, and I reached the floating dock in record time.

I pushed myself up to sit on the dock in my dripping clothes.

And then, my heart pounding, I pulled the buoy up by its chain.

It had never crossed my mind to look in it—it had never

even occurred to me that buoys could open. But as I looked at the white and blue halves, I realized that they unscrewed, and I twisted the bottom until I pulled the two halves apart.

A double Ziploc bag fell onto the dock, and I felt a surge of triumph as I picked it up, knowing that—whatever it was—I had found what my mother had led me to.

"*Another* map?" Diya groaned as she picked up the piece of paper.

"Shh," Hattie and I said together. It was the next morning, and we'd taken ourselves to the far end of the long breakfast table to go over what I'd found in the buoy.

And we normally would have just done this on the dock, but it was gray and drizzly outside, and I didn't want to risk anything getting ruined—even though this was *very* well packaged. It seemed like my mother had learned her lesson from the fireworks fiasco.

"Let's hear it for the buoy!" Max said.

Diya shook her head at him. "No. Just no. I think Uncle Byron is starting to be a bad influence on you."

I saw Holden step inside and look around. I motioned him over, and he slid onto the bench next to Max, across from me. "Morning," he said. He looked down at what was spread out on the table in front of me, and his eyes widened. "You found it?"

I grinned. "It was in the buoy."

"The *buoy*," Holden said, leaning forward to look closer. "Of course."

"I can't believe it's *another* map!" Diya sputtered, so loud that some of the adults glanced over at her.

"Shh," Hattie, Max, and I hissed.

"How long is this going to go on?" she continued, a little quieter now. "Is this one going to lead to another map, and then another, and another? Like those nesting dolls? And never any treasure?"

"I love those dolls!" Hattie enthused as she took a bite of her bagel. "I have them of the cast of *Hamilton*, but we got it from this kind of weird site, so I don't think it's *official* merchandise—"

"I think it's the end," I interrupted. We'd all learned that when Hattie started talking musical theater, it was best to cut her off early. I carefully pulled out the other two pieces and lined them up. Now that the three of them were together, you could tell it was one piece of paper that had been torn into thirds. "See? Look."

With the pieces together, the whole camp was revealed—the woods, the lake, the floating dock, our dock, Holden's house across the lake. The message along the bottom was complete now—and it read, *Protect the things that matter most even if it's hard!!* There was a tiny drawing of a ship surrounded by a bubble. And there was an *X*—right by the picnic table. But it was next to a pine tree that didn't exist.

"There's no tree there," Diya said, tapping the drawing of the pine.

"I know," I said. "Maybe she was using artistic license? But this is the end. It has to be. It's where we're going to find the deed to the camp." I saw Max and Hattie exchange a look. "What?"

"Just . . . ," Max started. "If we find something and it's *not* the deed to the camp, I don't want you to be disappointed."

"Yeah, maybe it's just regular treasure!" Hattie pointed out.

"What's 'regular treasure'?" Diya asked her skeptically.

"I'm not saying it's not that," Max said. "But I just think we should be open to the possibility that it could be something else."

I looked to Holden for backup. "What do you think?"

"Um. I mean, I think it absolutely *could* be. But do you really think your mom would have hidden something so important in a place where she might not be able to find it again?"

"What would you do," Hattie asked, reaching over to steal a strawberry off Diya's plate, "if you had something super important and secret? Where would you bury it?"

"Don't *tell* her," Diya yelped as Holden took a breath to answer. "She's obviously going to dig up your buried treasure!"

Holden laughed. "I don't *have* buried treasure."

"Oh." Hattie nodded. Then her eyes narrowed. "Or *do* you, and this is just your way of throwing us off the scent?"

"If I did have treasure, I wouldn't bury it."

"What would you do with it?" I asked, curious.

Holden thought for a moment, running his hand along the wood grain of the table. "I feel like I'd give it to a friend. Right? Because you never know if someone else is going to come along and find your treasure. But if you had someone you trusted—someone you had faith in—you could leave it with them and know it would be okay."

Diya scoffed at this and slapped Hattie's hand away as she reached for another berry. "Safe-deposit box. It's the only way."

"What are you all talking about?" Grams asked as she wandered past.

"Nothing," Holden, Diya, and I said together.

"Okay," she said, shaking her head as she walked over to the coffeepot.

"So," I said, carefully gathering up the papers and looking around the table, "what do you think? Should we start looking?" Just as I asked this, there was a *crack* of thunder from outside, and a second later I could see sheets of rain start to pour down—soaking Archie, who was walking up to the lodge. He yelped and began to run, sliding a bit on the gravel.

"Maybe when it's not raining?" Max suggested.

"Good call," Diya said.

Thunder boomed again, and like it was a cue everyone had been waiting for, Hattie got up to get more berries, Holden went to get breakfast, Max walked over to Uncle Dennis to talk about sandcastle plans, and Diya went to laugh at Archie, who was dripping in the doorway and ranting about sudden Pennsylvania monsoons. So for just a moment, I found myself alone at the table, my mother's map in front of me.

Protect the things that matter most even if it's hard!! This felt like encouragement, just for me, and I looked at this sentence for a long moment. "I'm trying, Mom," I said quietly as I folded up the pieces of the map carefully. "I'm trying."

CHAPTER 21

I had just gotten the coffee brewing when Max strode through the doors of the mess hall and announced dramatically, "The day is upon us."

I exchanged a look with Gramps. Usually it was Hattie who would make those kinds of proclamations. "Um, what day?"

"Yeah," Gramps said as he set the fruit plate down, then plucked a blueberry off it for himself. "I was under the impression it was a regular Wednesday."

In the week since we'd found the third part of my mother's treasure map, we'd dug all around the spot the map had indicated but hadn't found anything. And even digging up a small area had left us with blistered hands (again), broken plastic shovels, and a lot of annoying questions from the grown-ups, like *Why are you doing that?* Diya had to pretend to be suddenly interested in geology, even though, as she kept telling us, she found rocks incredibly boring.

The fact that we hadn't found it yet had been disappointing, but if I understood anything about my mother's clues by now, it was that it wasn't going to be straightforward. Something was there—we just had to find it.

But when it had rained for three days in a row, nobody had complained—I think we were all secretly glad to have a forced break from the digging. And I'd discovered how *different* it felt here when it rained. It was darker all day, and the air smelled woodsy. I'd run up through the rain in the morning to help get breakfast ready, and there was now a stack of towels by the mess hall door so you could dry yourself off. We all needed them because the whole camp was designed for sunny weather, and when it wasn't sunny, you got drenched just trying to do basic things like brush your teeth or get breakfast. I'd gotten used to hearing thunder rumbling, the sound of rain on the cabin roof, and the sight of lightning flashing across the lake, so bright that it could have been daylight.

And since we couldn't do any of our outdoor things, we'd all started spending time inside the lodge. It was the week that both Aunt Katie and Uncle Byron took off from work, so they got to be here the whole time, not just on weekends, making everything a little more busy and crowded, but somehow in a good way.

Gramps usually had a pot of hot chocolate going on

the stove, and Aunt Abby had declared herself Fire Captain, which meant there was usually a fire going, starting in the midafternoon. We'd read or play games or do puzzles, and then usually at night, we'd watch a movie. There was one day when Max had pulled a board game called Dominion off the shelf. It was a worldwide battle game, and we'd started playing it casually, just to see what it was about—only to get utterly pulled into it as we formed teams and started plotting the downfall of our teammates. When we all waved off lunch and then dinner, not wanting anything to interrupt the game, Grams intervened and upended the board, and that was the end of Dominion.

But even though it had been fun to have a change of pace for a few days, when I'd woken up that morning and seen that the rain had stopped and the sun was shining brightly, I was thrilled. You can only drink so much cocoa and plot the takeover of Fiji for so long, after all. We had a clue to find—and a camp to save.

"It is *not*," Max said as he grabbed his plate and started to fill it up, "an ordinary Wednesday. Do you know why?"

"No," I said, glancing at Gramps. "That's kind of what we just—"

"Because conditions are perfect!"

Gramps raised his eyebrows. "Well now, that sounds exciting. Perfect for what?"

Max grinned, and I could see now that he was practically vibrating with excitement. "Sandcastles."

"Max!" Uncle Dennis burst through the door, his eyes wide. It was the most awake I'd ever seen him in the morning; usually he required three cups of my coffee before he stopped growling at people and starting using actual language and full sentences. He held out his hand, and I could see there was sand clenched in it. "Did you see it?"

"I did!" Max said, doing a little hop. "I was just telling them about it!"

"Why are conditions perfect?" I asked.

"Look," Uncle Dennis said, spilling his handful of sand out on the table. Gramps moved his plate away just in time. "This is the best sand to build with. It's damp but not soaked. Excellent clumping, good consistency . . ."

"Great," I said, giving Max a smile. I'd been hearing about this sandcastle project all summer, so I was glad it was finally going to happen. "Good luck. I can't wait to see how it turns out."

Max and his dad exchanged a look. "You're going to be part of this, Ryanna," Max said, like it should have been obvious. "It's an all-hands-on-deck situation."

"Or all hands on dock," Uncle Dennis said, and Max raised his hand for a high five.

"I'll get everyone," Max said, taking his bagel off the

plate and dashing out the door with it. "Meet on the beach in ten!"

Uncle Dennis hurried toward the bagels, leaving the sand in a pile on the table, and I turned to Gramps. "I'm part of this?"

"We all are." He grinned at me. "Don't worry. You're going to love it."

I had thought I understood what it meant to build a sandcastle. I'd built some of my own over the years, and when we'd be on the beach in Santa Monica, or Venice, or Malibu—or on vacation in Mexico—there would usually be someone attempting a sandcastle.

But I wasn't prepared for this.

The whole beach had been raked, and there were buckets and shovels and wooden tools lined up. There was an oversized diagram, on thin blue architect paper, held down with rocks. And there were Max and Uncle Dennis, pacing around it, both with serious, intense faces.

"Oh no." I looked over and saw that Diya had appeared next to me, her hair in a messy topknot. "It's sandcastle day?"

"We should have known," Pete said around a yawn, running his hand through some truly impressive bedhead. "It's the perfect dampness after it rains."

"Hey!" Max yelled from the beach. "We're getting

started before it gets too hot. Grab some breakfast and then circle up. We're going to need everyone."

An hour later I understood why. This was *not* a normal sandcastle. In fact, it wasn't a castle at all—we were building a sand version of the camp. Camp Van Camp, in sand form, a perfect scale model of it.

"Max and I just thought," Uncle Dennis said, clapping his hand on Max's shoulder, "it would be a nice gesture to do this here, while . . . while we still can."

After that, we were put to work—all of us. One of the rotating jobs was keeping buckets filled and making sure there was enough "muddy sand" on hand for binding. I was learning a lot about sandcastle construction—that you can't do anything with dry sand, it has to be wet, and you want to shape things with really wet sand, let them dry, then transfer them over. That a solid base was crucial—and that you had to be well on your way before the sun got too hot.

But everyone had a job—Grams, Gramps, all of us, Archie, all my aunts and uncles. Holden had kayaked over after we'd gotten about an hour in, and Hattie had tried to wave him off.

"Turn back," she called to him, looking grave. "Or you're going to be put to work and you'll never escape."

"Tell Holden to get over here and help," Max called from where he was focused, with Uncle Dennis and Aunt

Katie, on the second floor of the lodge. "We need everyone. Tell him to bring Ella, too."

"Ooh, yes, please," Archie said. He took a step toward Holden—and his foot went right through what had been S'mores Hill. "Oh, bloody hell," he said. Then his eyes widened as he looked at us. "Sorry for swearing."

"I feel like you can British-swear all you want," Aunt Abby said as she carefully shaped the side of the cabin she was working on with a wooden tool.

"Seriously," I said to Holden. "If you don't leave, you're going to be a part of this."

"What's so bad about that? It looks fun," he said as he rolled over in the kayak and then swam out from under it, steering it toward shore.

And as the day progressed, I had to admit that Holden was right. It *was* fun. All of us were together, for the whole day. We each had our own jobs, and Uncle Dennis was really good about delegating, so it felt like we were working as a team. My job was piling the wet sand up to make foundations so that Max could smooth it out with precision. And after a few hours, I could see it taking shape—a small version of the camp. There was the lodge, and S'mores Hill (rebuilt), the cabins, the lake, the dock.

We stopped for lunch—everyone had to spend extra time trying to get the sand off our hands before we basically came to the same conclusion—that our food would just be a little sandy today. "They're called *sand*wiches for a reason!" Uncle Byron said, and everyone groaned.

Max and Uncle Dennis had us all on a break schedule, so nobody burned out. I'd taken my first few breaks in the lake, swimming or floating, but it turned out it's not really that fun to do on your own. So when my midafternoon break came, I just decided to take a rest, out of the sun . . . and my gaze landed on the picnic table.

I walked over to it. Since my mother had apparently loved lying under here, maybe I would too. It was something that never would have occurred to me—to sit under a picnic table—but after seeing all the pictures of her here, and learning that it was where she'd liked to spend time, I knew I had to give it a shot.

While Holden and Pete ran back and forth with their buckets of water, and Hattie and Diya bickered over who was doing a better job with making sharp angles on the cabin roofs, I crawled under the picnic table.

And I was . . . under a picnic table.

I looked around, expecting something more. I didn't really get what the big deal was. It was cooler under here, and there was shade . . . but there was also a *lot* of old gum stuck underneath it, which was currently much too close to my hair for my liking.

I leaned back—both to get away from the old gum and because in all the pictures I'd seen, my mother hadn't been sitting under the table—she'd been *lying* under it.

I immediately felt something hard digging into my back—something on the ground. I moved around it so I wasn't lying right on top of it. I looked up at the unfinished wood planks, the old gum (ugh), and the writing people had carved into the underside of the picnic table.

It was peaceful under here, but after a few minutes of just looking at the underside of a picnic table, I had to admit I didn't get what the big deal was.

I started to crawl out when something caught my eye, and I lay back down, to try to get a clear view of it. RYAN LOVES ANNA was carved across two planks, the names separated. I stared at the two names, suddenly seeing something.

It was my name.

My name was contained in those names.

I stared up at the carving and let my eyes go slightly out of focus. Like one of those magic eye pictures, RYANNA was formed from the two names on the planks. I sat up in excitement—and bonked my head on the underside of the table. "Ow!"

"You all right?" I looked over to see Aunt Abby bending down to look at me.

"Yeah," I said, rubbing my head.

"Let me get a picture of you, okay?" Aunt Abby asked, pulling out her phone and walking backward, bending down to get the shot. I took a breath, about to excitedly explain what had happened, what I'd found out—but a second later I hesitated.

This was almost like a secret my mom and I were sharing. I'd solved a mystery that not even my dad knew the answer to. It was like there was now an understanding between us, across all those years, linking me and my mother.

I glanced at the table, where my mother had seen the words RYAN and ANNA and had decided, right then and there, what her future daughter—me—would be called. I'd never loved my name more.

"Smile, Ryanna!" Aunt Abby called.

And I looked straight at her and grinned.

By the time the sun was starting to go down, we were done. There it all was, in much more detail than I ever knew could be achieved with sand and water—the main lodge, the field, the archery targets. The cabins, the dock, tiny sand canoes and kayaks, the lake. It was wonderful—a monument to the camp.

Max put the ceremonial final scoop (I hadn't known this was a thing, but apparently it was a *big* deal) on the rendering of S'mores Hill, and then we all clapped, and Max and Uncle Dennis took a bow, both looking exhausted but happy.

And even though we were done, nobody really wanted to leave. We were taking pictures and admiring it and walking carefully around all our hard work.

Since everyone had been working all day, nobody had cooked anything for dinner, so Quinn drove into town and picked up a bunch of pizzas from Humble Pie. She piled the pies on the picnic table, and we ate our slices sitting on the dock, all of us still admiring what we'd built—together.

It got later, and darker, but still nobody left. The fireflies winked on and off as we ate our pizza, looking at the tiny version of the camp, the big version looming behind it, and I couldn't help feeling like we'd pulled off something special.

Nobody wanted to go inside—and none of us wanted to go to bed—but finally we were ordered to, in no uncertain terms, by Aunt Abby. Holden got into his kayak and waved as he started paddling across the lake, the moon shining like a spotlight above. Archie followed behind, paddling Ella back in our canoe.

Everyone started drifting off to their cabins, but I took one last moment.

I stood on the beach, and by the light of the moon, I looked at what we'd made. And then before Aunt Abby could yell at me, I hurried off to the Hummingbird Cabin.

. . .

When I opened my eyes the next morning, I could tell by the light it was earlier than usual. I knew I could have just rolled over and gone back to sleep—but I didn't want to. I wanted to see the sand camp and then get to the mess hall before Gramps for once, and have the coffee waiting for him.

I got dressed in the closet—bathing suit, a pair of Quinn's old cutoffs she'd given me, an old Camp Van Camp shirt of my mother's—and tiptoed barefoot across the Hummingbird Cabin. I closed the door behind me and then ran down toward the beach.

The sand camp was still there—looking a little less pristine than it had yesterday, but still standing. I smiled, looking at it—but then felt my face freeze as I saw what was across the lake.

They were in a row next to Holden's dad's house. They were huge and menacing and the only thing I could seem to see.

A line of bulldozers.

PART FOUR

THE HUNT

CHAPTER 22

I thought we had until the end of the summer!" Diya said, looking equal parts scared and furious.

We were in the mess hall, all of us kids at the end of the table, speaking low even though it wasn't a secret—everyone had seen the bulldozers as they'd headed up to the lodge. They were pretty hard to miss. All the happy vibes from yesterday had been wiped away in a moment. And everyone seemed pretty shaken—barely anyone was eating.

"I thought that too," Max said, rubbing his hand over his face. "Why are they here *now*?"

Gramps passed by carrying a fresh mug of coffee—I'd made it in a state of shock after I'd seen the bulldozers. Luckily I could practically make it with my eyes closed now. "Gramps?" I called, and he detoured over to us. His smile, for the first time, looked a little forced.

"Hi, kiddos," he said, taking a sip of coffee.

"We don't understand why the, um . . . bulldozers," I said, getting through the word quickly, like it was a bad word I knew I wasn't allowed to say, "are here already."

"I thought," Hattie said, "that it wasn't until the end of the summer? That we had that long before they pulled everything down?"

I heard Max draw in a sharp breath when Hattie said this. It hit me then just how much all of us—even the grown-ups—had been pretending that this wasn't happening. That this day wouldn't actually ever come. Like if we somehow had enough fun and built enough sandcastles, we could outrun this deadline.

"We have until the end of the summer for *our* land," Gramps said, and he wasn't even trying to smile now. It sounded like every word was hurting him to say. "That's the agreement. But Rick—Holden's dad—can do whatever he wants with his land. And I guess he decided to start clearing it."

"It's awful," Uncle Benji said from down the table, shaking his head. "Tearing down all those beautiful trees."

Diya looked over at her parents, her expression stormy. "I can't believe you're just going to let this happen."

"There's nothing to be done," Aunt Abby said. She gave Diya a sharp look. "Like we talked about before—there's no secret solution here, and I don't want you meddling. Agreed?"

"Abby's right," Gramps said with a nod. "I know it might

be hard, but just try to ignore them and enjoy the time we still have. Okay?"

"*Not* okay," Diya said ten minutes later out on the dock, where we'd all decamped, so we could have a private conversation.

"We're not listening to them, right?" Max asked, his face worried. "We're still going to try to stop this."

"Of course we're not listening to them," Hattie said dismissively. "We have to get this shut down—"

"If we could just find the third clue," I said. Between the rain and now the epic sandcastle building, it felt like we'd lost way too much time.

"No offense," Diya said, "but I think we need to focus on stopping this *now*, and I'm not sure we should take the time to dig for no reason."

"It's not *no reason*! And if the clue leads to the land deed—"

"But this is about to start! Like, any day now!" Diya interrupted me, her voice shaky. She glared across the lake. "What happens once they begin? What if they just keep going and start tearing down our trees and buildings too?"

"Also," Max said gloomily, "how are we supposed to enjoy what's left of the summer with the sounds of construction and trees being ripped out of the ground?"

I winced and looked away from the line of bulldozers. "We need to talk to Holden."

"Good timing," Hattie said, nodding toward the lake. "He's coming over."

I turned and saw that Holden was kayaking over from his side of the lake to ours.

"I know," he said as he pulled the kayak onto the sand and rested his oar inside. He turned around and glowered at the bulldozers. "I woke up to them today."

"You didn't know?" Diya asked, a touch of suspicion in her voice.

"No! I had no idea—I swear."

"What did your dad say?" Hattie asked.

"He's not even here. He's coming in later to 'oversee this next phase.'"

"So what does this mean?" I asked. I didn't want to say it out loud, but the presence of these bulldozers seemed really ominous. I had a feeling they weren't just going to *sit* here for another three weeks. "Like—when does this . . . happen?"

"I don't know," Holden said slowly. He looked back toward his house. "But I bet we can find out."

Holden's dad's office looked the same as it had before—desk, computer, wall of ships in bottles.

"Let me see what I can find," Holden said as he pulled open a desk drawer and started rifling through it.

Max looked at the door, nervous. "And you're sure he's not going to come in, right?"

"His flight doesn't get in for an hour," Holden said as he pulled out a pile of paper and started flipping through it. "So we're in the clear, I promise."

I walked behind the desk and saw that, sure enough, the computer now required a password—clearly Holden's dad didn't want a replay of the email incident. I looked up at the wall of bottles, still amazed that there were so *many* of them. I tilted my head back to see the older ones, up at the top. You could tell the very first ones had been made when Holden's dad was a little kid—they were the simplest ones, the masts and sails crooked and off-center. But the next row, from what I was able to see of the dates, looked like he'd made them around when he was our age, and they were starting to look better. I noticed the same one I had before, the one with the white sail that seemed to have writing on it. I stretched up on my toes, trying to get a better look—

"What's this?" Max asked. I glanced over to see that he was flipping through a leather-bound photo album— but instead of photos inside, there were cutout newspaper clippings.

"Oh," Holden said, "that's my dad's scrapbook. He's,

like, obsessed with how he gets covered. He never wants bad press."

I met Diya's eye and she sat up straight. "Interesting," I said.

She grinned at me. "Very."

"What?" Hattie asked, looking between the two of us. "Do you have an idea?"

Diya nodded. "I think we might."

"Because if Holden's dad hates bad press," I said slowly, starting to smile, "I say we make sure he gets some."

We made a plan to regroup in ten, and I went to the Hummingbird Cabin to grab my phone—only to realize that I was running on phone battery fumes. I plugged it in to charge, and while I was waiting, I sat down on my bed and slid the box I'd gotten from Grams—the most precious thing I owned—out from underneath it.

Here was where I was storing the maps, and the photos of my mom, and even the letter Grams and Gramps had sent to me in California—back when I hadn't known who they were. I realized it was hard to even remember that time now.

I looked at the map again—I'd taped it together so that it was no longer in pieces. I was only half hopeful I'd see something new there. I spent time every morning, before I made coffee, and every night, before I went to bed, just looking at the map. Trying to see if there was something I was missing. Something I wasn't understanding.

I studied the ship in the bubble that was drawn near Holden's house. After looking at it for a few minutes more and getting no answers, I took out the picture of my mom. I looked at her smiling twelve-year-old face. I drank it all in—the spray of freckles across her nose, the pink-and-purple tackle box thing on her lap, the padlock keeping it closed, her cheerful peace sign. At least now I knew why she was sitting right by the picnic table. I knew now that it had been her favorite place to go and think—and it was the spot where she'd come up with my name.

I looked at it for a moment more before I carefully returned everything to the box. And then, not wanting to keep everyone waiting too long for me, I unplugged my phone and ran out to the south lawn.

By the time I got there, Max, Diya, Hattie, and Holden were all sprawled in a circle. I flopped down next to Holden, and Diya immediately reached over and grabbed my phone.

"Okay," she said, already typing into it. "I think we should start with the *Pocono Eagle*."

Hattie frowned. "Really? I was thinking maybe the *New York Times* . . . or the *Times* of London . . . or the *Wall Street Journal*. You know, really hard-hitting news."

Max shook his head. "I'm not sure how much the *New*

York Times cares about a construction issue in Pennsylvania."

"But they should!" Hattie smacked her fist into her open palm. "It has all the elements of a great story. Family legacies . . . a son betraying his father . . ."

"Hey now," Holden said.

"Money! Real estate! Trees! A whole David-and-Goliath angle! But in this case, Goliath is a real jerk."

"Uh . . . no offense," Max added to Holden after a moment.

"It's okay," Holden said, though he was starting to look uncomfortable. "But I promise that my dad's not all bad. I know, deep down, he has good memories of this place and really cares about it."

Diya snorted. "I don't buy *that*. I think he wants to make a lot of money and is willing to bulldoze our camp to do it."

"Well, that too."

"So we're doing this?" Hattie said, grabbing for the phone. Max snatched it up before she got to it.

"Wait," he said. "What's the plan? What exactly are we going to say?"

"Well," I said, leaning back on my hands, "I think we should say that he's beginning construction illegally. And over the objections of the people who live there . . ." I suddenly remembered what took down my dad's first business manager. "Does your dad pay his taxes?"

"Um. I think so?"

"Really?" Diya fixed him with a look. "*All* of them?"

"Why don't we say there are *questions* about his taxes?" I suggested. "Because there are! *We* have them. And . . ."

"Ooh! Maybe say something about my frog!" Max said.

Diya shook her head. "There is no frog."

"But *they* don't know that."

"All right," Diya said, taking the phone back. "I think we've got enough to start with."

She put the phone in the center of the circle, pressed the number to call the *Pocono Eagle*, and put the phone on speaker. I allowed myself just a moment of imagining how it all might play out—Holden's dad opening up the paper, his face going white as he read the article all about how terrible he was. How he'd promise to stop construction, if only we'd stop the bad press. The line of bulldozers would all leave, the camp would be saved. . . .

"Hello, *Pocono Eagle*." A bored-sounding woman answered the phone, interrupting this daydream. And it was in that moment I realized that we'd never decided who was going to do the talking.

I looked around the circle, and from the panicked expressions on everyone else's faces, this had just occurred to them as well. "Hello?" the woman said, this time with a sigh.

"Um, hi," I said after another pause. "Hello." I tried to

deepen my voice so that I sounded older. "We have a . . . tip. Information about a construction project. And the truth about Rick Andersen."

"Yes!" Diya joined in, also lowering her voice. "We have it on good authority that he doesn't pay his taxes. And that he's building on land he doesn't own, and that the people who live there have *strongly* objected, but he doesn't care."

"Plus, there's a frog!" Max broke in, clearly too excited to try to disguise his voice. "An endangered frog, the Northeastern Dotty-Frog. It's real, you can look it up. And Rick Andersen doesn't care and is destroying its habitat. Which it totally has, because it's real."

"But also," Holden said, leaning forward, "I've heard from, um, reliable sources that he's a good father who's never missed a soccer game!"

"Plus," Hattie broke in, now using a British accent for some reason, "there's all these construction lorries that 'ave rolled up, with hardly a do-you-mind, it's like Bob's your uncle, wot? And—"

"What . . . ," a voice said. We all whipped around to see Aunt Abby standing behind us, looking furious. "Do you think you're doing?"

I hadn't gotten in trouble since I'd come to Camp Van Camp.

I mean, there had been little things. Like, one of the

adults would yell at us to pick up our plates or stop running on the dock or tell us in no uncertain terms that we couldn't do archery practice with flaming arrows, but for the most part, it felt like it had been a while since I'd gotten *in trouble*.

Aunt Abby had told us all to meet in the lodge in ten minutes. Then her gaze had landed on Holden, and she'd hesitated. "Holden," she said, "I think maybe you should call your dad and have him pick you up."

He nodded, but I could see that his eyes had gotten big. "Are you going to tell him what we did?"

"*I'm* not." She gave Holden a level look. "But I think *you* should."

Holden borrowed my phone and texted his dad, looking resigned as he did it. "Holden could just kayak back over," Max pointed out. "Why does his dad have to pick him up?"

"Because I'll have to explain why," Holden said with a sigh as he handed my phone back to me. "I think it's your aunt's way of making sure he knows I was in trouble."

Diya nodded. "She's not messing around."

"So what happens now?" I asked in a low voice, even though Aunt Abby was out of earshot.

"We have another tribunal," Max said, and Hattie and Diya nodded. "To decide consequences for us."

"Yeah," Hattie said. "It happened last summer, when Quinn's annoying ex-boyfriend J.J. was visiting. And he was trying to tell us how to paddle the canoes, and getting it wrong . . ."

"What happened?" I asked.

Diya shrugged. "We declared mutiny," she said, like it should have been obvious. "It was the only thing to do, really. He got out on the floating dock, and we saw our chance. We took over the canoes and paddled away so that he could think about what he'd done."

"He could have swum in," Max said, sounding defensive. "But anyway, Quinn wasn't happy that we'd stranded her boyfriend, and all the adults weren't happy about the mutiny. So they held a tribunal to discuss what should happen."

"What did happen?"

"We had to set the table *and* do the dishes every night for the rest of the summer, and we had to write a formal apology letter," Diya said with a sigh.

"Dad told me there's no point in grounding us because the adults want to enjoy their summer too, and not have to be disciplinarians," Hattie explained. "So hopefully this will go the same way?"

When ten minutes had passed—it felt like forever—we trudged up to the lodge.

Holden sat down on the steps outside to wait for his dad. As we went in, he gave us a smile I could tell he didn't feel.

I blinked as I stepped inside—it always took a second

for my eyes to adjust after the bright sun outside. But as they did, I could see, lined up on and standing behind one of the squashy couches, waiting for us, was . . . everyone else. Aunt Katie, Uncle Byron, Grams, Gramps, Aunt Abby, Uncle Benji, Uncle Dennis, Uncle Neal, Quinn, and Pete.

We'd already had one tribunal this summer—but at least in that one, we'd all been on the same side.

"Jeez," I muttered as we walked through the mess hall.

"Told you," Diya said under her breath.

"Sit," Grams said, pointing to the couch opposite.

"Did you *all* have to be here?" Max asked as we sat down on the couch, his eyes wide.

Pete shrugged. "There's nothing else to do."

"You're welcome to leave," Diya snapped at her brother. "This doesn't need to be your entertainment—"

"Okay, young lady," Uncle Neal said, and Diya quieted down immediately. "I wouldn't press your luck right now."

"Let me get this straight," Aunt Abby said. "We just talked to you at breakfast about not meddling. And rather than listening to any of us, all of you cook up a plan to smear Rick Andersen in the paper?"

"I have to say, as a journalist, I'm particularly offended," Quinn said, shaking her head. "A newspaper is not the place to settle scores and defame people."

"Totally," Pete said. "Use the internet for that."

Max nodded. "Good to know."

"No!" the adults said, practically as one.

"Pete, you're more than welcome to leave," Uncle Neal said pointedly.

"I'm good," Pete said.

Uncle Neal gave him a look. "It wasn't a suggestion."

Pete sighed, then pushed himself up to standing and headed out of the lodge, picking up his soccer ball where he'd left it by the door on his way out.

"Kids," Gramps said, his tone softening slightly. "I know you're trying to fix this. And it's a lovely instinct."

"But," Grams said, her tone no-nonsense, "there's nothing to be done, except make things worse."

"We don't want to get sued for slander," Uncle Dennis pointed out. "Which is what making things up about people and printing them is."

"He might *not* pay his taxes," Diya pointed out. "We were just *raising the question*."

"Well, please stop," Aunt Abby said. "In case we weren't clear enough this morning—I need all of you to stay out of this."

"Rick technically didn't *have* to let us stay here this summer," Gramps said, and I felt my stomach clench. "So if we aggravate him, he could kick us off this land at any minute, and then the summer will be over like *that*."

"Are we making things clear?" Grams asked, and we all nodded.

"I understand," Quinn said, leaning forward, "that you're not happy about this. I'm not either. But there's nothing we can do to change it. So let's just enjoy the time we have. Okay?"

I nodded and saw Hattie, Max, and Diya doing the same, even if Diya looked very reluctant.

"So," Aunt Katie said. "Ready? Dish duty for the rest of the summer." I heard Hattie let out a barely audible groan next to me. "And it's lights-out a half hour earlier every night this week." She looked around at us, and I held my breath, wondering if there was more. "Sound like a plan?"

"Can we say no?" Diya asked.

"No," Aunt Abby said with a laugh, and it broke some of the tension in the room. She slapped her hands down on her knees, like she was signaling this was over.

"Good," Gramps said with a nod. "The tribunal has spoken!"

"Why do we need to have these every summer?" Uncle Benji asked, shaking his head.

Grams raised an eyebrow at him. "Would you like me to tell these kids about the stuff you and your siblings got up to when you were their age?"

"No, no," Uncle Benji said quickly. "It's all good. I'm sure we've all learned something here today. See you at dinner!" He gave Hattie a *behave yourself* look and hurried out, clearly eager to get back to writing his book.

"That wasn't so bad!" Max enthused as we headed for the door. "I was worried they'd take away lake privileges."

"Things have to be *really* bad for that to happen," Diya said. "Like, I don't even think Pete lost them when he crashed Gramps's car into the garage."

I stared at her. "He did *what*?"

We stepped outside and Holden jumped to his feet. "Well?"

"Not the worst," Hattie told him. "Dishes and earlier bedtime."

"Way better than it could have been." Holden gave us a smile that faded immediately as he looked out toward the driveway.

"Is your dad coming?" I asked, realizing that while we'd just gotten our consequences over with, Holden had been sitting out here this whole time, waiting for his.

"Yeah, he's just—" But whatever he said was lost in the roar of a sports car's wheels as a bright red, low-slung car screeched into the driveway, sending up a spray of gravel. "He's here," Holden said with a sigh.

We all watched as the gull-wing doors lifted up and a guy with thinning blond hair and a red face pushed himself up out of the car. "Holden!" he snapped.

Holden grimaced. "Gotta go."

"Wait," I called as he started to walk across the gravel, "what about your kayak?"

"I'll swim over for it or something," he called behind him, giving us a tiny wave.

Holden's dad looked at us for a moment, then shook his head and got back into the car. "You know what my day is like today," I could hear him already start to lecture. "You think I have time for this? Seriously?"

The doors lowered, and the car sped out as fast as it had sped in, leaving flying dust and gravel in its wake.

"So that was Holden's dad, huh?" I asked in the silence that followed.

"Unfortunately," Hattie said.

"I totally think he doesn't pay his taxes," Diya declared definitively, already heading down the hill to the lake. "I think we really should have had someone investigate that. Last one to the pizza float has to do the dishes!"

I looked at Hattie and Max, trying to see if they were in on this too. A second later Max grinned, and then we all took off running at once.

"What are you doing?" Hattie asked, and I looked up from where I was studying my mother's map before bed.

Even though we hadn't lost lake privileges—and had

spent most of the afternoon trying, and failing, to figure out an aquatic version of ActionBall!, called AquaBall!— everything that day had felt a little bit off.

Holden hadn't come back, even though we'd expected him to. It was strange that he hadn't returned to the lake all day, and I was worried that maybe he had confessed to his dad and was being grounded.

And even though we were having fun, it was hard to ignore the bulldozers lined up across the lake.

And now we were going to bed *much* earlier than we would have liked. I hadn't even pulled out *Cara Vanessa Cole and the Surprise Party Snafu*; I had just reached for the map instead. After all, I had an *actual* mystery to solve and should be focusing on that right now, not invented mysteries.

I held it up. "Just looking at the map."

Diya dropped her head down over the top bunk to look at me upside down. "Find anything new?"

"No," I sighed. I focused on the tiny words at the bottom—*Protect the things that matter most even if it's hard!!* And then next to it, the drawing of the ship in the bubble. But why a ship in a *bubble*?

"We will figure something out, though, right?" Hattie asked, real doubt creeping into her voice. "We're not going to just . . . let him win?"

"Lights out!" Aunt Katie called.

Hattie squinted, took aim, and threw her flip-flop across the room, hitting the light switch and sending the cabin into darkness.

I leaned over and carefully placed the map in the box under my bunk, then hit my pillow twice to fluff it up and closed my eyes.

"Guys," I heard Diya whisper after a moment, her voice smaller and more scared than she ever would have let herself sound in the light, "what are we going to do?"

I didn't reply, and neither did Hattie.

What was there to say?

After a moment I heard Hattie's breathing turn slow and even, and Diya sigh the way she always did before falling asleep.

But I lay awake, my eyes wide open and my mind racing, for a long, long time.

CHAPTER 23

I was almost out the door the next morning when I noticed my phone lighting up.

"Hi, Dad," I said, walking away from the cabins. It was a foggy, chilly morning, and I was glad I'd put a sweatshirt on over my usual uniform of bathing suit, shorts, and T-shirt.

"Oh—hi." My dad sounded surprised. "I didn't think I'd get you."

"Why not?" I started walking down toward the dock where I could see the mist rising off the lake.

"It's just early. Early there, I mean. Here it's lunchtime."

"I'm always up early here." I stood on the dock and looked out at the lake, and Holden's kayak from yesterday still resting on the grass. It was bothering me that we hadn't heard from him, and I wondered if we should arrange some kind of reconnaissance mission to go make sure his evil dad wasn't keeping him locked up. "Wait." I turned away from the water, trying to concentrate. "Why did you call if you didn't think you'd get me?"

"Well," my dad said. I noticed for the first time that he sounded nervous. "I was going to leave a message for you to call back when Ginger and I can talk to you together."

"Why?" That didn't sound good. I'd been talking with my dad and Ginger separately all summer—why did they suddenly need to talk to me together? "What's going on?"

"Why don't I try to patch Ginger in?" My dad sounded more flustered than ever.

"It's four a.m. in California."

"Oh. Right." I heard my dad sigh, and I could practically picture him on set like I'd seen him a million times—pacing around the trailers, stepping over cables without even having to look down. "Look, I'm heading back to New York tomorrow for my meetings, maybe we just—"

"Dad, tell me." I was getting more nervous by the second. "Is everything okay with you and Ginger? Are you two . . . ?" I hesitated. My thoughts were racing. Was this the reason they'd been apart all summer?

"No, nothing like that," my dad said hurriedly. "Everything's fine. It's just . . ." I heard him draw in a breath. "Ginger and I . . . We're going to have a baby."

"Oh," I said. And then a second later, what this meant

hit me. *"Oh."* The world seemed to shift under my feet, like someone had just yanked the ground out from under me. I sat down on the dock, my thoughts racing. A baby. They were going to have a *baby*?! I'd be a sister! But . . .

"What do you think?"

What did I *think*? What if this made everything different? I'd only just gotten used to it being three of us, and now that was changing. But it would be fun to have a baby— and Ginger and I could decorate the nursery! On the other hand . . .

What if this made everything change all over again? What if they forgot about me now that they would be a family of their own? And how was it fair that this baby was going to grow up with two parents all the time? I shook my head. The baby wasn't even *here* yet, and I was jealous of it? But . . .

"Ryanna?"

"Was this why Ginger was sick?" I asked, finally putting it together. "That flu she had—it wasn't really the flu?"

"No. She was having morning sickness because of the baby."

"Why didn't you just tell me then?"

"We had just found out. And we didn't want to drop all that on you right before you left. We wanted to tell you now so that you'd have some time to process before you came home. How . . . are you feeling about this? Are you okay?"

"I'm really happy for you." I tried to make my voice sound excited.

"Really?" My dad sounded unsure. "Maybe you should talk about this. Want me to book you an appointment with Dr. Wendy?"

"No!" My voice came out sharper than I'd intended.

"Are you *sure* you're okay with this, Ryanna?"

"Would it make any difference?" I snapped.

"I . . . well . . ."

"It's like you just want me to say I'm okay. And so, fine, I'll say it. I'm okay."

"But *are* you?"

"Dad!" I exploded. My voice echoed across the lake, and some birds in a nearby tree took flight. "You've been keeping this from me because you think I can't handle it. And then you spring it on me and want to hear that it's fine. You keep *doing* this!"

"Honey." My dad sounded shocked, like this wasn't the way he expected this conversation to go. "What are you talking about?"

"I never even knew about this place!" I was yelling now, like something inside me, something raw and tender, had just been hurt. "You never *told* me, Dad. All these years. You never told me I had all these cousins and aunts and uncles.

You kept it from me. And now that I'm finally here—getting to know everyone and learning about Mom and being a part of this family—it's all going away. Everything's changing, and all you want is for me to say it's okay. But it's not okay! None of it is!"

I hung up the phone with shaking hands, then immediately turned it off in case he called back. I tried to take a deep breath, but my breath was coming shallowly. I had never yelled at my father like that, ever.

I looked across the lake again—the mist was starting to burn off. I could see, emerging like monsters in a scary movie, the bulldozers.

I tried to get my thoughts in some kind of order, but I couldn't do it, not with the bulldozers hulking across the lake at me. Finally I pushed myself up to my feet, grabbed my phone, and walked up to the lodge.

I could feel Gramps looking at me, concerned, as I made the coffee on autopilot. But I didn't want to talk to him about it—I didn't even know what I would say. That everything was changing and nobody had even asked me? So I was grateful when Aunt Abby showed up early, fresh from her run, with Quinn right behind her.

"Morning!" Archie strode through the door of the lodge with a smile on his face, carrying a green box from the bakery in town, Borrowed Thyme.

"Ooh," Gramps said, leaning forward. "Whatcha got?"

"Donuts," Archie said, placing them on the long buffet table. "Thought it was the least I could do after eating your food all summer."

Quinn jumped up and hurried over to the donuts. "Why are you in such a good mood?"

He smiled. "I'm just in love," he said happily as he made himself some tea.

As though they could somehow sense the presence of donuts, everyone seemed to be up at the lodge a lot earlier today. I was grateful for it—the loudness and chatter. It meant that nobody noticed that I was quieter than usual. My thoughts were scattered and spinning.

I tried to join in as the day went on. We played Action-Ball! and kickball. Even though nobody said anything, it was clear we all wanted to avoid the lake. But I had a churning, angry, nervous feeling inside me that was only growing as the hours passed. I barely ate lunch—Pete formed all the leftover donuts into a giant sandwich; it was actually very impressive—and when we came back to the archery targets afterward and everyone started arguing about how far away you had to be for an arrow to count, I couldn't hold it in anymore.

"Why are we doing this?" I burst out, and my cousins turned to look at me.

"Because otherwise there's no way of knowing who really won," Hattie explained.

"We don't have time for this!" My voice was rising. Why didn't anyone *understand?* "We don't have time for archery and ActionBall! We have to keep digging, find this deed . . ."

Diya shook her head. "I think we need to stop. I think maybe my mom was right."

"How can you say that?"

She pointed around at us. "Have you seen Holden today? I bet it's because he got in trouble."

"But we can do something else. We can stop Holden's dad . . . somehow . . ."

"No." Max sounded tired. "Ryanna. We can't. We probably shouldn't have been messing around with it to begin with. But we can at least enjoy ourselves now."

"We still have some time," Hattie said, and it sounded like she was trying to look on the bright side. But for all her big talk, she wasn't quite a good enough actress to pull it off.

"So you don't even want to try?" I asked. "You don't want to do everything we can—"

"We've *been* doing that," Diya said. "And we haven't gotten anywhere except in trouble and with blisters on our hands. I don't know what Aunt Casey buried, but I don't think it's going to save this place. So I think we should have fun for the rest of the summer."

"But it's my *last* summer!" I blurted this out, and my voice broke. "I'm probably never going to be able to come back again, or see any of you. The only reason it happened at all was because this place was going away. And you guys had it for years and years and I didn't, and *everything* gets taken away from me, always—"

"Um." Hattie looked at me with wide eyes. "Are you okay?"

"No, I'm not *okay*!" I yelled. "Of course I'm not! Can't you see that? Are you *stupid*?" I saw all three of them draw back, hurt. I could feel tears in my eyes, and I knew I was crossing a line—and that I should walk it back, make this right. But instead I snapped, "Just leave me alone!"

I turned and ran from the field.

I crossed the camp, running as fast as I could, like maybe I could outrun everything I was feeling and the fact that I knew I was making a mistake but didn't seem to be able to do anything to stop it.

I wasn't even looking where I was going, but when I found myself down by the dock, I decided it was as good a place as any. I grabbed the nearest one-person kayak and pushed off in it, paddling hard, barely able to see through my tears.

The problem with running away to a lake is that there's nowhere to *go*.

I had spent the first hour or so paddling the circumference, channeling all my rage and hurt into choppy oar strokes until my arms and shoulders were aching and I could feel my nose getting sunburned. I'd paddled over to the floating dock and then just kind of sat next to it, bobbing in the water, trying to figure out what to do.

I knew I should just paddle in, find my cousins, apologize.

But it felt like there was a mountain in front of me preventing that from happening. I wasn't sure if it was pride or embarrassment or what, but I couldn't seem to get past it.

I looked around and decided that maybe I would just live here now. I really didn't seem to see any other options. There was plenty of water. I would be fine.

The sun was just starting to set—and I was beginning to get cold—when I saw the small group make their way out to me.

Hattie was on a stand-up paddleboard, Max was in a canoe, and Diya was on Slice of Pizza, being towed by Max's canoe.

I drew in a breath when I realized they weren't just hanging out on the lake—they were coming to get me. Just like they'd come to get me in the woods the last time I'd done this. I was suddenly ashamed of myself. My cousins were braver and better than me. They were giving me chances I wasn't sure I deserved.

Because even though I'd run away and yelled at them and told them to leave me alone, they'd come to find me. And I realized I could at least meet them halfway.

I started to paddle toward them, realizing that the obstacle that had seemed so big—keeping me from doing just this—actually didn't exist at all. It had all been in my mind.

I stopped paddling when we were all just a few feet apart from one another. I saw Hattie take a breath, but I jumped in first. "I'm so sorry," I blurted. "I just found out my dad and stepmom are going to have a baby, and the bulldozers are here, and everything is changing. . . ."

I stopped and took it all in for a moment—the camp, lit by the setting sun. *Magic hour*, we called it on set.

"I thought I could find a way to stop it. I thought I could save the camp. Because I couldn't just let it go." I looked around at all of them—my *family*. "It's like the fireflies. I know they exist now. How am I supposed to go back to summers in California and not have them?"

"Wait, *what's* like the fireflies?" Hattie whispered to Max.

"It's a metaphor," Max whispered back.

"Yeah," I said, giving Hattie a smile. "I just meant it's the same with all of you. And the summer here. I don't know . . ." I stopped and shook my head. My voice was starting to tremble. "I don't know how I'm supposed to just go back to my old life now. Knowing that this one exists."

"We can figure something out," Diya said, a look of fierce determination on her face, one I'd gotten to know all too well. "We can petition Grams and Gramps. You can talk to your dad. It doesn't have to be over, okay?"

I nodded and gave her a shaky smile. She gave me a smile back. "The camp's gonna be gone, though. I don't think we can fix that."

"Well," Max said, looking at Hattie and Diya. "We talked about it. We decided no more trying to interfere with Holden's dad. But we *will* help you try to find whatever it was your mom left."

Diya nodded. "Even if it's not the deed, it's still something of your mom's. And we should try to get it before it's too late."

"I appreciate it. Thank you." The dinner bugle sounded, but none of us moved right away.

"Are you okay, though?" Hattie asked me, tilting her head to the side. "It's kind of wild that you're going to be a sister."

"I know." Now that the shock of it had worn off, I was starting to get excited. Having a sibling hadn't been in any of my plans for how I pictured things. But if I'd learned anything this summer, it was that maybe that would be okay. Not only okay—more fun than I ever could have imagined.

All at once I felt just how long the day had been . . . and how hungry I suddenly was. I grabbed my oar and started paddling. "Last one to the dock forfeits their dessert!"

I wasn't sure what time it was when I awoke with a start. My mind was going a hundred miles an hour. Fragments of the dream I'd just had were still lingering, and I closed my eyes, trying to concentrate. It was something important— the ship in the bubble, and hidden treasure, and Holden—

I gasped out loud, then clapped my hand over my mouth so I wouldn't wake my cousins. I was wide awake now, and for good reason.

I'd finally figured out what the map meant.

CHAPTER 24

I waited until it started to get light out before I got out of bed. I hadn't been able to go back to sleep—I'd just been lying awake, turning it over in my mind. I was *sure* that I was right.

My mother loved mysteries, just like me—and so I should have known that *X* never marks the spot. That there was always going to be something else hiding—another twist before the end—and my mother had given me a big clue with what she'd drawn on the map.

When I couldn't stand it anymore, I crept out of bed and got dressed in the closet, then took my mother's map and carefully tucked it into my shorts pocket.

Rather than going up to the lodge, I went down to the dock, debating my next move. Now that I'd realized where the treasure was, I wanted to get to it as soon as possible. I didn't even want to wait for my cousins to wake up.

And given the tribunal, I didn't want to get them in trouble. When I found the treasure—recovered the deed—everything would be fixed. But to get it, I'd have to break the rules we'd agreed to.

It would all be worth it when I saved the day.

I hurried to the dock—Holden's kayak was still there. I dragged it down to the water, got in, and pushed off.

I paddled across the empty, quiet lake as fast as I could. It was an overcast morning—a little foggy—and cool on the water. I was extra glad I'd put on my sweatshirt. I was so focused on getting across the lake, and thinking about what was going to come next, that it wasn't until I was dragging the kayak up onto Holden's dock that I realized I wasn't sure how to get in touch with him.

I'd left my phone back in the cabin like usual. I could ring the doorbell—but I knew Holden's dad was not going to be thrilled to see me. Also, it *was* really early. I was starting to think I'd made a mistake when I saw Holden walking down the dock toward me.

"Hi!" I called, tucking the oar inside the kayak and running to meet him. But then I saw his face. "What's wrong?"

Holden looked despondent. His dark red hair was standing up in all directions, like he'd been running his hands through it.

"It's my dad," he said with a sigh. "He's really mad. Between calling the paper and the email thing . . ."

"What did he say?"

"He said I can't hang out with you guys for the rest of the summer."

My stomach dropped. "He can't do that!"

"And then *I* said I didn't want to be here if I can't see my friends, and then he said in that case I should just go back to my mom's . . . so I'm going to go back to Connecticut. I told him I don't want to be here if I'm just going to have to watch trees get torn down."

"But you might not have to!" I pulled the map out of my pocket. "I think I figured it out last night—"

"Ryanna. I mean, no offense, but we've had this for a while, and we've been digging, and all we have are more dead ends. And even if we *did* find something, I'm not sure it would be enough. I'm sorry. It was a good try, but—"

"I know," I said hurriedly, waving this away. "You're right. *Except* I think we missed the biggest clue of all—and you were actually the one to say it."

"I was?"

"What did you say when we were talking about where we would hide our treasure?"

"I said that I would give it to a friend," he said slowly. "Someone I trusted."

"Exactly! I think that's what my mom did with the deed to the camp."

"You think she gave it to—my *dad*?" Holden asked, his voice going high at the end.

"They were best friends," I reminded him. "She knew that Gramps was always losing everything, so she gave it to the person she trusted most to keep it safe. And if she were . . . still here"—I hesitated only for a moment—"she would have been able to tell everyone where it was as soon as they started looking for it. But she wasn't, and the secret disappeared with her. And so all of this happened."

"And then of course my dad would try to take the land away," Holden said, talking faster. "Because he knew he had the only copy of the deed!"

"Exactly!"

"Okay, I totally buy that. But we still don't know where it is. Right? We're back to square one."

"Maybe not. There's one ship in your dad's collection I've noticed. According to the plaque, it would have been made at the right time. And the sail is made of what looks like paper. Paper with *writing* on it."

"But why would you think that's the deed?"

I pointed to the tiny ship drawn next to my mother's words. The ship in a bubble—or a *bottle*. "What does that look like to you?"

"Okay," Holden said, whispering as he motioned for me to follow him down the hallway. "My dad's on a bike ride, so we have a little window, but we have to be fast."

"What about Ella?" I whispered back.

"She doesn't get up until, like, ten. I usually end up making *her* breakfast. I don't think she's actually a very good nanny."

"Au pair."

He grinned. "Right. So we'll probably have twenty minutes. But if my dad came back and found you here—and us in his office . . ."

"*Big* trouble."

"Exactly. He would not be happy."

"I mean, he's not going to be happy when we tell him he's not going to be able to build on our side of the lake."

"Good point."

We'd stopped outside Holden's dad's office. Holden reached for the handle, and for just a moment I panicked. What if the office was locked? And then we'd have to try to figure out how to be cat burglars *really* fast. But the handle turned, Holden stepped inside, and I followed.

This time I didn't look at anything else—I just focused right on the wall of ships in bottles looming above me. I couldn't believe that the answer had been here all along—that while everyone else had been tearing apart our house and we'd been digging next to the picnic table, the document had been here, waiting for us, protected behind glass in an impossible bottle.

"Which one?" Holden asked.

"That one," I said, pointing to the ship on the second shelf from the top. The first row of ships—the ones that had clearly been made when his dad was a little kid—were the closest to the ceiling. I was looking right at the one with the writing on the sail—in the center of the second shelf. It was too far away for me to be able to make out the writing, but I knew that was it. It *had* to be.

"Whoa."

"I know." We just stood there looking at it for a moment.

"Well, let me grab a ladder. There's one in the garage that should be able to reach."

"You need help?"

"I'm okay," he said, hurrying out of the office. "Be right back!"

I turned to the wall of ships, clenching and unclenching my hands. We were so close—this was torture.

I glanced at the desk chair, then back at the wall, sizing it up. I could stand on the chair and, if I stretched, be able to pluck the bottle off the shelf. And if I hurried, I could do it all before Holden even came back.

After all, I rationalized as I pulled the chair out from under the desk and wheeled it over, we *did* have to move fast. If Holden's dad came back and realized what we were after, he'd probably have the document destroyed so that he could build his ugly condos. Time was of the essence.

I pushed the chair up as close to the shelves as I could, then climbed onto the seat carefully. I didn't want to set it rolling. I straightened up and looked at the ship in the bottle. It was still a little bit out of reach, but I was sure that I could get to it. I knew I could wait for Holden to come back with a ladder—but I was *so close*. And I couldn't wait even a second longer.

I rose up on my toes and reached for the bottle. I was so near—just a hand's length away. I stretched out for it—and then things happened very fast.

The desk chair went rolling, sliding out from under me, throwing me forward. I grabbed out for what was in front of me—the shelf of bottles. I looked down at the ground and was about to jump when I heard the creaking sound. Before I could move—or react—the shelf cracked, and I was falling backward, and there was a red flash of pain in my arm and, all around me, the sound of breaking glass.

I remember thinking that I was going to be in a *lot* of trouble—and then it all went black.

When I woke up again, everything hurt.

"Owwww," I muttered to myself, trying to figure out what was going on. I opened my eyes—even that somehow hurt—and immediately squinted against the bright white light. I was in what looked like a hospital, in a bed with scratchy sheets and an unfamiliar blue blanket.

My left arm was all wrapped up with gauze and a splint, and when I tried to move it, I got another blast of pain. I could see that there were little cuts all over my arms and hands. And I had the worst headache in history.

"You're up!" Gramps hurried over to the bed, looking like he'd somehow aged since I'd seen him yesterday. "How are you feeling?"

"Bad," I said, trying to remember what happened. I tried to lift my arm again and winced.

"Careful there. You've got yourself a broken arm."

"I do?" No wonder it hurt so much—I'd never broken a bone before.

"They think you must have landed on it when you fell." All at once it came back to me—Holden's dad's office, the ships in bottles, the shelf coming off the wall. "I guess you were trying to look at one of Rick's ships?"

I nodded—this seemed like the easiest explanation at the moment.

"You bonked your head, too, and have a lot of cuts from the glass. They don't think you'll need any stitches, though."

"Oh—that's good." My head was still pounding. I tried to think clearly. "So how did I get here? I mean—"

"Holden and his dad called me, along with an ambulance. We're in Stroudsburg, at the hospital."

"Was Holden's dad mad about the ships?"

"He seemed more concerned about making sure he wasn't going to be sued," Gramps said, rolling his eyes at me in an exasperated way.

"Wait." I tried to sit up straighter, then winced again. "Did Holden say anything? Is he here?" The thought that I could be the one to tell Gramps that we'd solved the problem was almost making the pain in my arm and head go away.

Gramps shook his head. "They stayed behind. He did ask me to give you this." He reached into his pocket and pulled out a paper, handing it to me with a puzzled expression.

I took it with a grin—but then my smile faded as I looked at what it was.

The paper was just a flyer for the annual Lake Phoenix fireworks show from 1993.

There was a Post-it attached to the top, and I pulled it off with a sinking heart.

Ryanna—this was what was in the bottle.
Sorry we couldn't find it.
Feel better soon.
Your friend, Holden

"No," I said, half whispering, turning the paper over in my hands. This *couldn't* be what the sail had been made of. I'd been sure—I'd been *so* sure. I was wrong? This was just . . . over?

I went to push off the blanket and get out of bed—but as soon as I moved my arm, I had another flash of pain. "Ow!"

"Easy," Gramps said. "The doctors said they're going to put it in a sling so you won't be tempted to use it. And then when you're back home, and the swelling has gone down, they'll put it in a cast."

"Wait—what do you mean 'back home'?"

"Ryanna." My grandfather let out a long sigh. "We had to tell your dad what happened. We caught him on the plane—he was on his way to New York. I guess for some meetings? Anyway, as soon as he lands, he's heading up here. He's very angry—saying that we failed to keep you safe. Which is true, of course . . ." Gramps rubbed his hand over his face.

"You didn't do anything! It's my fault, no one else's. I can talk to him. I don't have to leave."

Gramps shook his head, looking sadder than I'd ever seen him look before. "I'm afraid it's been decided. You're going with your dad back to California."

I felt tears flood my eyes. I hadn't been able to fix

anything. I hadn't been able to find anything. I'd only made things worse.

"So that's it?" I felt the first hot tear hit my cheek. "There's nothing else to do?" Gramps didn't say anything, just shook his head, but I knew what that meant.

It meant my summer was over.

CHAPTER 25

Gramps pulled into the driveway of Camp Van Camp, and I had to swallow hard to keep from crying again. When he put the truck in park and I looked up at the lodge, I couldn't help but remember the first time I'd pulled up here, with Kendra the driver, and no idea about the summer I was going to have—and how long ago that felt now.

I thought about that first night, and how I wanted to leave. But now that I had to go, it was the very last thing I wanted. I was supposed to have more time here. It felt like it was being ripped away from me.

"Well," Gramps said, giving me a smile that didn't meet his eyes as he killed the engine and twirled the keys around his finger. "I guess you better get to packing, huh?"

I nodded, even though I was considering just barricading myself in the truck and refusing to get out.

"Your dad thought he'd be here around dinner," Gramps said, checking his watch. I leaned over to look, and he turned the face so I could see it—it was a little after four. It had taken longer than I'd anticipated to get discharged from the hospital. And then when we'd driven back from Stroudsburg, the valley surrounding Lake Phoenix had been foggy, slowing us down.

The whole time, I'd just been watching the car's clock ticking down the time I had left, helpless to do anything about it. "And you're *sure* he said I have to leave?"

"I think if he's coming all the way up here, you're going with him."

"Yeah," I muttered. I knew, deep down, that this was true. The very fact that he was coming on his own and not sending someone to get me let me know just how mad he was about everything.

"Okay," Gramps said, clapping his hands together. "You pack, and maybe if you do it quickly enough, we can do a s'mores send-off for you before your dad arrives?"

"Really? S'mores before dinner?"

He winked at me. "Special occasions call for special rules. So hurry, okay?"

I nodded and had to get out of the car carefully, trying not to jostle my arm in its sling. It was *very* annoying, only having the use of one hand, and I wasn't at all looking forward to the next six (or possibly eight, depending, according to the doctors) weeks of it.

I walked to the Hummingbird Cabin, knowing I should hurry, but at the same time, wanting to freeze all of it in my mind. Why hadn't I taken more pictures? Why hadn't I realized that one day I'd have to go?

I wanted to remember it all, the twisting pathways and the smell of woodsmoke and the ripples in the water from a canoe on the lake—it looked like it was Aunt Abby and Uncle Neal paddling across it. What if, when I was back in California, I forgot the way the leaves shook in the wind, or the sound of the birds in the trees, or the ferns that sprouted just outside the woods? I looked as hard as I could, trying to capture it in my mind, not able to believe it might be the last time.

I pushed open the door of my cabin and then instinctively jumped back. "Ryanna!" three people yelled at once. Max and Hattie and Diya all jumped up to greet me as soon as I stepped inside.

"Are you okay?" Hattie asked, rushing forward.

"What happened?" Max asked, his brow furrowed. "Nobody will tell us anything!"

"Did you really go to the hospital?" Diya asked. She was scowling, which I'd learned by now was what she did when she didn't want to express any emotions.

I nodded, then took a deep breath and filled everyone in—about my theory, how I was so sure I was right, and then going to Holden's this morning to finally get the deed. "But this happened instead." I gestured to my sling.

"And this was really what was inside?" Max asked, turning over the paper Holden had given Gramps.

I sighed. "Yep." I went to the foot of my bed and flipped open the lid of my trunk. If I'd thought about having to pack at all—which I'd done only in the vaguest of ways—I'd thought we'd all be doing it together, me and Hattie and Diya, laughing and arguing about whose jean shorts were whose. Not like this. Not me alone.

"Then why was there a ship in a bottle on your mom's map?" Hattie asked.

"I have no idea. Maybe it was just a doodle?" As I opened my drawer and grabbed an armful of clothes, I realized I probably should have known better. After all, in every mystery I'd ever read, there was *always* a red herring. Sometimes a literal one, like in *Cara Vanessa Cole and the Fresh Fish Fiasco*.

"You really have to leave?" Max asked.

"Yeah." My throat tightened around the word. "My dad's on his way to come get me."

"He is?" Hattie suddenly looked a lot less gloomy. "Like, in person and everything?"

"Jeez, Hattie," Diya said, tossing my pillow at her. "Can you not think about your acting career for one minute?"

"I can be sad about Ryanna leaving and still want to give her dad my headshot, can't I?" She threw the pillow back at Diya, but it missed and hit Max instead.

"Well," Diya said, scowling more fiercely than ever, "if you have to leave, we better take advantage of the time we still have."

"Gramps said we can maybe do s'mores before dinner," I said, feeling like I should at least give them a little bit of good news.

Max went to go collect s'mores sticks while Hattie and Diya helped me pack. This meant just dumping all my things into the trunk, not bothering to fold anything, and putting my toiletry bag from the bathroom on top. The last thing I packed were all the things I'd gotten this summer that had been my mom's—the mysteries, the T-shirts, the sweatshirt. I had her necklace on—I hadn't taken it off since I'd gotten it, and I slid the heart and key charms on the chain for just a minute before I tucked it back under the neck of my sweatshirt. Then I latched the trunk, and Diya nodded.

"Good," she said. "That's done. I say we try to get one more ActionBall! game in before it gets too cold. Maybe we'll all play one-handed to make it fair for Ryanna. And then we still should have enough time for s'mores. Sound good?"

I nodded, suddenly feeling like it was too sad to be in the cabin with none of my stuff around and a packed suitcase.

We headed toward the field, and my eyes rested on Grams's bird-watching platform. If my dad really was coming in the next few hours, this might be my last chance. And I didn't want to waste it.

"I'll meet you on the field," I called as I started hurrying up toward the lodge.

I was running out of time, after all, and I needed to get some answers.

Which meant I needed to talk to my grandparents.

CHAPTER 26

I found them both in the mess hall, Grams sitting at the table and Gramps setting out what we'd need for s'mores—a giant bag of marshmallows, a box of graham crackers, Hershey's bars.

"Hey, Ryanna," Gramps said, giving me a smile. "You want to give me a hand with this?"

"How's your arm?" Grams asked, frowning as she looked at my sling. "Did they wrap it properly? I knew I should have gone along—"

"I need you to tell me the truth," I said, and watched them both freeze, their expressions startled. "I need you to tell me what you and my dad fought about all those years ago. Because this . . . might be my last chance to hear it from you."

They exchanged a look. Neither one of them said anything.

"I have to leave"—my voice broke on the last word—"in

the next few hours, and I don't know when I'll see you two again or talk to you . . . so I need to know."

"Why don't you make us one last pot of coffee?" Gramps suggested. "For old times' sake. And while you do, we'll talk."

I hadn't understood why he wanted me to make coffee now—it was getting close to dinnertime—but as I started going through the familiar movements, spoon, coffee grounds, water, I realized that it was actually good to have something to focus on, something to do while I listened to my grandparents. And it was so familiar to me now, I could do it one-handed.

"You came to stay with us the summer you were three," Grams started off, a faraway smile on her face. "You and our Casey. For the whole summer." She paused here and looked up at me. "Your parents had decided to take some time apart."

My hand froze where I was stretching it out to press the button to make the coffee. "They were going to get a divorce?" I could barely get the last word out. I'd never heard anything about this—never even a hint of it.

Gramps shook his head. "I don't think it ever came to that," he said. "I think they were just . . . spending some time apart to sort things through. They met when they were very young, you know, and even the best marriages go through rocky times."

"You came up here with your mom for the summer, and

it was wonderful," Grams said. "Casey was getting to spend time here, with us and her brothers and sisters, and we were so thrilled to have you—"

"But then she died," I interrupted, my words catching in my throat. Because however great that long-ago summer was, I knew how the story ended. On a New York City street, at the end of August, a cab speeding through a red light. I'd always known that—but I'd never bothered to ask, until now, just why my mother had been on the East Coast in the first place. And why my father hadn't been with her.

I could read all the mysteries I wanted, but I was a terrible detective.

"We were just heartbroken," Gramps said. Grams wordlessly handed him a tissue, and he dabbed his eyes with it. "Our little girl. And she was so young. She had so much ahead of her. And then there was you. . . ."

"Your dad was wrecked too," Grams said, patting Gramps's hand with her own, then leaving it on top of his. "Just absolutely thrown for a loop. Devastated. And we . . ." She looked at Gramps, then took a breath. "We weren't sure that he was up for being the single father of a three-year-old. He was working all the time, traveling all over the world for his job. . . . It didn't seem stable to us. And especially since they had been taking time apart, we weren't sure what your mom would have wanted. . . ."

The machine started to burble, the coffee smell filling the mess hall. "So what happened?"

"We told your father we were intending to seek joint custody."

"What?" I whispered.

Gramps shook his head sadly. "In retrospect—it was a huge mistake. I think we were trying to hold on to Casey the only way we had left. We told ourselves we were doing it for her—but we were doing it for us. We weren't ready to let go."

"We had a fight. . . . Terrible things were said, on both sides. It turned into such a mess . . . your dad was furious, and rightly so. And he decided, because of what we'd done, that there should be no contact between the families. That it would be best not to have any communication."

"Best for who?" I asked.

"For no one," Gramps said with a heavy sigh. "It was our biggest regret. That you weren't here every summer, getting to know your cousins, your aunts and uncles . . ."

"And so," Grams said, "when we found out about what Rick was going to do—that it was our last summer here—we wrote. We knew we at least had to try to let you see this place before it was gone. And your dad was kind enough to let you come."

"And here we are," Gramps said. He nodded to the coffee maker. "I think it's just about done."

Sure enough, a second later, the *ding* that signaled the coffee was done went off. Using my good arm, I pulled down Gramps's favorite mug and poured him a cup, then set it down in front of him. He took a long sip, then smiled at me. "Delicious."

Grams rolled her eyes. "You know you're going to be up all night now, right?"

I'd come to the end of the mystery. This was why I had been so estranged from them for so long. I tried to figure out if I was mad, but I wasn't, really—I was just sad. Sad about how everything had gone. Sad that we'd wasted so much time when we didn't have to. And sad because I had a feeling that this separation would have been the last thing my mother would have wanted.

"Hey!" I looked over to see Diya standing in the doorway with a cricket bat and a Super Ball, a quiver of arrows over her shoulder, looking annoyed. "Are we playing or not?"

I glanced at my grandparents—but I wasn't sure if there was more to the story. We'd arrived back at the beginning, after all—the summer my dad let me spend with them, and how I'd wrecked it by going snooping and breaking my arm.

"Yeah," I said. I gave both my grandparents a quick one-armed hug, and then a smile, and hurried to meet Diya at the door.

"Don't forget about s'mores!" Gramps called, gesturing

at the table. "We'll get the fire going. We'll have to start soon if you're going to spoil your dinner!"

"What was that about?" Diya asked as we headed out and she handed me the cricket bat.

"Just tying up some loose ends."

"Everyone else is out on the field," she said as we started half walking, half running in that direction.

"Any sign of Holden?" I asked, even though I knew it wasn't likely.

"No," Diya said with a sigh. "But we have a whole rescue mission planned tomorrow. Max is going to—" She stopped short, like she'd just remembered that I wouldn't be here tomorrow. "Anyway. Race you to the field?"

We'd made our pre-dinner s'mores—Max helped me assemble mine—and eaten them around the fire and argued about who won the last game of ActionBall!, but my dad still hadn't shown up. So I'd gone in to have dinner with everyone else—grilled chicken and corn on the cob and fries. Uncle Benji, who'd cooked, grumbled about how cold and windy it was getting outside, and that we should be extra grateful that he grilled. But after we'd finished dinner and my dad *still* hadn't shown up, I was starting to get nervous. Had something happened? I kept checking my phone, but I didn't have any messages. And whenever I tried to call him, it went right to voice mail. I could see the adults exchanging glances, like they were also wondering what was happening.

"Maybe he changed his mind!" Max suggested, pushing his empty plate away.

"I don't think he changed his mind," Aunt Abby said.

"But if he did," Diya pointed out, "then Ryanna could stay."

"We can try to call him again," I heard Grams say to Gramps in a low voice. But before he could respond, there was the sound of tires crunching over gravel, and I knew that my dad had arrived.

Everyone looked at me, and I nodded and stood up. "I'll go too!" Hattie said, jumping out of her seat, but Diya yanked her back down.

"This is *not* the time to audition!"

"This business is all about who you know," Hattie said. "And I don't know anyone, and I'm trying to fix that!"

"Just not *now*."

I could hear them still bickering—the soundtrack to my summer, practically—as I walked out the lodge doors. As soon as I did, I realized what Uncle Benji had been talking about—it was *cold* out, and the air was damp, like it was about to start raining at any minute, the wind blowing hard. I saw a blue sedan parked around the circle in front of the lodge, and my dad standing next to it, looking up at the house. He was just staring at it, like he was seeing a ghost.

"Hi," I called. All at once I remembered the fight we'd had—how I'd yelled at him and then hung up on him. Was he still going to be mad about it?

"Ryanna," he said. A series of emotions broke over his face, one after another—fear, relief, happiness. He crossed over to me and gave me a careful hug, avoiding my arm in its sling. "Are you okay? How's the arm?" He hugged me again, half laughing. "I missed you!"

"I missed you too," I said, hugging him back, breathing in his familiar dad smell, and realizing that I really had. Seeing him here, it was like my worlds were colliding. And it hit me, all at once, how much I wished he could have been around all summer, with the other parents. I knew it was impossible—but now that he was actually here, it was all I wanted.

"I'm so sorry," I said, my words rushing out in a tumble. "I'm so sorry for what I said, and I shouldn't have yelled at you like that. And I never meant for this to happen—"

"It's okay," he said, hugging me a little harder. "I'm sorry too." He took a step back and gently touched my arm in its sling. "Does it hurt a lot?"

"I'm okay."

My dad shook his head, his voice sounding angry. "I can't believe this. I never should have trusted them—"

"This was all my fault. Nobody else's."

"We can talk about it at the hotel. Where's your stuff?"

"Hotel?" I asked.

"Hotel?" I looked over and saw Grams and Gramps step out onto the porch. A second later Hattie appeared, smiling wide, only to be yanked back inside again, the screen door bouncing once on its hinges before it shut.

"Hello, David," Grams said as she gave my dad a half smile, her tone cautious.

"Vivian," my dad said, his voice cold. He nodded at Gramps. "Cal."

"What do you mean 'hotel'?" Gramps asked, taking a step closer. "I thought you were heading back to New York tonight."

"That was the plan. But the whole drive here was fogged in. That's why it took me so long. I was just crawling along, barely able to see. . . . I don't want to do that again, not with Ryanna in the car. So we're just going to get something around here and head down in the morning."

"Yeah, the fog can be rough," Gramps said, already easing into what I knew was his reminiscing voice. "In fact, a few years ago, Byron was trying to come up from the city—"

"There's no need to stay at a hotel," Grams interrupted him. "We're happy to put you up."

"That's not necessary," my dad said crisply. "Ryanna will get her things, and we'll be out of your hair."

Grams raised an eyebrow. "Not sure you're going to find

anything. It's the high season; things book up. And if you're going to go all the way to Stroudsburg or Blakeslee, you're going straight back into the valley where the fog is."

"I'm sure we'll find something," my dad said, giving her a curt nod, then pulling out his phone. He looked at me as he started typing into it. "You want to get your stuff?"

"We can just stay here," I suggested, clinging to this like a lifeline. The idea that I wouldn't be driving away, possibly *forever*, was too good not to try to hold on to. "We wouldn't have to find something else."

"Ryanna." My dad stopped typing and gave me a look that let me know he wasn't in the mood for a discussion. "I'm not in the mood for a discussion."

"But—"

"I need you to act your age right now, okay?"

"Did you say *act*?" Hattie burst out of the door again—I saw a hand, presumably Diya's, grab for her but get only air. "What a coincidence, because *I* am an actress!" She bowed with a flourish. "Hattie Vivian Lowenstein Van Camp. My age range is eight to eleven, or even twelve if the twelve-year-old is really short for some reason! Would you like to hear my list of special skills? I have a monologue prepared, comedy *or* drama!"

My dad just blinked. "Um."

"Hattie, leave Ryanna's dad alone," Grams said. "He

needs to concentrate and look for a hotel room he's not going to be able to find."

"He might." Gramps was looking on the bright side as usual.

"It's okay," my dad said, scrolling through his phone. "Because I'm . . . going . . . to . . . get . . ." There was a long pause while he typed into it, his face slowly falling. He lowered his phone and looked up at us. "There's nothing available."

Grams smiled, looking satisfied.

"Great," I said. "So we can just stay here. I'll put my stuff back in my cabin. . . ."

"No." My dad shook his head. "We're going to leave first thing in the morning, so let's stay somewhere we won't bother anyone." He turned to my grandmother, and when he spoke, it was like every word was painful to say. "I would like to accept your offer to stay. I will of course pay you a commensurate rate."

"No need. We don't charge family." Grams gave my dad a long look. "Which we all are here, in spite of everything. We'll get Ryanna's suitcase, and I'll set you two up in the Phoenix Cabin."

"I'll come too!" Hattie said, but Gramps put a hand on her shoulder.

"Maybe not *just* right now."

• • •

My dad drove his rental car around so that it was parked near the other cars and pulled a huge suitcase out of the back. "Need a hand?" Hattie called, but my dad grimaced and shook his head as he hauled it out.

"You moving in, Dave?" Gramps called with a chuckle.

"I've been living in Budapest," my dad called back, sounding like he was nearing the end of his patience.

Gramps nodded sagely. "That's what they all say."

I'd left my trunk in the Hummingbird Cabin, and we—Grams, me, my dad—walked the familiar path down to the cabins to get it. Grams and I walked easily down the path, my dad more cautious, his feet sliding. He looked at my bare feet and shook his head. "The gravel doesn't bother you?"

"Nah," I said. "Not for weeks now." A gust of wind picked up, and I pulled my sweatshirt around me more tightly.

"It's gonna rain," Grams said, nodding, and I could see a dark cloud over the lake.

"Well, hopefully that will get rid of some of the fog," my dad muttered as he stumbled over the stones that marked the path.

"Careful there," Grams said. She shot me a look that clearly said *newcomers*. I grinned back at her.

"I can't believe how much this hasn't changed," my dad said, sounding slightly out of breath from hauling his suitcase behind him. "Like, this could almost be the first time I saw it, when we were here to shoot *Bug Juice*."

"Almost," Grams said, the flinty tone coming back into her voice. She stopped and pointed just below us, toward the picnic table. "Remember when you cut down the tree that was there without asking our permission?"

"I didn't cut it down—"

"Just chopped down that beautiful pine—"

"I was twenty-one and the *writer*—you think I was making decisions about trees?"

"And it wasn't even clean. They left the stump, and we had to move the picnic table over it because people kept tripping—" Grams started walking, and my dad followed, hauling his suitcase, both of them still arguing, but I was standing stone-still, looking at the picnic table.

So there *had* been a pine tree, like on my mother's map, after all. And just like that, I remembered when I had been under the table. I had felt something hard digging into my back—it must have been the tree stump. Which meant I knew exactly where the pine tree had been.

In a flash, I realized what all this added up to.

It meant we'd been looking in the wrong place.

PART FIVE
THE TREASURE

CHAPTER 27

"Did you bring them?" I asked as Diya hurried up to me, a bag over her shoulder. I was trying to speak loudly enough that I could be heard over the wind, which had seriously picked up, but quietly enough that we wouldn't wake anyone.

I had waited in the Phoenix Cabin until my dad fell asleep. It didn't take long. He was in the bunk across the room from me, and the lights had only been out a few minutes before he started snoring. I waited a few minutes after that, then put on a sweatshirt over my pajamas—this proved harder than I'd expected, and finally I just pulled it on over my sling so that one sweatshirt arm was hanging empty—and crept outside, grabbing a flashlight from the cabin's porch.

I'd had to keep my head down against the wind as I ran over to the Hummingbird Cabin, just crossing my fingers that no adults would see me.

Neither Hattie nor Diya was initially thrilled to be awakened—Hattie had flung a pillow in my direction, which had hit the light switch, which had woken Diya up—but as soon as I explained, they jumped into action, pulling on sweatshirts and arguing about who was going to do what.

Finally they decided that Diya would grab all the sand tools from where Max and Uncle Dennis had left them in the equipment shed, and Hattie would go wake up Max and let him know what was happening. We'd all meet by the picnic table for the last chance at solving this mystery, once and for all.

"Yeah, I brought them," Diya said as she set her bag down on the picnic table. I looked through it and saw all the sand tools, plus a spade and a gardening trowel. "And some other stuff I thought might be helpful." She pulled a Coleman lantern out of the bag and turned it on.

"Genius," I said. I had my flashlight, but this was much more practical.

"So it's under here, huh?" Diya peered under the table.

"We were just digging five feet in the wrong direction."

"So let's get started."

We tried to lift the picnic table—but found, after multiple attempts, that we couldn't. It turns out, picnic tables are heavy. "I'm sorry. This stupid arm is slowing everything down."

"We'll just wait for them," Diya said as she glanced back at the darkened cabins. "I don't understand what's taking them this long."

"I'm sure they'll be here any second." All Hattie had to do was wake up Max and bring him down here. What was the holdup?

"You know"—Diya's voice was uncharacteristically cautious—"even if we dig where the map says . . . there's still a chance there's nothing there. You do know that, right?"

"I know." I'd been disappointed too many times to not understand that this might be one final dead end. "But I think we have to try, right? Otherwise, in a couple of months, there's a terrible condo built right over this spot, and then we *never* know. And if my mom left something here . . . something she said needed to be protected . . ."

I might not have her with me. I might have had to say goodbye to her before I was even really old enough to remember her at all. But it felt like I'd somehow gotten to know her this summer, and I owed it to her. Even if the terrible condos were built, my mother's treasure wouldn't be lost along with the camp. I could do that much, at least. "We just have to try this one last time."

Diya nodded, then shivered. "God, it's really cold out."

"Grams said she thought it was going to rain."

"She's usually right about that stuff."

I looked back at the cabins. "Want me to go try to find Hattie?"

Diya grinned. "No need."

"What do you mean?"

She pointed, and I saw what she was looking at. A two-person canoe was coming across the lake with three people inside it—Hattie, Max, and Holden at the front, holding up a lantern like he was in a Revolutionary War painting.

Diya and I ran down the dock to meet the canoe, which was tipping from side to side, like it did *not* like that it had one more person in it than it was supposed to.

I grabbed Max with my good arm and helped him onto the dock. Hattie took a leap from the canoe and landed with a spin as Max pulled the canoe onto the dock.

"How did you get Holden?" Diya asked as she helped him onto the dock, then gave his arm an affectionate punch for good measure.

"It involved his window and throwing rocks at it," Hattie explained, looking proud of herself.

"And then continuing to throw them even after I'd opened the window," Holden said, wincing and rubbing his nose.

"Sorry! But it worked, didn't it?"

"How are you doing?" Holden asked me. "Does your arm hurt a lot?"

"It's not so bad," I said, even though my arm was basically emitting a low-level hum of pain that had been there ever since I'd reached for the ship in the bottle. "Is your dad big mad?"

"Yeah," Holden said. "He made me clean up all the broken bottles and glass, and then told me I was doing it wrong and sent me to bed while it was still light out."

"So he'd be *super* big mad if he found out you snuck out, huh?" Max was starting to look nervous on Holden's behalf.

Holden shrugged. "I know. But I figure at this point, he's sending me back home anyway. So what do I have to lose? I left him a note, so he knows I wasn't kidnapped or anything."

"Even so," Max said, glancing over his shoulder, back at Holden's darkened house, "let's do this quick before anyone finds out we're all out of bed." Just as he said this, a crash of thunder sounded.

"That seems kind of like a bad sign," Diya pointed out.

"It's not a sign," Max said as thunder crashed again. "But maybe we should hurry before it starts raining."

"Good idea," I said, and we all hurried off the dock and stood around the picnic table. I pointed underneath it, where the tree trunk was—and, hopefully, whatever treasure my mother had buried. "Let's dig."

• • •

It was a lot easier to move the table once there were five of us (even if I could only use one of my arms). We lifted it and carried it a few feet away, then got to digging. We decided we shouldn't dig *right* next to the tree trunk—since the roots would be in the way—but fanned out in the area just around it. We'd only been digging into the dirt for a few minutes when I felt the first drop of rain.

"Was that rain?" Hattie asked.

"And to think you made fun of my windbreaker," Holden said, flipping the hood up over his head.

"Let's just dig faster," Diya said as lightning flashed across the lake, making everything as bright as daylight for a moment. "Okay," she said, her voice getting serious. "Anyone with a metal tool, toss it far away from us."

Max tossed the spade and Hattie tossed the trowel, and then they both took plastic and wooden tools out of the bag. "This is going to slow me way down," Hattie grumbled.

"Better than getting electrocuted," Holden pointed out.

"Does anyone have anything?" I asked, shivering as I brushed my wet hair out of my face. I'd dug a hole straight down, but it was hard going with my plastic shovel, and I was worried that, given the weather and that it was getting increasingly miserable, everyone else might be on the verge of giving up.

"Nothing here except worms," Max said, squinting

against the rain that had started to blow in sideways with the wind.

"It has to be here." I started to dig faster, even as the dirt was slowly turning to mud. "Somewhere . . ."

"Ryanna!" I froze and looked up. My dad was standing on the path just above the beach, sounding frantic, looking around in the rain.

My heart sank.

"Um." Hattie pointed across the lake, and I could see that every light in Holden's house was now on and shining brightly across the water. "Is that something we should be worried about?"

"Ryanna!"

"Here, Dad," I said, standing up and waving, realizing that the jig was up. He looked in my direction and then stumble-ran down toward me. When he reached us, he stopped, his eyes wide.

Whatever he'd been expecting, I had a feeling from his expression that it was not seeing me and four other people digging with sand tools in the rain.

"Find her?" I turned and saw Grams and Gramps—Grams in a windbreaker and Gramps holding an umbrella.

"We're down here," Diya called.

"What is going on?" Gramps asked as they reached us, standing behind my dad. He sounded genuinely confused as he looked at us and the holes we'd dug that were slowly filling up with water.

"Holden," my grandmother said sharply, "does your dad know you're here?"

"I left a note," he said weakly.

Diya pointed across the lake. "Well, if he didn't know, I think he does now."

Grams sighed. "I'll drive you home," she said, "before we're accused of kidnapping."

"But seriously, what is going on here?" my dad asked as he looked around at us. "I don't understand this."

"That makes two of us," Gramps chimed in.

I dropped my head, knowing that this was over. It was raining, I was soaked through, and we were all going to get in trouble (or even more trouble, in my case). And we hadn't even found anything. Holden's dad would probably be so mad, he'd kick us out early, and then whatever the map led to would never be found.

I'd let my mother down—there was no other way to look at it.

In frustration, I threw my shovel into the hole I'd dug—and that's when I heard the *thunk*. The sound plastic makes when it hits plastic.

I could hear Diya and Hattie explaining about the treasure map, and Max was attempting to draw it in the dirt, only to keep stopping as it got rained on, but I wasn't paying attention to any of that right now. I was digging, faster and faster, until I could see it—purple and pink amid all the mud.

"Hey," I whispered, my voice shaking. "Hey!" I said louder, and everyone looked over at me. "I think I found something."

CHAPTER 28

I set the purple-and-pink box with its padlock on the table in the mess hall, and we all crowded around it, dripping onto the wood floors. I recognized it as soon as I'd pulled it out of the ground—it was the one my mother had been holding in the picture Grams and Gramps had sent with the letter. I'd had a clue all along, right from the beginning.

Grams had ordered us all out of the rain and, once inside, had given Holden her phone so he could text his dad and let him know where he was, and that he'd be getting a ride back. But even Grams didn't seem to want to drive Holden over right away—like us, she clearly wanted to see what was inside.

"What even is it?" Diya asked, brushing some of the dirt off the lid.

"'Caboodles,'" Max read, sounding out the word.

"And you found it from . . . a treasure map?" My dad closed his eyes for just a moment.

"It was Mom's," I said, and my dad opened his eyes.

"Your mother's?" he asked, a hitch in his voice.

"I found a map she left in the Goldfinch Cabin."

My dad frowned. "Wasn't that the one that was supposed to be haunted?"

"I think she actually *started* that rumor."

"That sounds like Casey," he said with a laugh. "My goodness . . ."

"So what's in it?" Holden asked.

"How are we going to open it?" Grams asked. "Bolt cutters?"

"I don't think we need them," I said slowly. I pulled my necklace out from under my sweatshirt and looked at Diya. She nodded and unclasped it for me. I picked up the key charm. It had been too small to open any of the doors here—but it was the perfect size for a padlock.

I brushed the dirt off the padlock, then fit the key inside. It turned, and the lock popped open. All this time, I'd had the key—I just hadn't realized it.

I rested my hand on the latch, giving myself a second before I opened it up. I couldn't help but think that this would be the last gift my mother would ever give me. For just a moment, that thought was enough to make me want to keep it closed forever—so that I could keep on imagining what was inside.

But then I realized this was missing the point. I'd imagined a quiet summer with my grandparents—and instead I'd gotten something a thousand times better. If something stayed unknown, unopened, the possibilities could be endless, and you wouldn't be disappointed—but it also wasn't real.

And feeling like I was in every final drawing room scene of every mystery I'd ever read—I opened the latch on the caboodle.

I leaned forward to look inside.

The caboodle was half full, and I started pulling the objects out one by one. An orange-and-pink Koosh rubber ball. A Cara Vanessa Cole mystery—*Cara Vanessa Cole and the Babysitting Bandit*. A tube of Dr Pepper–flavored Lip Smacker. A tiny ship in a tiny bottle, and three Polaroids.

I laid everything out on the table, like they were priceless objects—which, I realized a second later, they *were*. These were the things my mother had cared about so much that she'd buried them to keep them safe.

The pictures all looked like they'd been taken here—I recognized the camp in all of them. "That's us," Grams said, picking up one of the pictures, a little quaver in her voice. I leaned over and saw that *Family* was scrawled along the bottom part of the picture, along with a heart. Grams and

Gramps were standing together on the lodge porch, with my aunts and uncles—when they were kids!—clustered around them and what looked like a young Uncle Benji jumping up to give Gramps bunny ears.

"Where's Quinn?" I asked, squinting at the picture.

"Not born yet," Gramps said with a smile as he picked up the second Polaroid. "She would be here the next summer." The picture showed my mom, looking around my age, sitting on the dock and grinning widely at the camera. I realized with a thrill that she was wearing the Benneton sweatshirt Grams had given me—the one I was currently wearing.

The third Polaroid was of my mom and someone I didn't recognize, even though he looked familiar. It looked a little like Holden, even though that couldn't be possible. . . .

"That's your dad," Grams said, holding out the picture to Holden.

Holden blinked at it. "Really?"

Grams nodded, and I leaned over to look at the picture—my mom and Rick Andersen, both freckled and sunburned, laughing hysterically about something. "They were insepa-rable, you know."

My dad made a huffing noise, but when I looked over at him, he just picked up the Koosh ball and threw it in the air. "What?" I asked.

"I wasn't the biggest fan of Rick Andersen."

"We're not either," Diya assured him.

"We've heard he doesn't pay his taxes!" Hattie said. Grams shot her a look and she shrugged. "There are *questions*, at least."

"And he's tearing down the camp," Max said with a sigh.

My dad frowned. "He is?"

I looked in the caboodle and realized there was still one last thing lying on the bottom—a piece of paper. I picked it up carefully and set it on the table. *The Things That Matter Most* was written across the top in what I knew was my mother's handwriting.

The Things That Matter Most
#1 My family!
#2 My friends
#3 Camp Van Camp—getting to come here every summer and be together with my family. We need to be able to keep coming here!! I want to come back when I'm all grown up with my husband (Jonathan Taylor Thomas) and daughter (RYANNA!) and five dogs.

I looked down at my mother's writing, tracing over my name that she'd written years before I was ever even born. "Who's Jonathan Taylor Thomas?" Hattie asked. "Did he live around here?"

"He was an actor," my dad said with a smile as he looked down at the letter.

"So *this* is the treasure?" Diya asked. "A toy and a lip gloss and some pictures and a letter?"

"Yeah," I said, picking up the Polaroid of my mom again and smiling at it. "This *was* treasure, to her. They're the things she cared about most."

"And a Koosh ball," Max added.

I looked at the letter again, reading over number three and feeling like somehow my mother was giving me a message, reaching out across decades to let me know what I had to do, right now.

"Look," I said, pointing to the list. I looked at my dad, and then at Grams and Gramps, across the table from him, on opposite sides. "*This* was what was important to Mom. The most important thing to her was family." I gestured at the four of us. "I don't think she would have wanted this." My dad took a breath, like he was about to say something, but I continued on. "Dad, I know what went on after Mom died—why you guys fought."

"Wait, what happened?" Diya asked Max in a loud whisper.

"And I understand," I went on. "I get why it happened. But I think this has to stop, right? It's not that I believe in signs—"

"I do," Hattie said fervently.

"But . . ." I gestured down to the paper. "It's right here. She wanted her family to be together. And I think for this to continue—it's going against what she would have wanted."

My dad looked at me for a long moment, his eyes bright, then wrapped his arm around me in a hug.

Grams and Gramps exchanged a look, then Gramps stepped forward. "David," he said to my dad, his voice shaky, "we were wrong to do what we did."

"What did they *do*?" Diya asked. Hattie and Max, watching with rapt attention, shushed her.

"Yes," Grams said. "I think we told ourselves we were doing it for Casey, but that wasn't it. We were just sad and scared. And having Ryanna here this summer has just been the greatest gift."

"You've done a wonderful job," Gramps said to my dad, and his chin started to tremble. "And you've done it all on your own. Casey would be so proud."

"Ryanna's a great kid," Grams added.

"Yeah, I think we'll keep her," my dad added, even as his voice broke.

"I'm so sorry," Grams said, shaking her head. "We both are."

"I'm sorry too," my dad said. He took a step forward and held out his hand, but then Gramps pulled him into a hug, then stepped back, and Grams hugged him too. And I felt my heart swell—with happiness and relief and sadness, too, that we'd wasted all these years, that it had taken so long to get here. But mostly happiness.

Hattie burst into tears—and I could tell they were real tears, not just showing how well she could cry on cue.

"I'm so confused," Holden whispered.

"Me too," Diya whispered back. Then, at full volume, she yelled, "Will someone please tell me what is happening?"

"We'll fill you in later," Grams said, half laughing.

"Wow," my dad said, stepping back and wiping under his eyes. "You guys sure do know how to have an exciting Thursday night."

"Okay!" Gramps said, clapping his hands together, trying to sound like his normal hearty self even though his voice was still wobbly. "Hot chocolate all around, I think?"

"*Yes,*" Diya and Hattie said in unison, just as the door flew open, letting in a burst of wind and rain—and a very damp, angry-looking Rick Andersen.

"What in god's name is going on here?" he demanded, his face bright red.

"Dad!" Holden said, walking over to him. "I can explain—"

"I have had it up to here," Rick fumed. He raised his hand near his shoulder and then, seeming to think better of it, lifted it so that it was by his ear. "Up to *here*. I don't know what you people are doing, but—" He stopped short and squinted at my dad. "Dave?"

"Rick," my dad said. Neither one of them sounded thrilled to see the other.

He wheeled around, turning back to the door. "We are *leaving*!"

"Listen, Ricky," Gramps said. "We didn't know Holden was coming over here tonight. We were going to drive him back—"

"Enough! I'm done with all of this." He gestured around at us. "I've gone out of my way to be accommodating, to let you have this last summer. But given what's been happening . . ."

"Wait!" I cried, suddenly seeing an opportunity. I pointed at the table. "We just found these things that my mother—Casey—had hidden away. The things that were the most important to her. And you're in here."

As if we'd rehearsed it, Holden picked up the Polaroid and showed it to his dad, and something softened in his face. His eyes ranged over the table, and he picked up the tiny ship in its bottle. "I made her this," he said slowly.

"And look," I said, holding out the letter to him. I watched him as he read it, and I crossed my fingers on both hands. Hoping that he would see . . . that he would understand he couldn't tear the camp down after all.

"Wow," he said softly as he looked at it. "That's really something."

I exchanged a look with my cousins. "So . . . you won't build condos here after all?"

He shook his head. "Nice try. The plans are still on." He pushed the paper back at me.

I carefully folded it and picked up the Cara Vanessa Cole mystery to tuck it inside.

Which was when I saw that there was already a piece of paper inside the book.

I took it out with shaking hands and a pounding heart, not quite able to believe this was real, and started to read.

I, Robert Andersen, being sound of mind and body (and music!), do hereby sell land parcel #PA121919 in Lake Phoenix, Pennsylvania, to my dear friend Cal Van Camp, with the intended purpose of having a summer camp across the lake from Camp Somerset.

It was the paper we'd been looking for all summer.
The buried treasure.

"Maybe this will change your mind?" I asked, holding the paper up to Rick.

Rick's face went pale as he read it, and Gramps started laughing, and everyone crowded around to read. And Max gasped so hard he started coughing, and Diya took a picture with Grams's phone so that Rick couldn't destroy the document, and Hattie started doing wobbly cartwheels up and down the length of the room.

"What's going on?" my dad asked, looking utterly lost.

I gave him a hug, not sure if I wanted to laugh or cry or do some combination of both. "I'll explain later."

In the end Gramps declared that a giant batch of hot chocolate was needed after all—to warm us up, and to celebrate. Hattie got permission to wake everyone else up, and all my aunts and uncles and Archie stumbled into the lodge, looking bleary-eyed and confused.

My dad re-met my aunts and uncles—and met some of their spouses for the first time—and there were awkward handshakes and half hugs all around.

Rick Andersen had stormed out, trying to get his lawyer on the phone, yelling about unfair tactics and eleventh-hour surprises. Before he followed his dad, Holden had turned to me, his face alight. "We did it," he said to me with a grin.

"I know," I said, smiling back, still not quite able to believe it. "We did."

"I'll talk to him. Hopefully I won't have to leave after

all!" Holden gave me a quick wave, then hurried after his dad, who was yelling into his phone about documents.

But mostly, it felt like it was all too much to take in— too many good things happening to even wrap my mind around. There was my dad talking quietly to my grandparents, nobody yelling, everyone with a mug of hot chocolate. My aunts and uncles celebrating, Archie trying to tell us about the British legal system, and nobody listening. Everyone passing around my mother's letter and looking at the pictures and telling stories about her until it was almost like she was here too, celebrating with us. And we got to tell the story—with Hattie acting it out—about how we'd found the treasure map and then, against all odds, the treasure.

It felt like it could have gone on all night—and I would have been happy for it to—but at two thirty in the morning, Grams whistled and decreed that it was bedtime for everyone, but especially herself. "Good idea," Gramps said around a yawn. He looked at me and gave me a wink. "After all, Ryanna has to be up to make us coffee in the morning."

My dad looked at me in surprise. "You make coffee?"

"It's not that hard. I can show you how."

Back in the Phoenix Cabin with my dad, it felt like there was too much to say. But it also somehow felt like now we'd have enough time to say it.

"I'm sorry I kept you away all these years," my dad said with a sigh. "If I hadn't been so proud . . . you could have been here all along."

"But I'm here now," I said. "Thank you for letting me come."

My dad nodded, then laughed. "They're really something, aren't they? This place . . . it's really special. And they get to keep it, thanks to you."

"And Mom." My dad nodded, his expression faraway.

"Dad," I said before I lost my nerve or missed this moment. "I want you to talk about her more. About Mom."

"Okay. We can do that. . . ."

"And I *don't* want to talk to Dr. Wendy," I said, my voice firm. "You always ask me if I want to talk to her. But what I really want is to talk to *you*."

"I guess I thought," he said, his voice unsure, "that someone else would be better than me. Someone who . . . knew what they were doing."

"I think you're doing great," I said, my chin wobbling. But that was okay, because my dad's was too.

"Your mom would be so happy to see the person you've turned into. She loved you so much. Did you know that?"

I felt my eyes fill with tears—but they were somehow happy and sad at the same time.

"And she would have loved what you did here this summer." He laughed, even though his eyes were glistening. "Finding her map and digging up the camp and breaking all Rick's bottles and not stopping until you solved her mystery. She would have been so proud."

I smiled and let the words wash over me. "I wish she could be here too." It would be the one thing that would make all of this perfect. "I'd just love to see her again. But I know it's impossible."

"Well," my dad said slowly. He had a thoughtful expression on his face. "You know what? Maybe not."

CHAPTER 29

The next two weeks were maybe the best of the whole summer.

Three days after my dad arrived, Ginger came too, with a tiny belly and a suitcase full of new maternity clothes. She got all set up with my dad in the Goldfinch Cabin (it was the biggest, and plus, we no longer had to worry that it was haunted), and I was back with Diya and Hattie in the Hummingbird Cabin.

Holden was back as well—his dad was apparently so busy now dealing with lawyers and contractors and angry buyers that he no longer seemed to remember he'd barred Holden from hanging out with us, so he was back in the group again.

Which was good, because there was a *lot* to do before the summer ended. My dad and Ginger had to be introduced to ActionBall!, and to s'mores nights, and to float-versus-kayak races around the lake. I couldn't swim, unfortunately. Five days after I'd broken my arm, I'd gone back to Stroudsburg Hospital and had gotten a cast—bright pink—along with dire warnings about what would happen if I got the cast wet. When I got back to camp, everyone descended on it with markers, signing it and drawing pictures, so that an hour after I'd gotten it, it was totally filled up.

My dad's editor, the one who cut his movies together, arrived a few days after my dad and was installed in the Phoenix Cabin. He and Archie bonded right away. And whenever I heard my dad's editor grumbling about being stuck here, and how there was nothing to do, Archie would enthuse about the hidden wonders of the Poconos and how great it actually was here.

I wasn't sure why the editor had come—he didn't seem sure either—but when I asked my dad, he just promised that all would become clear soon, and that there would be a big surprise for all of us.

But while I waited on whatever the surprise was, I was getting to have what would have, only a week earlier, seemed impossible—my dad and Ginger, hanging out with my aunts and uncles and cousins, everyone having a good time. Ginger and Aunt Abby got along right away, and when Grams found out Ginger was a pediatrician, she deputized her to be in charge of any cuts or bruises that cropped up in the remaining days of summer.

And we were all determined to make the most of it. There was kayaking around the lake with my dad (my arm wrapped carefully in a trash bag), the once-a-summer kids-versus-parents game of capture the flag, ice cream runs, and s'mores up on the hill.

But best of all was knowing that this *wasn't* the last summer. That we were going to get to do this again next year. Because of the paper we'd found, Gramps had gotten an injunction (whatever that is), and Rick Andersen had been forced to stop his development plans for our side of the lake. He was still making noise about handwriting experts and people who could date paper and ink, but Grams and Gramps were pretty sure it wouldn't come to anything. When we'd heard that construction had to stop, we'd all cheered so loudly that Grams had told us to pipe down because we were scaring all her birds away.

"It's going to play out for a while with the lawyers. But it can't move forward. So I think Camp Van Camp is safe." We all cheered again, and Grams shook her head. "He's still going to be able to do whatever he wants on his side."

"Condos?" I asked.

"Afraid so. But at least there won't be any over here. Thanks to you."

"And thanks to Mom," I pointed out. I had kept my mother's caboodle—it now had a place of pride in the Hummingbird Cabin.

Quinn had written up an article describing everything that had happened—the twists and turns, the family drama, the improbable discovery. And she'd told us one night over burgers that she'd sold it to a major magazine—which meant getting a job at a paper wasn't seeming so impossible after all.

Most days, while we were either on the beach or the dock, I'd see my dad in the shade, talking to Uncle Benji. Hattie had blurted out his secret pen name, and my dad had immediately gone into superfan mode—getting his Sven Svensson collection sent from California so that Uncle Benji could sign them all.

I had no idea what they were always talking about, but I'd catch words here and there—about movies and adaptations and pseudonyms.

And finally, a week after my dad's editor had arrived, we got to see why. My dad stood up at dinner and announced that there was a special treat for all of us waiting on the beach.

I'd changed into the one fancy dress I'd brought, and we'd gone out to find that blankets had been set up on the sand, and a giant screen in front of the water. My dad announced, with a hitch in his voice, that this was the first annual Casey Van Camp Film Festival.

I sat on a blanket with my dad and Ginger, and everyone quieted down as the movie began.

It was a montage—my dad and his editor had cut

together all the things my mom had ever acted in. There were the kid-appropriate parts of *Bug Juice*—we all cheered when the camp showed up on-screen. There were her old commercials, the TV show about witches who were also vampires, the indie movie where she played a country singer.

And then her acting work ended, and the home movies began. I stared, trying to take it all in—there was my mom, at all stages of her life. When she was little, when she was my age. Running full speed off this very dock and landing with a splash in the water. Arguing with her brothers and sisters, paddling a canoe with panache.

There was her wedding day with my dad; there was me in her arms as a baby. My mom holding my hands tightly as I took wobbly first steps, and smiling at me as I stuffed bananas into my mouth with chubby fists. The three of us at Disneyland, my dad's arm around her shoulders, all of us smiling at the camera.

There she was, larger than life, here among us at last. The movie ended on a freeze-frame of her face, smiling wide. We all clapped, and when I looked around, I could see I wasn't the only one wiping away tears.

And I knew it was a night I'd never forget—feeling like my mom was right there with me, here in the place that she'd loved best.

My whole family, together at last.

• • •

I couldn't ignore the fact that it was getting a little colder every day. That the days were starting to get shorter, that twilight wasn't stretching on for hours anymore, so we needed flashlights and lanterns with us when we made our s'mores.

Summer was ending.

And while everyone else was going to be driving home, we had a flight back to California with a fixed date—one that came much too soon.

The morning we were leaving, I woke up even earlier than usual and got dressed in the closet for the last time. My suitcase was mostly packed—just a few odds and ends, and my mother's caboodle that I would be taking on the plane with me as my carry-on. I pulled on her Benneton sweatshirt—we'd had to cut the arm a bit to fit my cast in, but Ginger had assured me we could get it sewn up when the cast was off, and it would be good as new. I reached for a sweatshirt automatically now in the mornings, since it was always chilly—reminding me that it got cold in the fall and winter in Pennsylvania, and they were coming faster than I wanted them to.

Gramps was already there when I made it to the lodge. "About time," he joked as I stepped inside.

"Thought I was going to beat you for once," I said, smiling at him as I walked to the coffee maker.

He laughed. "You're going to have to get up earlier in the morning to do that. Literally!"

I started spooning coffee grounds into the filter. "I'll get you next summer." Even though nothing was definite yet, we'd all already started to talk about next year. How I would be able to come for the whole summer this time. And maybe my dad and Ginger could join at some point too. Diya had big plans for an ActionBall!/AquaBall! hybrid, and Max was determined to build the world's best tree house. And every time we talked about these plans, it was like a thread was stretching out, from this summer to next year, meaning that this wasn't over—that there was still lots and lots to come.

"About that," Gramps said, his face getting a little more serious as he set down the bagel plate.

"What?" I asked. My heart pounded. "Did something happen?"

"Well . . . yes and no." I hit the button to start the coffee brewing and turned to face my grandfather. "Here's the thing. Rick is giving up on claiming our land—"

"That's good—"

"But he's saying that if the document is valid, we have to obey the terms of the sale."

"What does that mean?"

"Well, since in the document, Robert said that he was selling the land to me so that it could be a camp, Rick is arguing that unless we operate as a camp for at least two weeks a year, we're in violation."

"Whoa." I started to smile as it hit me what this meant. "So it's going to be a summer camp again here? With, like, counselors and other kids and everything?"

"For two weeks, at least," Gramps said. He smiled at me, and his eyes were twinkling. "What do you think? Still want to come back, even if it's going to be a camp again? I was thinking maybe you and Diya would be old enough to be CITs—counselors in training. How does that sound?"

I grinned at him. It sounded *great*—like there was going to be a whole new way to be here, one I hadn't even thought was a possibility. I wasn't sure what a counselor in training *did*, but I was sure I could figure it out. I nodded. "I'm in." I poured him a cup of coffee in his favorite mug and handed it over to him. "Just as long as I can keep this job."

Gramps smiled at me and took a long sip. Then he raised the mug to me in a toast. "Your best one yet."

Three hours later, the car was packed, and we'd all said our goodbyes and hugged everyone.

When even Diya started to get weepy, my dad declared that it really was time to go, that we had a plane to catch, and we all piled into the car. But as my dad drove around the circle and then down the long driveway, I didn't look away.

I leaned out the window as far as I could, not wanting to lose sight of them, everyone who had meant so much to me this summer—an intern, an au pair, a friend, my cousins and grandparents and aunts and uncles. Everyone spilled out onto the street, following our car, waving and waving as we drove very slowly.

I waved back with my good arm, trying to keep looking at everyone for as long as I could. I caught Diya's eye, and she grinned at me. Gramps's eyes were wet, but he was smiling wide, and Holden gave me a nod that I somehow just knew meant *see you next summer.*

Our car rounded the bend, and everyone got smaller and smaller, and I waved one last time—but then I couldn't see them anymore.

I would miss them all more than I could say. But I'd see them—all of them—next summer. And we'd have a whole new adventure ahead of us. Campers! Counselors! I couldn't wait.

Maybe my new brother or sister could even come. Because I wanted to show them this place. I wanted to tell them all about it.

"You okay?" my dad asked. Ginger turned around and gave me a sympathetic smile. I thought about it as I pulled my mother's sweatshirt closer around me and breathed it in. I might not have been able to smell her in the sweatshirt—

but I knew somehow she was with me. That she always would be. That she always had been.

I thought about the summer. The things I'd done, the things we'd found—the wrong we'd righted. The fun we'd had. And I met my dad's eye in the rearview mirror.

"Yeah," I said, "I'm great." I gave him a nod, then leaned back against the seat and smiled. "Let's go home."

The Hollywood Edit
OPTION ALERT!

In a move that sent shock waves through the industry late last night, screenwriter Dave Stuart has secured exclusive movie rights to reclusive Swedish author Sven Svensson's latest bestselling thriller, *The Stockholm Syndrome*. This is particularly noteworthy because the author, based outside Malmö, has never before allowed any of his work to be adapted for film or TV. When contacted to ask how this came about, Stuart replied, "I have long been a great admirer of Sven's work. I was able to spend time with him this summer at a lake house, and we developed a great rapport. He has kindly agreed to entrust me with his work." When asked follow-up questions—like how he got in touch with Svensson, and where exactly he lives—Stuart said that he had to catch a plane and hung up.

We eagerly await more details of this exciting development.

The Pocono Eagle

Camp Van Camp to Return!

After over thirty years as a private residence, the *Eagle* has learned that next summer, Camp Van Camp—which operated as a sleep-away camp in Lake Phoenix for decades until it closed operations in 1993—will be back in business.

According to a just-launched website, it will offer a three-week stay in the Pocono Mountains, with a lake, swimming, arts and crafts, and something called ActionBall! (?).

More to come.

Acknowledgments

First and foremost, I'm incredibly grateful to my editor, Justin Chanda, for helping me tackle this brave new middle-grade world. Thanks so much for your wonderful notes, tireless editing, and belief in this story from the start. You're officially the absolute best.

Thanks and gratitude to Emily Van Beek, Sydney Meve, Melissa Sarver White, Katherine Odom-Tomchin, and the whole team at Folio. Thank you to Corrine Aquino at Artists First and Austin Denesuk at CAA for always taking such good care of me.

Thank you so much to the wonderful and brilliant people I'm so lucky to work with at Simon & Schuster—Daniela Villegas Valle, Alyza Liu, Amanda Brenner, Chava Wolin, Anne Zafian, Chrissy Noh, Brendon MacDonald, Ashley Mitchell, Nadia Almahdi, Lisa Moraleda, Morgan Maple, Hilary Zarycky, and Lizzy Bromley. And a huge thank-you to Celia Krampien for the cover and illustrations of my dreams.

I'm so lucky to be part of a wonderful community of writers in LA—and am beyond grateful for the work sessions and brainstorm walks and friendship. Thank you to Adele, Anna, Jen, Julia, Julie, Kate, Maux, Max, Rebecca, Sarah E., Sarah M., Siobhan, Stu, and Veronica. And a special thanks to Diya and Sonia for letting me borrow their names.

And finally, thank you to my brother, Jason Matson, my Redwood Terrace partner in crime, and my mother, Jane Finn, for making all those magical Pocono summers possible.